CW00858284

The Girl Who Wasn't Min

The Girl Who Wasn't Min

The Black River Chronicles Book VI

LG Surgeson

Copyright (C) 2017 LG Surgeson
Layout design and Copyright (C) 2017 Creativia
Published 2017 by Creativia
Cover art by Cover Mint
This book is a work of fiction. Names, characters, places, and incidents are the product
of the author's imagination or are used fictitiously. Any resemblance to actual events,
locales, or persons, living or dead, is purely coincidental.
All rights reserved. No part of this book may be reproduced or transmitted in any form
or by any means, electronic or mechanical, including photocopying, recording, or by
any information storage and retrieval system, without the author's permission.

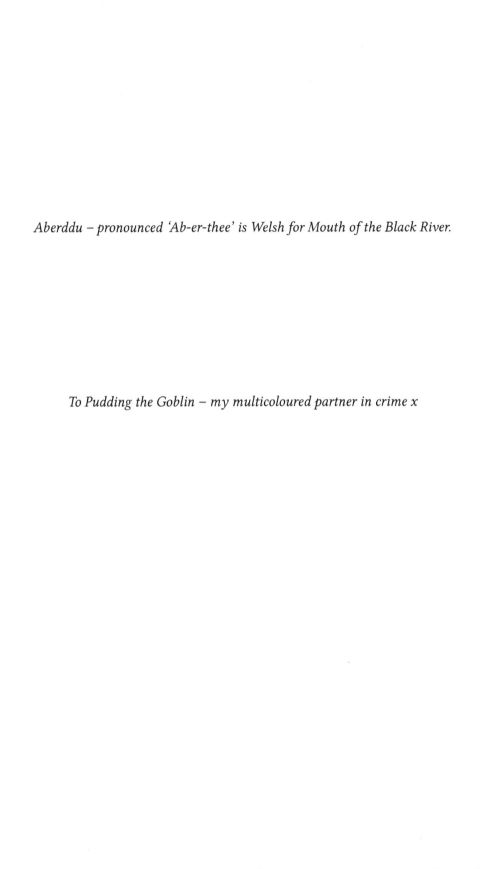

Aberddu – pronounced 'Ab-er-thee' is Welsh for Mouth of the Black River.

To Pudding the Goblin – my multicoloured partner in crime x

Contents

Chapter 1
The Game

A tight-laced whale-bone corset meant that she had no choice but to sit bolt upright in the polished leather side-saddle of her fine bay mare. The beast was beautiful, glossy and lean - sleek, nimble and small - as a town horse ought to be. Her russet and brown riding attire was made from top-grade damask and lace; most likely authentic Alendrian lace at that. These elegant, slightly understated women were always dressed in the finest fabrics. She had a pile of thick mahogany hair swept high up on to her head and held there by three or maybe four glittering combs. Most likely paste rather than diamonds, but still worth more than a sneeze to the sifters on the Black Market.

If that was her real hair colour and her actual nose or chin, then Luce would happily have eaten her hat - if she'd had a hat to eat. They'd really done their homework on this one. She was Lady Something, Duchess of Somewhere - the names were unimportant. She was had been widowed during the Summer of Fire and rumour had it she had once been desperate for children. Perfect. Luce doubted that she would think so well of children tomorrow.

Luce had quite literally fallen into the Guild Below six or seven years earlier, through an open sewer hatch in the Trade District. No one seemed bothered by her loss, so the Guild kept her. She vaguely remembered a very large family, an empty belly and a bad-tempered mother but she didn't miss any of them at all. Lying in the shadows of the roof, she didn't think about the past, she just kept her eyes on Min.

She really had to hand it to Min, the girl was a true artist. How she got her nose to run on cue like that Luce had no idea. The grubbiness was real, as was the suggestion of a bruise of her cheek and the lice were an unavoidable occupational hazard. But whilst the whole package made Luce and the others look like something you would leave town to avoid, it made Min look beyond vulnerable in an absolutely heart-breaking way. As far as Luce knew, Min was the youngest. She had been dumped, swaddled and squalling, in a tavern in the Government District, not so much a foundling and a leftling.

The Quizzical Cat was well-known for having no connection whatsoever to the Guild Below, and the tavern keeper, a very stout, short man called Harald, was not in any way a Guild sympathiser, nor did he have a hatch in his back-room under two surprisingly light ale barrels that lead straight down into the sewers. His scrawny wife Ruby had taken one look at the child and pragmatically decided that this wasn't the miracle she had been praying for; this was someone else's disaster and the Guild could deal with it. They had paid her to care for the child until the little girl was old enough to care for herself and then Min had gone to live Below. Harald had named her Mini because she had been tiny even as a baby, and even though she was at least ten still looked only six or seven. Luce watched as Min wandered, barefoot, out of the end of alley way straight into the path of bay mare. She heard the expected whinnying and refocused herself on the job in hand.

A waxed fish-line garrotte was the most easily concealed physical weapon in the City. It was light, and small so it didn't affect the line of your clothes, plus it could be safely swallowed if you knew how to knot it. Luce's garrotte had been adapted slightly with a strip of chamois. Whatever Luce was, she wasn't a murderer. She peered over the edge of the low roof, careful not to be seen. Down on the street, she could see Angel preparing the cotton cloth with knock-out vapours.

Angel was perhaps the most tragic of the four of them. She was white blonde, milky pale and grey-eyed. She had a face like a porcelain doll - admittedly a sour-looking one that had been sitting in a gutter for a month - but still. Unlike the others, she clearly remembered her life before the Guild. She had been snatched by slavers as a small child and sold to an odious woman she only ever referred to as Mistress, although she spat the word with such venom that it made Min shudder. She had been traded to the Guild as part of a settlement on the Mistress' debts. Luce sometimes wondered if one of the reasons Angel seemed so bitter was that she'd been only part of the payment. She'd never dared ask.

Min's performance was reaching a crescendo; she was whimpering and clinging to the woman's skirt. Luce was relieved to see that the mark had dismounted from her horse - unlike the previous two who presumably didn't have enough compassion to spoil their shoes, only to not kick out at the wailing, snotty urchin hanging on to their saddle strap. This woman was actually crouching down, one hand on Min's shoulder when Luce and Angel made eye contact, counted to two and sprung.

Once the woman had been downed and dragged into the alley, Clara appeared from a puddle of darkness across the street. She was ostensibly the brains of the operation; meaning that she had most of the ideas, the biggest mouth and hated climbing up on to roofs. She had been orphaned sometime shortly before the Summer of Fire, and had been living in the Trickster Temple when it had burnt down during the invasion. She had been found by Lady Iona, Duchess of Pringle, who had forced her to wash and taken her to the Guild Below for what she styled as 'further' training. She liked to make sure people knew she'd had contact with Lady Iona, as she was convinced it helped her standing in the Guild Below. It didn't.

Clara was in charge of gathering up their harvest greedily and shoving it into four potato sacks that she had brought for this very purpose. She had a good eye for what would sell.

"I feel almost bad," said Min tugging the combs out of the woman's mahogany locks, "She was actually lovely."

"You're not turning soft I hope?" grunted Angel who was trying to heft the woman's skirt free without touching the body.

"I said almost," returned Min, looking a little wounded. Angel didn't notice.

"You know what," said Luce, cutting the lacing on the corset with a single run of her blade, "this is the best scam yet." She watched the whale-bone and fabric relax as the tension suddenly released.

"They silk?" said Clara distractedly pointing to her stockings. Angel gingerly ran a rough finger over the sheer white fabric and nodded,

"She's even got matching garters, with pearls on."

Angel sounded disgusted. Of all of them, she was the only one who actually despised the rich. The other three just saw themselves as wealth farmers, harvesting the ripe pickings from whichever unwitting soul came their way next.

"Right," said Clara, "let's have 'em. She'll do in her chemise and bloomers, unless they'ze silk an' all."

"Nope, just cotton," snorted Min, as she took the fine gold chain from around the slender neck, " She can find out what it's like to walk in this alleyway without any shoes on." Min had been quick to shove her own feet back into the stiff boots she had proudly re-appropriated during the last plague.

"I swear," said Luce, checking that nothing had been missed before they dragged her further down the alley, "if Min ever grows breasts we're in trouble."

"If I ever grow breasts," retorted Min handing three rings to Clara, who stuck them in the least wholly sack. "I'm going on the game. It can't be much different from this."

"Luring people into alleyways, taking their clothes off and leaving them well and truly screwed?" said Angel dryly, making them all laugh as they rolled Lady Whatnot, Duchess of Thing on to her back and watched as her sagging and suddenly unrestrained bosom wobbled to a stop.

They didn't hang around contemplating the pros and cons of prostitution versus street robbery for very long as they were well aware that they needed to be swift in retreat. Leaving Lady Whosit, Duchess of Whatyacall sleeping soundly on the damp alley floor they disappeared down the sewer hatch not ten feet away. Each one dropped in to the darkness with a sack slung over one shoulder and headed off without a pause. It was straight to the Black Market with this lot. Then, when they each had their share, they could peel off and spend it how they wished.

Chapter 2
The Other Guild

Aberddu was a renegade city free-state that had ripped itself from the clutches of mother Albion only a few years previously. In such an anarchic and treacherous place, where the laws only really existed to let the ruling council prosecute the people they didn't like, it was small wonder there was a rich and thriving underworld.

In fact, underworld was an extremely accurate term for it because the Guild Below were exactly that. Beneath the city were several complex networks of caverns and tunnels, chambers and hidey-holes that had sprung up almost organically like a clutch of hollow octopuses, tentacles running into every corner of the city.

Any passer-by haplessly opening a sewer hatch would be forgiven for thinking that this world must be foetid and desperate and at a glance, they would be correct. The first layer of the tunnels were a catch-all for the rainwater, slurry, blood and other detritus that washed from the streets of the city. Here the rats grew fat on the pestilent effluent and the bloated cadavers that floated in it. The cloying sweet-sour smell of waste and decay made the air unpleasant. Strong tidal surges swelled the water, if you could really call it water, backing it up and pushing it to the surface in spewing plumes. Heavy rain filled them up so they raced and roared around blockages, carrying the worse of the city out to river Ddu and on into the unsuspecting delta.

The practical minds of the Guild Below never ever sought to change this. It was the perfect barrier between the city and their world below it. They never lingered there - unless they were desperate, or worse lost. They simply cut through it, dropping down to the layers below using cleverly placed slips and tunnels, ropes and ladders - all designed to keep the water from getting any further down.

Even though they were in a part of the sewer was firmly Guild territory, the girls didn't take their safety for granted. Guild loyalty in a Guild with only one real rule doesn't stretch very far - particularly not when that one rule is basically 'don't get caught'. (In truth it wasn't the only 'rule' but it was the only one that actually mattered). Whilst some people were protected by status, like the Guild heads or some of the more prominent assassins, no-one would question the disappearance of four sewer brats. It would probably be weeks before anyone noticed they'd gone and even longer before they could find anyone who cared.

The girls didn't splash far through the muck before they found a narrow slit in the top of the tunnel - a recent favourite of theirs. It was narrow enough that only someone the size of a child could use it and it was a safer route than their last cut through. Luce still had the grazes from the altercation that had occurred the last time they used the previous gap and after that the girls had learnt about the importance of varying their behaviour.

Deftly, Min jumped up and grabbed the brick, and hung from the gap by one hand. A moment of acrobatics and she had wedged herself securely in front of the gap. Reaching out a hand, she pulled Angel up so that she could check for any unwelcome company on the other side. After a brief glance, Angel slithered through the gap feet first. Quickly, Min posted the sacks through to her one at a time. Once all of their takings were on the other side, she helped Clara and then Luce up to the gap. They wriggled through frantically, Luce's rapidly developing frame was almost too large for it now. Carefully, each girl dropped neatly on to the pile of stolen clothes below. Min was the last through, she hit the brick floor moving and they carried on without a pause. This new tunnel wound down towards a hatch and monkey-rope that would put them well on the way to the Black Market, or it had done three days ago at least. Hopefully no-one had decided to slash the rope, that would mean a substantial detour.

Mulligan watched with a self-satisfied leer as the girls shimmied down the heftily knotted monkey-rope, dropping sacks of takings to one another, staying alert all the time. They were pros, no question. He'd heard about them but he had to admit he'd been sceptical. It hardly sounded like a slick criminal outfit; four foundling girls working a tired old angle fleecing rich women. However, as they scuttled off down the tunnel away from him, their eyes darting everywhere, he could see that this was a million miles from hanging around barefoot the rich district with your shoes hidden in an alley whining 'ere missus, spare us a florin, I aint eaten for days and my feets is cold'. They were exactly what he was looking for. And if they were the pros they appeared to be then it should be easy to sell the plan to them. It wasn't like he wasn't paying well. He treated himself to an indulgent snort and dropped noiselessly down from his perch in the tunnel roof. They were heading for the Black Market and so was he, but he had no intention of going the same way they were.

Mulligan was not quite arrogant enough to see himself as a criminal mastermind, but he did like to flatter himself that he was a cut or two above a simple petty crook. He had had, in his career, one or two ingenious plans that had made him quite a lot of money, and more importantly were still being talked about by people who couldn't put any of his names to his real face. As he trudged down the tunnel he congratulated himself that this scheme was in fact his best yet. These girls were perfect.

When he'd first hit on the idea of using a small girl as a patsy to gain access to the finer homes and gardens, he'd originally intended to pop along to the Temple District and see who he could find at the Life Temple Orphanage that looked the part. For all their caring, the overstretched Sisters could be remarkably gullible when it came to well-dressed benefactors looking to adopt. A few silvers and a kindly smile and they'd hand over a girl, no trouble at all. But he had abandoned that plan when he'd first heard about these girls, reasoning that a bath, some clothes and an elocution lesson or two were far easier to organise than a crash-course in cat-burglary. He could also pretty much guarantee that as long as their cut appeared to be generous, these girls would have no qualms about doing pretty much anything he asked of them.

The Black Market was not nearly as exciting as it sounded. Clara had never quite recovered from the disappointment of that. Held in one of a handful of locations, the market was like a giant back room of a very dodgy bar except that the beer was worse and it had significantly fewer on-duty prostitutes. People didn't come to the Black Market looking for that kind of entertainment, and the hookers that did come down here were looking to trade in entirely different commodities. In fact, Clara had been most disenchanted to discover, that people didn't come to the Black Market looking for any sort of entertainment at all.

This was just as well, because there was none to be had, it was very strictly business.

She had imagined a bustling bazaar with stalls peddling all sorts of dark curios, cages of strange looking and undoubtedly poisonous creatures and exotic characters of every stripe. She had entertained dreams of jugglers and mummers and fortune-telling gypsies with talismans and curling nails, plumes of incense and flashes of magical light. Too much time listening to the bards had left her with a highly-coloured view of the underworld.

In truth it was a subdued gathering of people whispering in corners, showing each other surreptitious suitcases and exchanging cash purses on the quiet. No-one set out their wares, except the food vendors, with good reason – pretty much all the clientèle were skilled pick-pockets. It also didn't do to let people know what you had unless you knew they wanted to buy it. If you wanted to buy something, you had to know who was selling and you had to hope they were in the mood to talk to you.

Clara had been to the Black Market four times before she managed to find anything other than pastries for sale. It had been quite intimidating, even though she would never have admitted it. Several years on and the four of them knew nearly everybody and people knew them. They had a regular fence, Johnny (almost certainly not what anyone else called him) who paid fair prices for 'finely-made ladies' essentials'. None of them were completely sure what he did with them when he'd bought them and Angel didn't care. Luce had once told Clara that he sold them to the poshed-up hookers in the Government District, which Clara had found hilariously funny until Min pointed out that they had better hope that none of the girls tried to service a gent whilst wearing his wife's stolen pearls. Angel had merely grunted at this comment, which had stopped the others flat in the middle of a howl of laughter.

A good fence was two steps from point of sale making them, as his source, a fair way from being collared if one of the posh doxies was unlucky enough to get caught. Johnny whatever-his-name-was was probably not a very good fence, the girls had no real way of know, but he was happy to deal with street-robbing sewer brats and they hadn't been caught yet.

The girls let Angel do the deals with Johnny. She got the best prices, they didn't ask how. While she was negotiating the other three bought some food and found a corner to crouch in, although they did keep their eyes on Angel as she made the transactions. It wouldn't do to have her snatched - particularly before she'd handed over their share of the cash.

Mulligan was happy to wait for the opportune moment. He had thought this whole thing through carefully. The other advantage of finding the girls down here was that he didn't have to pretend to be a kindly uncle type. These girls had all been down here a couple of years or so and were as hard-nosed as any. They would be more likely to try to do him over if he came across as unctuous or in away well-meaning than if he were mean to them. He had considered that very carefully, kidnapping after all being one of his options - but that also had its drawbacks - four of them versus one of him where not odds he fancied. Better to offer them a deal, a percentage. Willing partners were more use than prisoners for a start, gold being a much more inviting master than fear or charity. And if it turned out that they were as clever as he thought they were, then he'd just have to make sure that he paid them their cut fairly. Almost.

It was the sound of Luce's voice raised louder than usual, cutting the buzz of the market, that caught Angel's attention.

"Piss off mister," she almost shouted. "I aint going on the game,"

Angel looked over and was unsurprised to see the man who was trying to talk Luce down from her growing anger. She couldn't hear him, or even see his lips - his face was in shadow - but she knew exactly who he was. Actually, in one context that wasn't true at all. She had no idea of the man's name, or his profession or intentions but she did know that the man she was looking at, with his nondescript ...everything, was the same man who'd been tailing them for three days at least.

At first, she had been scared that he was going to snatch one of them - but as the days past, fear turned to curiosity. If it had been a straight-forward abduction, then surely he'd have picked one off as they dropped down a hatch or rounded a corner. An ether rag in the mouth and ten seconds later you'd have a neat bundle over your shoulder. Who misses a street brat right? She'd stayed alert, even given him an opportunity to try it. When he didn't take it she had at first been confused, then intrigued. If he wasn't simply looking for a quick take, then he must have something else in mind.

Two days later, she'd seen him as they approached their last mark and she had been wondering all afternoon what exactly he was playing at. She doubted very much he was just a dockland pimp - they didn't spend nearly as much time observing their girls. However, she did have a gut feeling that this man had some kind of business proposition for them, which may or may not survive Luce shrieking that she 'aint no bleedin' docklands doxy,' at the top of her lungs. Angel snatched the coin purse out of Johnny's outstretched hands and, skipping their usual post-transaction badinage, jogged over to the others.

Twenty minutes later, Luce was shovelling butcher's pudding, pease pottage and gravy into her mouth so fast that you had to concentrate to see the spoon move. Apparently, she wasn't bothered if you were a pimp or not if you were paying for lunch. The others were a little more circumspect about their would-be benefactor, who had taken them up top to The Bird and Bottle for a 'spot of grub'. Judging by the way Luce was putting it away, it was going to be a very large spot. Min, who was the one of the four that could most accurately be described as shy of strangers, sat in one corner picking over a large bowl of stew that had been served with a lump of rock hard bread almost the size of her face. She wasn't going to speak to anyone in front of Mulligan, but she was listening.

Once he'd explained and they'd eaten everything in sight, including what seemed like a bath-tub of custard, Mulligan left them for an hour 'to mull things over'. It took the girls less than half that time to make a decision about his offer. There was no denying that his plan was certainly very clever and if he was telling the truth about their cut, it stood to take them into the big league. Well not the big league exactly, just a slightly bigger league with more sophisticated locks and fewer knocked-off ladies' undergarments. As Clara put it so eloquently and succinctly, if it took off the 'dockland strumpets will 'ave to steal their own bleedin' pearls'.

Chapter 3
Mulligan's Rooms

Mulligan lived in an insalubrious part of the North Wall Slums, down an alley-way behind a run-down knocking shop with the windows boarded over. This wasn't the part of the poor quarters where cheeky geezers with missing teeth looked out for tousled waifs and vast-bosomed matriarchs stood in their door-ways passing moral judgement on everyone's business. This was the rat-end of the city, where the nasty people really were nasty and nobody batted an eyelid at Mulligan trailing four young girls behind him like ducklings in the middle of the day. They followed him up the street and down the alley, each with their hand on their dagger-hilt, and in through the rotting front door at the bottom of the building Mulligan called home. His rooms were five storeys up, in the attic.

It was a tight squeeze into Mulligans rooms. To be perfectly honest 'rooms' was a very pretentious, and somewhat felonious description of Mulligan's living arrangements. It was in fact just a loft space which Mulligan had sectioned off into three areas. At the end where the roof sloped, behind a makeshift wall built precariously from about forty-five impressive looking religious tomes, was a saggy palliasse with a couple of moth-eaten blankets on it. This Mulligan had laughable styled his 'bedroom'. He may as well have thrown a piece of cloth over the chamber pot and called it the 'en suite privy' for all it impressed the girls. In the living area there was a small range in the fire place, a couple of knocked-about chairs and a smart looking gate-leg table. This was cluttered with bits and pieces. There was one grimy window, that let in a lot of draught but not much light. Mulligan hadn't even bothered to curtain it, presumably because he'd used the fabric to separate the other end of the space into what he pompously declared to be his 'training area'. When he firmly instructed the girls that they weren't to enter, he should have realised how stupid this instruction was.

Once he'd finished the 'tour', which took less than a minute, he sat them all down next to the slim-line fire place and deposited a battered old trunk in front of them. Judging by the slightly crazed smile on his face he was under the impression that he had presented the girls with something akin to the treasures of the ancients. The girls were more inclined to think it was a dirty old chest with a very shoddy padlock. None of them bothered to move to look at it and it was only after Mulligan grunted "go on then," with more than a hint of irritation that Angel crept forward and started to open it. She ran her hands over it suspiciously, checking for booby-traps and other nasty things before prizing the lid open. She found it was about half full of a seemingly random collection of items. A slightly grubby rag doll sat on top of the pile, which she started to unpack piece by piece. There were three absolutely ghastly shift dresses and a pinafore, all in different sizes and all far too big for Min. There was a pair of stiff lace-up boots stuffed with fleece to keep them in shape. Loose at the bottom were a cake of soap, a soft, slightly moth-eaten hair brush, a handful of ribbons - none of which matched any of the dresses - and a small silver bangle. Once she had laid it all out she looked back into the trunk to see if she'd missed anything. Mulligan - who had been watching her expectantly looked slightly disappointed by how underwhelmed she seemed to be.

"What's wrong?" he said and was rewarded with the first of many disparaging glares from Angel.

"Well," she said eventually when none of the other girls spoke, "the clothes are too big, these shoes are probably too small, the ribbons are horrid, the doll smells funny, that's not enough soap and do you really think that brush is going to do anything to that?" She pointed at the festering nest of hair on Min's head. Mulligan opened his mouth to retort but Angel filled the gap before he could, "It's fine - I'll make you a list."

About ten minutes later Mulligan found himself trudging down the stairs with a list in his hand. It included such items as a bone lice comb, a large onion, a stiff-bristled scrubbing brush, a flask of rough gin and a large bottle of Mrs Docherty's patent disinfectant and grime-remover. He was muttering under his breath about the cheek of it and wondering what would be left of his rooms when he got back. He'd taken them in off the street and this is how they acted? How very dare they.

When Mulligan returned from his errands several hours later, he had every intention of laying down the law. After all, he was a fully grown man, a master of certain arts and deserving of respect. They were four strays with a little skill and a lot of nerve. Hauling his bundle up the stairs to the attic, he was resolute but as he stood panting on the top step he could hear the sound of splashing through the door and low mumbled voices. Dropping the bundle, he snapped open the latch and pushed his way into the rooms, angry at the idea that they were in some way destroying his property. He was just about to shout at the girls when he was met with a harpy-like shriek and a flurry of flailing arms and cloth as Clara and Angel flew at him shoving him backwards out of his own door.

"Wait there," ordered Angel and disappeared back inside. Mulligan wanted to protest at being ordered around in his own home but she had gone before he could open his mouth. He was left gaping at the sopping wet face of Clara.

"We're givin' Min a wash," she said imperiously, as though that excused everything. Then having decided further explanation was needed added, "an' she's shy." Mulligan just stared back incredulously, so Clara carried on talking. "S'okay," she wittered, "we scrubbed out that old tin tub first like, and we managed to get the stove to light. Eventu'lly." The look on Clara's impish face when she said eventually didn't fill the still-speechless Mulligan with much hope as to the present state of his rooms, "and then it took most of the rest of the aft'noon to get the wa'er up 'ere. You wants another bucket really." It was then that Mulligan became aware of just how much water there was on the stairs. He opened his mouth to shout at her and then closed it again. He didn't really know what to say. There was an uncomfortable pause during which Clara didn't look in any way apologetic and then, far more calmly than he'd meant to, Mulligan said,

"Well, I can't stand out here all day."

After several minutes of faffing about, bickering and talking at cross-purposes during which Luce called Mulligan a 'bleedin' perv', the girls managed to construct a temporary screen around the still bathing Min, allowing Mulligan back into his own rooms.

The moment Mulligan had gone, they had pulled back the curtain to the training area and had a poke around. It was, in truth, quite an impressive arrangement. In a space no wider than two feet and about eight feet long he had managed to fit a trap making bench, a large wall-mounted map of the sewer network, a practice lock with changeable tumblers, a series of hand holds for climbing and hanging practise and a rope gym for flexibility training. The girls had spent a good hour playing with everything before they decided they'd better actually do something useful. They had really gone to work on Min. She was sitting folded up in the battered tin tub which Mulligan probably considered the 'main bathroom'. The range was lit, and she was trying not to splash the water on to the dirty rag rug. She had been rubbed down from head to foot with the bar of soap, which had successfully removed the top layer of dirt leaving the more permanent grime behind.

Mulligan unpacked his goodies onto the hearth rug.

"Hurry up," groaned Min from behind her modesty screen, folding herself even tighter, "this water's getting cold."

Mulligan grunted.

"S'also turned brown," said Luce, "and there fings floatin' in it,"

"Yeah," whined Min, "but that don't make it warmer,"

Mulligan grimaced.

"Look," he said as he plonked the stoneware bottle of Mrs Docherty's patent disinfectant and grime remover down on the floor, "I'll get some more water up if one of you sorts out the fire." No sooner had he said it than Luce had dived towards the bellows.

Leaving Min wrapped in a sheet and shivering by the fire, Clara and Luce emptied the tub carefully out of the tiny window and Mulligan went downstairs with the bucket and the hanging pan from the fire place to fetch up the clean water. Under the principle of all things being relative, things were looking up. Angel snatched up the bottle of Mrs Docherty's, pulled out the stopper and sniffed. It was largely an astringent aroma but there were hints of ginger and burdock that made her warm inside. It has to be said that Mrs D's wasn't normally used as a shampoo but the sewer brats swore by it. It had the ability to loosen and dissolve most things without creating a funny smell or a burning sensation and unlike quite a few of the other similar products, it didn't have the tendency to make your hair fall out in alarming chunks.

It turned out that when Min was liberally spread with Mrs D's and thoroughly scrubbed with the stiff bristled brush, that she was both freckly and blonde. She actually looked slightly less angelic when she was clean but still sweet enough to be instantly adored. She stood next to the pile of clothing she had stripped off to get in the basin and prodded them with a toe. Whatever colour they had been when they started they were now a grubby grey colour, more darning thread than any actual fabric. It was clear that she couldn't put them back on. The dresses that Mulligan had acquired for her were a variety of different sizes, none of which were small enough for Min. As Angel said as she held up the largest one, it was better than them being too small because at least they had enough fabric to sort something out, even if it was ghastly.

Mulligan sat folded into thirds in one corner with his knees under his chin, watching the girls in action. Min had made herself a dress out of a sheet and was sitting near the fire rubbing her arms for warmth as Clara ran the lice comb through her damp hair. She'd been given a second coat of Mrs D's and the smell was permeating through the whole room. Rumour had it that it was the odour alone that stunned the lice and Mulligan could well believe it.

Mulligan was taken in by the gentleness with which Clara pushed the comb into Min's slick hair and gently guided it downwards, patiently stopping to unpick mats and knots as she met them. She didn't tug or curse and Min didn't mewl or whine. Beside them, Angel and Luce were a flurry of activity, altering the dress that was closest to Min's actual size with a tuck here and nip there. They dipped into Mulligan's extensive sewing kit with such confidence and didn't seem to falter at all. To Mulligan, who was not an inconsiderable tailor himself, it seemed almost magical as suddenly they were holding up a slender russet-coloured shift dress delicately trimmed with brocade that had been carefully unpicked from one of the other frocks.

By this time, Min's hair was drying a soft blonde colour and had settled into a gentle wave after its assault by the lice comb. As she wriggled into the dress with the help of Luce and Angel, Mulligan found himself gaping in amazement. It was total transformation the squalid little sewer brat had vanished and been replaced by something far more hygienic. The other three stood back and looked at her with the critical gaze of artists trying to decide if they've finished their masterpiece. Angel gave a little dissatisfied grunt and dived into the suitcase. After a few moments of flailing that saw most of the case contents scattered on to the floor, she emerged looking triumphant with a thin strip of dark green satin in her hand.

"Sash!" she declared by way of explanation and the other two nodded their agreement as she rapped it around Min's tiny waist and tied it off with a modest bow. When she had been finally adorned, Min turned to Mulligan to show herself off. Mulligan was just about to add his approval when the girl smiled wide displaying her teeth or lack of them. Mulligan recoiled, no matter how cute the dimples they could not detract from the ghastly decaying mess in Min's mouth.

"What about her teeth?" was all the Mulligan could manage.

"What about them?" retorted Luce with definite affront in voice.

"Well look at them," returned Mulligan, "she can't go parading around the Merchant's District with a mouth like that." Luce was just about to open her mouth to give Mulligan some very choice instructions when Clara cleared her throat and said,

"No problem guv," Mulligan just looked at her, so she carried on. "Aint no problem at all, there's a chap down the market he'll do 'em for two florins, one and an 'alf if he's down on his luck and outta cider." Mulligan didn't understand. He was too busy staring at Clara, hoping for more explanation, to see Luce giving him a filthy look. When no further information forth coming and Mulligan realised, yet again, that he was the only one who didn't understand he said,

"Do them how?" Clara looked amused as she said,

"Wiv magic, he'll make 'em look all shiny and clean. And there. He does all the hookers on the docks when them big ships come in and anyone what's got a posh con on the cards." Mulligan nodded. Now she said it, he vaguely remembered hearing something like that but not being a front man, his work wasn't really bothered by his dental arrangements. "They aint real or nuffin' just 'llusion'ry like, but it's the look of the thing aint it? Just so long as she aint gotta eat no apples."

That night, as he sat in the living area by the last embers in the range, Mulligan had the feeling that his plan might just work out. However, some things were going to have to change. He looked mournfully over to his bedroom where the four girls had curled up on the palliasse wrapped in the blankets. He'd tried to send them home but he had met with a barrage of objects including Clara's well-reasoned point that there was no point in washing Min so thoroughly just to send them all back to the sewers for the night. That had been the clincher. As he lay down on the rag-rug, he groaned as he found several of the remaining damp patches with his back and legs. Then closed his eyes. Hopefully, it wouldn't take him long to get to sleep.

Chapter 4
The girl who wasn't Min

Mulligan gave up trying to lay down the law with the girls after three or four days and once he'd accepted that he wasn't actually in charge of them things became much easier. The only thing he'd managed to insist on was that the other girls washed as well. Mulligan, for all that he had been born and still lived in the city slums, was not a street-rat and he prided himself that he was generally free of lice, fleas, fungi and other obnoxious free-loading parasites that dwelt in the poor district making life unpleasant-smelling and itchy. Living in such close proximity to the girls, he had found it difficult to keep his distance and when he found himself faced with a single louse looking at him from his comb he had put his foot down. There was no humility or apology in them as they insisted he fetch the water for them. They gave themselves what Mulligan had started to think of as the Mrs Docherty treatment and sat dripping in front of the fire with the well-used nit comb. Ignoring Mulligan's objections, Clara and Angel had re-appropriated the curtain that hung in front of the 'training area' to make themselves dresses and Luce had helped herself to one of his shirts and a pair of his less shabby underpants. Mulligan had tried to get them to wear the spare dresses that still languished in the trunk, but they had insisted that they did not fit - Mulligan suspected out of sheer spite for being made to wash. He'd contemplated washing their old clothes, but in the end he burnt them.

It had taken a little over a week for life in the overcrowded attic room to become normalised. Mulligan had given up trying to evict the girls from his bed and acquired himself some extra padding and blankets. He found that whilst he wasn't overtly fond of any of the girls, having them around the house did have compensations. They didn't complain about things like being cold or hungry, and all the bodies meant the rooms had never been warmer. He had briefly entertained fantasies of the girls cleaning up the place and making it homely and comfortable but these were quickly dashed. None of them were natural homemakers, which in retrospect was unsurprising as none of them had previously had a home to practise on. They willingly did jobs like fetching up water and coal and when presented with food had no troubles cooking it but that was about it.

Angel was clearly the impatient one, already frustrated by the fact that they hadn't seen any action yet and not shy about complaining. Conversely, Luce and Clara had taken to the whole thing like ducks to the village pond. They seemed to revel in the level of detail that was needed to make the con convincing. Mulligan had the basic worked out, but now he could see that his original plan was merely the bare bones and these girls were adding layer upon layer of flesh until it became almost a living breathing entity.

If Mulligan's alter-ego was going to ingratiate himself with what passed for the gentry in Aberddu, then he would need more than just a clean-ish frock coat and a cheeky grin. The bored wives of the rich merchants and the scrag-end duchesses gossiped more freely than just about anyone else in the city and news of a newcomer would spread like fire through summer grasslands. Then, if they were particularly down on entertainment, the newcomer would be a source of almost morbid curiosity. His every movement would be scrutinised and analysed over and over again. The social circle he was trying to infiltrate was used to disgraced aristos and dishonest merchants and all sorts of other people who lie about their status. They knew the signs. For the scheme to work, Mulligan and the girls couldn't afford a moment's slip up - it was almost guaranteed that someone would spot the one time he let himself in through the back of his supposed house or stepped out ungroomed. With this in mind, it was crucial that at no time was the newcomer seen sloping off in the direction of the slums sucking on the arse-end of a roll-up.

To this end, they'd set about procuring a modest but spacious residence in the quiet end of the Merchant district. Mulligan had set aside a certain amount of cash for the set-up and he watched in awe as the girls set about squeezing every last drop of life out of each florin. Upstairs curtains were only needed at the front, and then only linings. The drawing room and dining room were to be furnished, and the corridor as far as the door to the privy in the back yard. If more became necessary, Angel pointed out, then it could be added.

The beauty of shopping at the black market was that generally nobody asked what you were up to - because that was a sure-fire way to be lied to apart from anything else. They called in every favour they were owed and bargained for everything. They skilfully collected all the items together, careful not to buy locally stolen goods - in case it turned out that Mulligan befriended their rightful owner. For his part, Mulligan held the cash and watched them carefully. Every groat was accounted for. He was too impressed by them to trust them not to cream off some cash - mainly because it was what he would have done given the chance.

Min had drawn the very short straw in all of this. Since receiving the Mrs D treatment which revealed her soft blonde curls and freckles, she had become much more recognisable and it was decided by the others that it was far too much of a risk to let her out during daylight hours. After all, how many seven-year-old daughters turn up in a town a month before their poor widowed father to organise living arrangements? She had been very quietly put out at first but after a couple of days, when the others would come back looking shattered and cold she started to almost revel in her enforced confinement.

To pass the time, she threw herself into developing their cover story and practising her reading, speech and elocution using some books that Luce had filched for her. This was particularly difficult because only Angel and Mulligan could read reliably and there had been several strops, one of them from Mulligan, before much literacy had been accomplished at all.

Min came up with endless details for herself and Mulligan to memorise and once all the major arrangements had been made, the girls ganged up on Mulligan - again - and forced him to spend a good portion of each day having 'daddy' lessons.

Nearly a month after they had first followed Mulligan home, the four girls were sitting in front of the glowing range fire. Angel was reading down their lists trying to find something, anything, that still needed doing. Every little detail was covered, right down to the practically empty travelling trunks that would accompany Min and Mulligan in the moving wagon, which Luce and Clara had put rock in to stop anyone picking them up too easily. Min was sitting on her feet to keep them warm, with Annabel her raggy doll tucked firmly under one arm, the way it had been constantly since she had named it just over a week ago. She had been habitually referring to Mulligan as Daddy, with the merest hint of a lisp for the last fortnight and the rest of the character had built up from there. For his part, Daddy Mulligan had at least stopped cringing when she said it.

They were just contemplating going to bed on the scratchy palliasse in the fake bedroom for the last time when Clara furrowed her brow, pulled her knees up to her chin and asked Min,

"Wha's your new name?"

The other three gaped. They'd taken care of every tiny detail. They'd spent ages picking and checking out a family name - Fortescue - that wouldn't draw too much attention. They'd come up with tales of how Min's fake mother Merielle Fortescue finally succumbed to the grips of a fever after her constitution had been weakened by a childhood case of influenza caught from a Jaffrian traveller who had been staying with her parents. They had gone to town on the details of how Min had come by Annabel and why she had picked the name. They had made up stories about the fact that her mummy always called her Tippy - short for tippy toes - and why she did. They'd even thought up what exactly Min would inherit when she reached majority. However, the one thing they didn't seem to have taken into account was that all this detail belonged to a girl who definitely wasn't Min. After several minutes of Clara, Luce and Angel suggesting names, which were getting more and more bizarre as their desperation increased, Min did something she had never done before and told them all to shut up. They were so taken aback that they did just that.

"I'll choose my own name, if you don't mind," she said with tone and confidence, neither of which belonged to Min. "And I shall tell you all in the morning. Good Night."

She got up and flounced off towards the bedroom with Annabel tucked under her arm. Luce was about retort with a mouthful of blunt unpleasantries when Angel poked her in the ribs,

"Leave it," she hissed, adding when Luce looked mutinous, "she's ready."

When Mulligan arrived home late that night he found Luce, Angel and Clara asleep in a muttering, wriggling heap on the hearth rug where he had slept since the girls had taken over. Min was all alone on the mattress with Annabel cuddled up to her chest and her thumb in her mouth. She looked so tiny and frail with her curls half covering her face that for one terrifying moment Mulligan was actually moved by it. He shook himself free before the sentimentality gripped him. Weighing up his options swiftly, he woke Min up and sent her packing, dolly and all, to sleep on the hearth with the others. As he lay himself carefully on the palliasse, and tugged the blanket up, he noted with interest the way the straw beneath him had shifted and reshaped itself to suit the bed's new occupants. It may well have been his imagination, but it seemed to be more comfortable like this. Although perhaps that was because the lumpy old straw mattress was a veritable luxury after nearly a month on the rag-rug and floorboards. He was surprised by how willing he was to sleep all of a sudden. He had expected a restless night, lying awake worrying about details - after all tomorrow morning was the big day when Maurice Fortescue and his daughter started their new life in Aberddu. Maybe Maurice slept more soundly than Mulligan. After all he slept in a feather bed…

Chapter 5
The Fortescue Arrival

Society in Aberddu was unusual, in fact it went beyond unusual in to downright strange. It was what the fashionable débutantes in Albion would probably have termed a 'funny goose'. It was both embryonic and of wildly mongrel origin. As its closest neighbour, Albion should have been the natural model for the fledgling gentry of the new city-state. However, those Albion that had remained after the coup and independence were not desperately enamoured of the Royal Albion Court and replicating it on a smaller and cheaper scale was not their idea of freedom. The next nearest country was Frisia, and as the fat dowagers of the Royal Court would have said, when it came to Frisian High Society it was definitely a case of 'less said the better'.

So, in the middle of the squalling bustling city state with its prosperous dock-lands and its rich, diverse population was an upper-class desperately trying to define themselves whilst forgetting completely about where they had originally come from. The mainstay of the social calendar had been imported from just about every other civilised nation on the continent - Grand Balls and Soiree, Ententes and Banquets of every kind to mark significant dates in pretty much every 'civilised' country but Aberddu. Whilst charming and entertaining, these occasions tended to be so authentically foreign that they did little to aid the floundering local gentry in defining their own traditions. They also had the downside that you simply couldn't guarantee the class of people that would be invited. As well as everyone who was anyone in the Rich Districts, people had an infuriating tendency to invite the great and the good, or sometimes not so good, from the Temples and Guilds of the City to these things. Whilst the

High Priests and their lackeys tended to be okay and had some semblance of decorum and hygiene, the Guilds provided far less reliable representation.

The more self-important establishments such as the Mages Guild and the Merchants Guild tended to trot out whichever minor nobles were not already invited. The Guild Master of the Weavers and Dyers Guild, and his small, round and upwardly mobile wife, attended everything themselves. However, the less rarefied guilds, who were related to more practical trades, tended to struggle; butchers, bakers and blacksmiths having better things to do that sit about in an over-warm room whilst some twiddly musicians mucked about on the lutes and lyres. There had been some horrifying incidents of class-clashing. It was perfectly possible to find yourself at dinner sitting next to a gigantic fowl-smelling oaf with a cauliflower ear and a nose the size of a small Middle Kingdom who had been rammed into a frock coat and given a crash course at eating with cutlery, only to have him lean both elbows on the table, chew with his mouth open and guffaw raucously and belch after each toast.

Rumour had it that the Adventurers Guild sent whoever could be bothered to go, the more unsuitable the better, or at least they had done until Angus the Bastard sat next to the wife of the Alendrian Ambassador, showed her his false teeth and caused her to faint. The Guild Master had received a very stiff letter from the Ambassador and a visit from the High Council. After that they were forced to vet their 'community liaison representatives' more carefully.

The upshot of all this lack of proper Society was that Aberddu didn't yet have its own social calendar, or a 'season' and that meant that unless there was a specific event on the horizon to occupy them, the Rich District was inhabited by thoroughly bored dowagers and twittering débutantes grasping for any social interest they could get hold of. There was basically no good time to make a discrete entrance into Aberddu Society.

To this end, Mulligan and the girls were forced to go to quite extensive lengths to make 'The Fortescue Arrival' feel as authentic as possible. They had acquired a small chaise in the preparations, which had been loaded and driven out of the city through the Poor Quarters - a sure-fire way to make sure none of the idle rich would spot it. They'd parked it up just outside the city walls, thrown a couple of oil-skins over it and slipped the gate guards on the Eastgate a few coins to keep an eye on it overnight. It had been agreed that Luce would drive the trap, because she had the most boyish features and could tuck her hair up to become 'Jack the stable hand'.

Before dawn, they were all up and ready. Min, Mulligan and Luce were heading for the Eastgate to reclaim the cart and change into the costumes already stashed in the back. They would meet Truvalle, the jobbing wizard who'd do the 'business' on their teeth - and the sorry looking nag they'd managed to rustle up for the cart - and drive slowly around to the Southgate. No self-respecting Albion Gent would arrive in Aberddu much before lunch time. They were to wait in the woods near the Southgate for the Noon-bell and then start out.

Clara and Angel had what was arguably the less enviable task. They were to head for the house and make ready without showing themselves. Clara had been elected to be the housemaid - who much to her disgust didn't get a name, never mind a back story as it had been decided this was an unnecessary complication. She did however get a dress and cap and was expected to look obedient, and should they ever have any company to actually wait on them. Angel had point blank refused to act as a servant which had left Clara with little choice.

They had calculated that what they needed to do was throw open the drapes sometime after the morning nine-hour - the furniture in the street-facing rooms had already been set up. Then, at just after ten, Clara in frock and cap, would appear on the step and shake out a rug. At eleven, they were expecting a delivery from a butcher's wagon - 3 hanging half-pigs and some parcels wrapped in paper. The pigs would come straight in to the yard to be taken back in due course, the parcels were all offal - so they stayed. At half past, the crooked wine merchants in Farthing Lane had agreed to deliver four empty crates; three with no wine in and one with no port in. However, as far as Clara was concerned, the piece de resistance of the whole set up would occur at Noon. Two of Mulligan's cronies from the Guild Below had been paid a fair sum to dress up fancy and hire a wagon. They were to arrive at the house at precisely noon and deliver a large parcel covered with a heavy cloth. It was in fact nothing more than a crate of potatoes but that was beside the point; it would have the gossip-mongers practically salivating.

As the morning drew on, and Clara found herself with very little to actually do, she entertained herself by poking around the mostly empty house, drawing patterns in the dust with her finger. The rooms at the back had been left unfurnished and largely ignored by the others. Clara liked to imagine who had lived in them before. The heavy beams smelled strongly of oil and the thick iron bolts that held them together had more than likely not moved for at least fifty years. Judging by the smell and taste of the air in the room, it seemed likely that the house's previous occupant had had little interest in this room. It wasn't an uncommon practice in the merchant's district for the upwardly mobile to purchase an address that they could ill afford, furnish only one or two rooms and move on when sudden wealth or bankruptcy visited them. Judging by the amount of furniture and personal items that had been left here when they moved in, the last occupant had left town in something of a hurry. Clara just hoped that they weren't going to find out why. She was just running her hands along the deep wooden window seat when Angel's voice shattered her imaginings.

"Clara, get down here," she screeched, "We're working not playing."

Glumly Clara trailed downstairs, sore that she had been dragged from her fantasy, Angel's voice ringing in her ears. She knew she was right but that didn't stop Clara grumping about it. It wasn't as though she didn't understand why Angel was so on edge. It was a big day, and also the first time in a long time that Angel had been surrounded by rich people – something she absolutely despised. It wasn't pleasant for her Clara knew that, but that didn't mean Angel had the right to take her discomfort out on everybody else.

She found Angel in the large basement kitchen. It was chilly and damp, the stone floor was cold under her bare feet. The pitiful little fire looked out of place in the heavy iron grate, and it warmed only a tiny area around the hearth. Angel was poking through the supplies with thought to supper

"Put these on," she grunted barely looking up at Clara as she kicked a sack across the floor to her. It contained a grey cotton bodice and an ankle-length brown skirt, as well as a pair of soft leather shoes and a cap that would cover her ears and hair – which had been cropped short the day before, much to Clara annoyance. She stood in front of the feeble fire and changed into the outfit, rolling the skirt at the waist so that it didn't drag on the floor. "Carpet beater's there," barked Angel, not even bothering to look up. "Don't bother waiting for the bells, just go beat a rug."

The party on the other end of the plan were having an equally tense time. They had reached the cart in good time and sorted everything out far quicker than expected. Truvalle had been spot-on punctual and didn't hang about. They'd parked themselves up in a small coppice about three miles from the Southgate and were supposed to wait until just after noon to start their journey.

However, they had been sitting there unoccupied since not long after dawn. None of them were used to inactivity and they were starting to get on each other's nerves.

Min had been in costume - and character- for nearly three hours. She had Annabel firmly wedged under one arm and was currently skipping about the cart playing some bizarre form of hopscotch that Luce didn't recognise. She was singing a silly little rhyme about cats, rabbits, hats and habits under her breath. Presumably she'd picked it up from one of the light-alliance temples.

It was the lisp that irritated Luce the most she thought, as she wound the reins around and around in her hands. Or maybe it was the pigtails, that made Min look so different from her normal, unkempt self. Luce had tried desperately to ignore Min but it wasn't easy, given that the only other thing she could distract herself with was Mulligan and he was so on edge that if Luce had breathed deeply he might well have tried to stab her.

Apparently he was utterly convinced that at any moment the entire plan was going to fall apart around their ears. He seemed to be slowly unravelling. So far everything had gone to plan and he seemed to be waiting for disaster at any moment. He had been twitching all over the place the entire time, apparently under the impression that a gang of off-duty Law Paladins were having a picnic with an unusually zealous militia patrol and a bunch of mind-reading mages just around the corner, and that any minute they would run out of sandwiches and sprint into view waving their swords and asking difficult questions. Perched on the edge of the passenger bench, he scanned the tree line constantly glancing over his shoulder every few minutes to check behind him. Luce would have laughed at him, but she didn't think she dared.

Naturally a placid creature, it took Luce a long while to get to the end of her rope but waiting in this clearing with Min and Mulligan was certainly doing the trick. She had tried every trick she could think of to distract herself but still the twitching and the skipping, lisping and pigtails were thoroughly irritating her. Without a word to the others, as neither of them had directed a word at her in the last forty-five minutes, she hopped down from the cart and wondered away into the trees. This unplanned movement only served fuel Mulligan's paranoia. He gripped the reins of the cart so tight in an effort to contain his temper that his knuckles actually went white. There was no way they could last until the noon-day bells.

Finally, not long after the chimes of the morning eleven-hour floated out of the Temple District and over the city walls, Mulligan cracked. He couldn't wait any longer for a confrontation with the Aberddu do-gooders annual seasonal picnic, it was time they went. Gruffly he barked Luce back into the cart and thrust the reins into her hands. He waved his hand indicating that they should go and without further explanation, they headed off towards the gate.

Mulligan needn't have worried. The tired gate guard let the well-to-do Albion gent and his daughter through on the nod from his sergeant and watched without interest as they turned down the road that would eventually lead them towards the Singer's Bridge. And with that, the Fortescues had arrived.

Chapter 6
Metcalfe

The first official Fortescue outing took place three days after their arrival. Prior to that, the weather had been a bit grim keeping the idle denizens of the Merchant District indoors, gossiping about the comings and goings of the new arrival. There had been plenty to keep them curious, as the girls had arranged for a steady stream of 'tradesmen' to arrive bearing cloth covered bundles that contained nothing of any actual interest. Mulligan, or rather Maurice, had done plenty of to-ing and fro-ing, mostly to the docks for a pint, but as yet Min had remained concealed. Min was going out of her mind with boredom and declared before bed on the second day that she was going out in the morning even if was 'pissing down'. She looked so adamant and cross that Mulligan didn't even bother to scold her use of unladylike language.

As it happened the next morning was clear and fresh, the cool sun throwing a slightly watery light over the city. This morning's outing had been carefully planned to gain the most attention possible amongst the merchant class without arousing any suspicions. First of all they were going strolling. Strolling was one of the very few social events peculiar to Aberddu. The river Ddu that ran through the city, carrying effluent and detritus into the delta and the sea beyond was not a sight to write home about. It was wide and the banks were anything but picturesque. Further upstream, the river ran through the Temple, Trade and Poor districts and its banks were bare earth and stones and usually populated by dozens of people with piles laundry, buckets and stoneware jugs. Across the water from the Merchants district was the Docklands, an even less attractive sight where several large gutters carried waste of all natures into the unsuspecting water. But in the Merchants District, and on the Summer Isle in the delta, where the rich people lived life was different - wizards supplied the water and the laundry was sent out to the trade district. There was no practical need to go down to the river at all and so the banks were lush and green. In a city as chock-a-block as Aberddu green space was a rare luxury, even these inelegant scraps of riverbank in full sight of the warehouse shit-pipes were greatly prized. As such, it had become a sort of custom for the Merchants, their wives and hangers-on to 'take the air' and stroll the bank whenever it was sunny first thing in the morning. Strolling took place between the morning nine and ten hours, a time at which the less well-off would be hard at work but early enough that it allowed the particularly pious to make it up to the Temple District in good time for mid-morning devotions. Therefore, what had started as a pleasant diversion for one or two had suddenly become a status symbol. 'Did you not stroll this morning?' implying that you were needed to work early, and therefore were not as rich or important as you claimed. And so, anybody who wanted people to think they were somebody must be seen strolling on the riverbank.

And so every morning when it wasn't raining, Daddy Fortescue and his little princess went strolling on the banks of the Ddu. The child chatted away and Daddy Fortescue quietly doted on her. No one spoke to them, but that did not mean that they had gone unnoticed. A new face that was growing ever more familiar had caused a certain deal of excitement among the noisy, idle women that filled their time with socialising. Newcomers were always a source of interest. A young man with a small daughter and an intriguing lack of wife had caused quite a stir. By the end of the first week, several of them were first-rate authorities on the tragic circumstances that had led to the reticent young father bringing his charming little girl to live in this big bad city. With extraordinary certainty they set about correcting each other's stories based on exactly zero actual information.

It didn't trouble Mulligan or the girls that so far all the talk had been about them rather than to them. They knew that that would come. Patience in this enterprise was the greatest virtue. They could hardly appear one day and demand dinner invitations the next. If this whole scheme was to work then they would have to conduct themselves with the utmost decorum to allay any possible suspicion. Wait patiently, and these silly socialites would open their doors to them gaily, welcome them warmly into their homes and show them their valuables.

After three weeks, their patience finally paid off. A feeble spring sun was just about visible through the thick woolly clouds that had drenched the City for the best part of a week. As such, the usual strollers had been confined to their drawing rooms and were in much need of amusement. Little Min was skipping along happily, singing to herself under the watchful eye of her father when Mulligan felt someone approaching behind him. He didn't tense he just held his breath quietly and managed to look pleasantly surprised when a delicate hand tapped him on the shoulder.

"Good Morning Mr Fortescue," said a surprisingly deep voice with a clipped Southern Albion tone. Maurice-Mulligan didn't bother asking how she knew his name. Tradesmen could usually be prevailed upon for that kind of information, and some of the ones that they'd used had been genuine. He just summoned up his resolve, smiled pleasantly and in a quiet, gentle tone said,

"Good Morning Madam." He gave a neat little bow and waited politely for the lady in front of him to speak, when she didn't he said, "I'm afraid you have the advantage over me."

This genteel response pleased the lady and she giggled in a manner she probably thought charming and said,

"Of course, I do beg your pardon," she said. "Please let me introduce myself, I'm Lady Metcalfe San Clear," she declared, offering him her hand court-style, palm down. She was medium height, pure-blood human by appearance with a generous round face framed by dozens of rich mahogany ringlets. Not a particularly handsome woman, but her eyes sparkled when Maurice took her hand gently and said graciously,

"Charmed. How may I be of assistance to you Lady Metcalfe San Clear?"

As he did so, Mulligan wondered rather unkindly why she hadn't asked the wizard who had clearly coloured and thickened her hair to remove at least one of her extra chins.

"Do call me Metcalfe," she said with an unwarranted level of familiarity which left Maurice smiling uncomfortably. She seemed oblivious as she went on. "I'm having a little get together tomorrow evening, just some supper and games, that kind of thing. Nothing formal. And what with you being new in town, I thought perhaps you'd like to join us."

"Oh, um," said Maurice clearly taken aback, "that's very kind of you." He paused and looked around for a moment. Min was a little distance away picking daisies. "I'd love to come if it's all right with my daughter."

"Of course," said Metcalfe sweetly as Maurice continued explaining,

"It'd be the first time I'd been out at night since we moved here," he said, "and I want to make sure she's happy to be left with my staff."

"Oh, of course," she said, clearly bewitched by the doting father.

At that point, as if on cue Min skipped over with a posy of flowers in her hand and stood by Mulligan's side. She looked up at Metcalfe wwith the kind of bold scrutinising gaze that only seven year olds, high-ranking priests and hookers can get away with. Then, having taken it all in she made a little curtsey and looked down at her shoes.

"This is Lady Metcalfe San Clear," Maurice told her and Min looked up again but far more coyly this time. "She's just asked me if I'd like to have supper at her house tomorrow night with some of her friends." Min nodded to show she understood. "Would that be okay sweetheart?" Min paused for a moment, frowned and then nodded deliberately.

"Then," said Maurice turning back to Metcalfe with a broad smile, "I'd love to."

"Oh wonderful," squealed Metcalfe, clasping her hands with delight. "I'll send the boy with a card when I get home, and let cook know." She was still babbling when Min pulled on Maurice's sleeve and beckoned to him. He bent down, and she whispered in his ear. Maurice straightened up and waited politely for Metcalfe to finish. When she paused for breath, he took his chance.

"Well," he said, "We really must be going."

"Of course, of course! I'll see you tomorrow evening!" trilled Metcalfe excitedly, bobbing a little to take her leave.

"I look forward to it," said Maurice with a neat little bob of the head.

"Here you go," said Min holding out her posy of slightly wilted wild-flowers and waving them at Metcalfe. "these are for you."

"Oh," said Metcalfe, totally taken aback, "thank you so very much." She took the flowers gingerly, clearly far warier of touching things found on the river bank than Min or Mulligan. "That's very sweet my dear."

"You're welcome," said Min, adding a touch of endearing lisp.

"Perhaps your Daddy will bring you to my house another time," she said in the manner of one who has to force themselves to be good with children, and then as an afterthought added "You really must tell me your name."

"Miss Tabitha Julieta Fortescue," announced Min proudly.

"Well," said Metcalfe, in the kind of singsong voice that most people would only use on a lap-dog, "Miss Tabitha, it's been very nice to meet you. Good bye!"

"Good bye," said Tabitha pleasantly, carefully saying nothing else and Metcalfe turned and wafted off into the crowd, a rich exotic floral scent trailing behind her. Maurice and Tabitha paused for a moment and watched her go, they could practically see her rubbing her hands together in glee – she had secured Maurice Fortescue's début occasion. For her, and all the other idle baggages on the social circuit, this was the social coup of the season.

For Mulligan and Min, it was far more important. Mulligan turned to Min and with uncharacteristic affection, squeezed her shoulder. As he watched the ample damask-clad backside hurrying away through the crowd, he lost himself for a moment and cracked a broad smile. They were in, the ball was rolling.

Min, Angel and Clara had been sitting on the kitchen hearth rug waiting for the news of Mr Fortescue's first official outing since Luce had left with the cart to collect him over an hour ago. Min, whose hair was still in the tight little pigtails she had been wearing all day, had drawn her knees up under her chin and was resting her cheek on them. She had her left thumb in her mouth, a habit that she taken to of late. It made Angel tut but she said nothing.

Both Angel and Clara were far more excited about the whole thing that Min, although Angel didn't show it. She just sat cross-legged on the hearth rug watching the door and waiting. Clara, far less reserved in her comportment, had sprawled over the remaining space on the hearth. Both Clara and Angel were desperate for this whole scheme to move forward. They had seen very little of the Merchant District and were forced to make themselves extremely scarce. The only outings they got involved daily chores, and most of those required nothing more interesting that a trip down the sewer hatch in the back yard. Finally, something more interesting seemed to be afoot and they were more than ready for a piece of the action.

It was about midnight when Mulligan finally returned from the Metcalfe San Clears, even though he had sworn up and down that he would make his excuses and leave just after the evening eleven hour. Luce was shivering and furious as she stamped into the house through the kitchen door. She had been forced to wait outside with the chaise for over an hour on the chilly spring night without a cloak. She dumped herself down in front of the fire, shoving Clara's legs aside to make enough space. Clara sat up expectantly as the girls listened to the sounds of Mulligan upstairs, entering the house through the front door and clumsily removing his frock coat and boots.

It seemed like an age as they waited for him to make his way down to the kitchen. It was by far the warmest room in the draughty house so they spent the majority of their time in there. When he finally did appear it was clear that he had been plied with wine. He was swaying and rosy, his eyes swimming as he concentrated on the steps down. In spite of his obvious inebriation he had still had the forethought to remove his elegant and expensive top layers, leaving him dressed in nothing but his wool combinations and thick grey stockings.

Clara snorted with amusement. It was hilarious how the posh-knobs alcohol didn't agree with those of the less elegant classes. Even massive dockers, who could drink a keg of cheap ale, rat tails and all, and still remember all the words to the much-loved folk ballad 'Well-boiled ham' would be found rosy-nosed, blood shot and weeping after even three or four delicate glasses of the Schlastz '89 or similar. Paravelian liquor was all the rage with the Aberddu posh-knobs because it was imported, sophisticated, expensive and most importantly lethally strong, which is presumably why it was bottled in thick glass instead of stoneware and stoppered with wax-covered corks. As Mulligan wove his way slowly across the room to one of the hard-backed chair at the table, all the girls turned to him with rapt attention, waiting for what he had to say.

Min and Clara listened with intense interest as Mulligan described who had been there and what had happened. They bombarded him with questions and hung on every word of his answers. Luce, who was still annoyed, didn't say much. She just kept shuffling closer and closer to the fire in an unsuccessful attempt to make Mulligan feel guilty about how cold she was. Angel, who had no interest in the lives of the rich, grew more and more impatient until eventually she snapped,

"So, did you do anything but guzzle yourself silly? Or was this all a waste of time?" Her sharp words deflated the mood like a pin stabbing a balloon and Mulligan seemed to sober up somewhat.

"Yes," he said tersely narrowing his eyes. His tone was cold and officious as he gave the details. "Whilst you were sitting here by the fire, I put my arse on the line and let myself be bored rigid by Metcalfe's spinster sister and some woman called Rosmalda whose husband died in the Summer of Fire. I have three more invitations including one for Tabitha and a very clear idea of where the Metcalfe San Clear valuables are kept. Anything else?" Angel glowered at him but didn't dignify him with a response. The excitement had crystallised into a chilly tension. Clara cleared her throat uncomfortably and muttered,

"Well, tha's good then, so when do we start?"

"Not yet," said Min with urgency.

"And why not?" retorted Angel coldly as though the thought the mere suggestion of waiting was ridiculous.

"Suspicion," said Min quietly but with confidence. Angel narrowed her eyes. "Think it through. We've only just turned up in the area. If there is suddenly a crime wave targeting our gracious hosts, it won't take a genius to join the dots and, in three months' time, point the finger at us." Min's accidentally patronising tone had clearly irritated Angel, her lips thinned and whitened.

"We're going to need to wait at least six weeks, maybe a little more. Until some great big fancy ball or something maybe. That'll give us plenty of cover." Clara sighed and Angel just looked away. It was easy for Min, she would have plenty to do in that time, whilst Clara and Angel were basically confined to the house. The worst thing about it was that both of them knew she was right.

Chapter 7
Ratatatat

Life in the Merchants Quarter started to normalise, just as it had in Mulligan's rooms. Over the next few weeks the five of them started to drop into routine as they waited for time to pass. Min and Mulligan were rarely at home these days. The handy thing about Maurice Fortescue supposedly being a widower was that no one expected return invitations, because clearly the poor man had enough on his plate with his daughter to care for never mind entertaining. As Mulligan had quite confidently stated the night after his first outing, he was well in with the women of the Quarter and at the top of everybody's social list. He had been to afternoon tea – a meal that none of them knew existed until now - with every notable woman in the District, he had been to supper with their husbands, been treated to liquor from across the continent and offered a whole array of different types of tobacco. Clara had been forced to mend the holes in his breeches caused by an ill-advised experiment with Jaffrian snuff.

He'd had more large meals in the last few weeks than he'd previously had in his entire life. Clara had taken to ribbing him about the fact he was starting to develop jowls and a paunch. Any more, she pointed out to him jovially, and she'd have to adjust his breeches. Mulligan took the jape in jest but it was clear that on some level he was unamused by it.

Min had, at first, thought of herself only as ornamentation. Like the others, she hadn't realised that the children of the Merchants Quarter had a fuller social calendar than most of the adults. Metcalfe, who had seized on Maurice Fortescue as new marriageable flesh, had set about inserting both of them neatly and deeply into her circle's social whirl. Initially Min had been forced to accompany

Mulligan on one or two outings during the afternoons, and had had to do little else but hold his hand and look charming in pigtails. She hadn't really paid attention to the people around her, only faintly aware of herself as a source of interest and intrigue, too busy making note of her surroundings and their potential value. She had been introduced to other children and shyly waved at them in greeting but amongst the adults they were seen but not heard, so she had not really made any acquaintances never mind friends.

However, yesterday she, or rather Mulligan on her behalf, had received the invitation - via messenger boy no less - to afternoon tea and entertainment in the nursery at the Town House of Lady Callingham-Henry. Min vaguely recalled that she was a rangy blonde woman with an unfortunate nose and a constant look of mild displeasure. She couldn't recall her daughter at all.

Min was actually nervous about Tabitha's first Nursery Tea - and it was a sensation that she wasn't used to and didn't much like. Having only recently discovered the existence of afternoon tea, she had no idea what to expect and considered for a fleeting moment pleading with Mulligan to make the excuse that she had chicken pox or scrofula or something else unpleasant and contagious, so that she didn't have to go. Then she took a deep breath and pulled herself together. It was a children's tea party; how difficult could it be?

She had carefully picked out a suitable dress for Tabitha, a simple but well-made green pinafore with a large pocket on the front and slightly ruffled sleeves. She'd even fished out matching ribbons. This dress was her favourite of Tabitha's wardrobe, far better than any of the others they'd managed to get hold or cobble together from scraps, some of which had appalling patterns on the fabric which were not for public display. She'd had a bath unprompted and persuaded Clara to brush and plait her hair with the matching ribbons. She skittered about the kitchen getting under Clara's feet until Clara told her off and sent her upstairs out of the way.

That was why she found herself sitting on a stool in the drawing room just as the afternoon one hour chimed even though they weren't due to leave until two. She filled the time by alternately twitching her leg and worrying about the fact she couldn't read very well and wondering whether it was acceptable to take Annabel the raggy-doll to the tea party with her. Mulligan, or rather Maurice, was supposed to drop her off between two and half past on his way to a gathering, in another house, for the parents of all the children who were at the tea. Mulligan seemed far more relaxed about his part in this outing and it made

Min feel slightly stupid when he appeared nonchantly about a quarter of an hour before they were due to leave. She had to concentrate to pull herself back into character, and much to Mulligan's irritation spent the last fifteen minutes before the two-hour bell singing the cats, rabbits, hats, habits nonsense rhyme that he was coming to despise. Trying not to lose his temper, he closed his eyes and visualised the money.

Tabitha hopped down from the Fortescue trap with blithe agility and scuttled up the stone steps to the open front door. There was an austere woman in a long plain brown dress standing in the doorway, she had a rigid smile and look of cool irritation in her eyes. She was not Lady Callingham-Henry and she did not feel the need to introduce herself to the diminutive guests. Judging by the sizeable chatelaine hanging from her girdle she was the housekeeper, and apparently felt that this particular task was beneath her. She ushered Tabitha, and a scrawny pale-looking boy who had arrived just after her, into the entrance hall where they were divested of outdoor clothes by two slightly more amiable maids who were showing them upstairs in batches of two or three. Tabitha let herself be uncloaked placidly and then waited patiently, thumb in mouth, for the boy, who kept coughing and wheezing and had to be extracted from several layers of outer clothing.

As they entered the nursery wing, via a discrete staircase tucked around a corner in a long plush corridor, they could hear that the 'entertainment' was already well under way. Even before she had stepped through the door, Min realised she was the world she was entering was far more complex and dangerous than any sewer tunnel she had ever set foot in - because down there no one pretended to be anything other than a crook and it was safe to assume everything was trying to kill you. Here, with all the fancy rugs on polished boards and sweet little painting, it was not so easy to tell.

"Go on," encouraged the smiling maid, who Min judged couldn't have been that much older than her although properly nourished and therefore fully grown. "Everyone's in there," she said kindly with a soft nudge to Min and her sickly companion - both of whom were hanging back reluctantly. Min let out a deep breath and took a few tentative steps into the noisy room, sniffing audibly and fiddling with his embroidered handkerchief her companion followed on. There were about a dozen and a half children already there, sitting in a large circle chanting a rhyme and clapping their hands on their knees, as one girl wearing a blindfold over her eyes stood in the centre of the circle. At the end of the rhyme everyone knocked enthusiastically on the floor with one fist and then fell quiet. One of the girls sitting behind the blindfolded one, speaking in a clearly assumed voice, said

"Ratatatat".

The blindfolded girl span around on her heal and paused, considering.

"Alisandra," she said in a clipped, decided fashion and the girl who'd spoken sighed and said,

"Yes."

"Ha!" said the girl in the middle triumphantly. "My go again." She adjusted her blindfold and the circle set about choosing another contestant. Actually, that wasn't quite right, thought Min as she surveyed the game that neither she nor her coughing companion had yet been invited to play. It wasn't the circle deciding, it was three or four girls who flapped between themselves and then pointed with condescending beneficence at their chosen victim - a freckly lad with a round spirited face and thick red hair. Clearly, they wanted to catch out the blindfolded player. He grinned broadly at the extended largesse and joined in as soon as the slighted Alisandra started up the rhyme.

"Ratatatat a knock on the door, ratatatat who is it for? Ratatatat come play at our game, here's the voice, now what's the name?" Then excitably they all 'ratatatat-ed' on the floor and the ginger boy spoke his piece.

It was clear from the sudden thinness of the mouth below the blindfold that player was displeased, probably because she was stumped.

"Carruthers," she said sharply,

"No," said the boy in the same voice he had used before. She paused then, to ponder,

"Hmm," she said, "Okay then, Alfric."

"No," said the boy, this time a gleeful chuckle in his reply. This displeased the blindfolded girl even more, a scowl taking over what was visible of her face.

"Fine," she retorted with a whine in her voice, folding her arms to indicate her irritation. Evidently she wanted to convey that she was not bothered by losing but managed not only to do the opposite, she also made herself look like a petulant, sore loser into the bargain. "Well, I don't know," she continued, "Aloysius then."

"No," said the boy in his real voice this time, "Aloysius isn't even here yet."

This was the wrong thing to say apparently, as the girl ripped off her blind-fold crossly and glared at the triumphant challenger. "Well, how was I supposed to know that," she sneered throwing the scarf at him dismissively, "I should have known it would be you Edgar." Clearly, there was some enmity there, Min noted, as the girl glowered at the boy before plonking herself inelegantly down between her cronies.

"Stop, stop," said a voice from the corner, and a soft-faced woman with danc-ing eyes stood up. Min thought this must be the Challingham-Henry governess.

"Let's all move around to let the newcomers in." At this point everybody turned to stare at Min and the coughing boy, who was recognised instantly.

"Hey, Al I thought you weren't coming!" called Edgar exuberantly, "come sit here." Apparently, this was the fabled Aloysius, who trotted off to his saved space without a second look. Tabitha, on the other hand who knew nobody's name - apart from Alisandra, Edgar and Aloysius - just stood there uneasily like the show-stopper at a freak-show, shifting her weight from foot to foot. No one beckoned to her, or even looked her in the eyes. All of the girls were looking at her, but not in a friendly welcoming way. They were examining every inch of her, comparing her clothes and appearance unfavourably to some commonly agreed standard. A couple of the bossy girls who had orchestrated the 'Edgar gambit' shot her a quick, vulpine smile that was not mistaken for a gesture of friendship by the street-savvy Min.

Tabitha didn't know what to do, she looked around for any familiar face and found none. Luckily, at this point the soft-face governess stepped in. Bending low so that her perfectly formed ear was on Tabitha's level she whispered,

"What's your name poppet?"

"Tabitha Fortescue," divulged Min in a hoarse whisper.

"Okay," said the Governess straightening up, leaving the fragrance of rose oil hanging in the air where she had been. "This is Tabitha Fortescue everybody," this information provoked no warmer response and the governess was forced to instruct two girls to shift apart so that Tabitha could sit down between them. After a brief dispute, that left Tabitha feeling distinctly uncomfortable they both moved up together leaving more than ample space for the strange girl in the green dress to sit down next to the ever-wheezing Aloysius.

By this point, Tabitha would quite have liked to burst into tears but she didn't, mainly because Min didn't really know how. She just sat down where she was bid and joined in slowly. Luckily, Min was a fast learner, although she had not picked up everything from the two repetitions she had seen and her ineptitude, as well as her plain dress and ribbons, was drawing unkindly amused looks from the 'in-crowd' girls. Min was well aware that her face did not fit, and that she wouldn't be getting a turn at this or any of the other games. Tabitha could do very little but play along and try to ignore them, which was probably more constructive than what Min had in mind - which made it necessary for Tabitha to sit on her hands when she wasn't clapping or knocking.

After this first unpleasant experience Min, or rather Tabitha, was invited to most of the events that followed. She simply created herself a persona that protected her from the harsh glares and snide whispering of the 'in-crowd' girls led by the Challingham-Henry heiress who turned out to be the stroppy blindfold wearing girl who couldn't identify Edgar. Her name was Grace, which Min considered to be extremely ironic, because she had absolutely none. There were, however, other children on the circuit glad of new company, particularly any that wasn't in favour with Lady Grace and her gang, because it meant fresh meat for the sneering and belittlement. She made a few acquaintances, but she was well aware that most of the underdog crowd stayed away for fear of being targeted for being too chummy with the girl in the cheap dress.

With outings to the park, picnics and playing in the nurseries of vast opulent houses Min was starting to find it increasingly difficult to snap out of her act as Miss Tabitha, the curious and delightfully vague seven-year-old daughter. She too had been introduced to the world of food served at tables, food you could identify.

After some initial confusion, she quickly developed a taste for what turned out to be the ultimate in nursery tea staples: fresh bread, butter and jam. These were three things that Min had never, in her life, encountered. She'd had bread obviously, but poor-quarter bread was flat, gritty and tough. It filled you up but it was best eaten at night because of the lethargy it produced as your body tried to digest it. Butter she'd heard of but never actually seen and jam was something that she had not even imagined. It was divine. Sweet mushy pulp with a slight piquancy she couldn't put her finger on, and – this had left her nearly apoplectic with delight – it came in different flavours and colours.

She too had noticeably put on weight, even in this short time. Clara hoped that she had been minding her table manners. Stuffing her face as though it was going out of fashion was something that would make others very suspicious. She had meant to mention it to Min in passing but she didn't really see her much anymore. Miss Tabitha tended to keep to the furnished rooms upstairs where the bright daylight streamed through the long windows in the mornings making the rooms pleasant, airy and sun-warmed. She would sit on the hearth rug even when the fire wasn't burning and entertain herself with whatever she could find. She still appeared in the kitchen at meal times, even though Clara found it hard to believe that she was hungry, or when it was cold enough that she required a fire.

One afternoon, when Min had been taken to see Violetta, the sulky younger daughter of Lord and Lady Van Garadi, Clara was in the kitchen with a pile of her dresses on the kitchen table. At least, she thought with resigned amusement, these are loose-fitting enough that she'll have to put on quite a substantial amount of weight before I have to let them out. She was heating a pan of water so she could wash them – Gods only knew was it was Min did in them but every single one was grubby and she couldn't very well go out in grubby clothes. Clara was hoping that once she'd pounded them clean, the water might be warm enough that she could have a quick once over in it herself.

As she waited, she idly checked for tears and holes. Given the state of these clothes, she wouldn't have been surprised if there were a few already and she wanted to keep up with them. Checking in the pockets of one of the better dresses she found that they were inexplicably sticky and sweet smelling. There was a light brown smear of something on the fabric, some of which had transferred itself to her fingers. She sniffed it, decided it was not poisonous and licked it. It was a sparse scraping but still enough for her to taste the delicious sweetness. If that was what they fed rich children, no wonder Min was getting fatter. She was almost loathed to wash it off and, whilst she waited for the water to warm up, gave in to the temptation to suck the rest of it from the cloth.

Whilst Mulligan and Min enjoyed the social whirl of being new in Town, life was not nearly as exciting for Clara, Luce and Angel. As stable-lad, Luce had taken on the duty of caring for the horse – such as it was. They'd had to have it re-enchanted by Truvalle on average once a week, which was an expense they hadn't accounted for, having naively assumed that once they'd arrived they'd be walking everywhere. The wizard did not take kindly to Luce suggesting he should give them credit and so they'd be forced to pay up front. This money was taken from the meagre funds with which Angel and Clara had been managing the housekeeping and was reflected in the food, or lack thereof, that appeared at meal times. Clara had hoped that Min and Mulligan, on the days when they were out socialising, would have the decency not to eat so much at home but she found this hope to be a false one.

Clara had taken to getting straight up into her maid's outfit after they had been caught out by something else they didn't know about the Rich: the practice of calling. Apparently, after lunch between the afternoon two and four hours, was 'calling time', during which it was perfectly accepted to show up at someone's house unannounced and expect to be greeted with mead, oatcakes and open arms. This was the time when the Merchant's Quarter gossip-engine really built up steam. Two or three times a week, children would generally be dispatched to one location, all the 'in-crowd' women would gather for tea at another house, and any gentlemen that were rich enough to be idle in the afternoons would join up for a couple of peaceful wife-free hours somewhere else again. They had learned this about two weeks after Mulligan's first outing, when Lord Metcalfe San Clears 'man' – whose name Mulligan could only hazard as 'Rubard' - appeared on the steps and rang the bell. This sent Clara and Luce in to a total panic as neither of them were correctly dressed because they hadn't expected to be on show all day. Luckily, Angel had kept a cool head and produced Clara's cap and skirt in time for her to hastily throw them on and answer the door. Mulligan, who'd had a skin-full of Paravelian Brandy the night before, was still in his room so Clara had thanked 'Rubard' profusely for the invitation and promised to convey the message to Mr Fortescue when he returned 'from busy-ness'.

After this, they done some research and concluded that it would be better if Clara was on duty all the time. Grudgingly she'd agreed – what else could she do. She was forced to leave the job of off-site errands, mostly to the Black Market, to the evermore stolid Angel.

It was a disparate existence, each of them enfolding themselves in their own little world and Clara was starting to feel strangely isolated. Mulligan and Min seemed to feel that socialising was hard enough work when it came to the sharing of duties and when he was in the house Mulligan tended to keep to his room. Angel was often out fetching things, navigating the sewer network alone was a complex business, and Luce seemed to have made looking after one decrepit horse into an art form that took nearly all day. Clara had plenty to keep her occupied –cooking, cleaning, washing, mending and of course answering the door, all fell to her. She had even organised things so that they could now take callers – callers who liked somewhat overdone oatcakes but callers none the less. She was often last to bed, so that she had to nudge Angel and Luce aside to make space for her on the large double mattress they all shared. Min had long since stopped sleeping with them and no one had questioned it, she had gained some extremely irritating habits of late and if she wanted to sleep alone wrapped in a quilt on the other side of the room then so be it.

It was fair to say that there was an atmosphere of tense boredom hanging over the house. It came to a head one night in the seventh week when Mulligan and Min were both in for supper. Angel had vanished down the sewer hatch not long after the morning eleven hour had chimed that morning and hadn't returned by sundown. Clara decided to serve dinner anyway – which was two day old pease pottage with bits of liver. She'd perfected the art of large pan cooking quite nicely in the last month or so, so it was plentiful and not exactly awful. Everyone apart from Angel was sitting around the table in the kitchen; a rare occurrence that actually made Clara smile as she dolloped the stiff pudding on to the plates and passed them out. Mulligan and Min, who hadn't quite vanished into the upper spheres just yet, set about their dinner with gratitude but less haste than Luce and Clara. There was enough left in the pan for Angel when she eventually reappeared, although Clara thought rebelliously, if that wasn't before bed time then she might lose out.

They didn't chat. They had never really chatted before they came to the Merchants District anyway. They had mostly talked business, which didn't need discussing now. Mulligan had an invite to the Al Rahiri Dinner the following evening and Min was to be accompanying him. They were ready, nothing more to say. They were half way through the meal when the back door banged open and Angel stomped into the kitchen looking damp and cross. She flung her heavy coat off in the corner and strode up to the table where she snatched up the empty wooden dish that had been left for her. Greedily she helped herself to what was left of the pottage, scraping the pan thoroughly and then dumped her plate down in front of the empty chair. She was clearly angry but none of the others really warned to pry, because she was likely to spew forth such a stream of bilious thoughts that it would ruin the companionable tranquillity.

The poorly repressed fury she exuded as she sat there managed to do that all on its own. After she had finished her portion of pease, she reached over and pointedly helped herself to some of what was still sitting on Mulligan's plate. He opened his mouth to object but, seeing the poisonous glint in her eyes, thought better of it.

"So," she started dangerously, "When do we start?"

"Oh," said Mulligan scraping what was left of his supper into a small pile in the centre of his dish. "Um, I hadn't really thought about it, a couple of weeks or so I guess."

"A couple of weeks?" whispered Angel icily, "A couple of weeks? What's the delay this time?"

"Oh, um, er," spluttered Mulligan, staring intently at the small pale mound of pease he'd made. "Well, you know…"

"No," snapped Angel, "no I don't know. I have no idea why you're still delaying except that obviously you're enjoying yourself." She said the words enjoying yourself with so much venom that they almost burned. "It's quite clear that you've more than settled in to your new life, must be lovely to see all that food, all that booze, all those lonely widows and comfortable, homely spinsters with buckets of money just dying for a husband, clamouring over you. Perhaps you've changed your mind about this whole thing, think it would be easier just to get married and ditch the rest of us?" Mulligan, who still hadn't finished his pease was just staring at her stupidly, totally speechless. It was true that he had been enjoying the high life, but he'd never thought of himself as anything other than a tourist. Now she mentioned it, marrying one of those soft and cuddly spinsters with their wobbly chins and wide eyes would have been a much more sensible plan, certainly much less effort than this whole palaver. Angel took his silence for capitulation. Clara looked away, not wanting to make eye contact with the enraged Angel and to her horror she saw that Min actually had tears in her eyes. She was blinking furiously and trying to hide her face but Clara wasn't fooled. Angel pressed on, either unaware or unbothered that she'd brought everything to a standstill.

"You're out tomorrow night aren't you? Some dinner or other no doubt," she scowled, "We'll start then." With that, she helped herself to the remains of Mulligan's dinner.

Chapter 8
The Al Rahiri Dinner

The Al Rahiri Banquet had been discussed at length. This was hardly a surprise as the Al Rahiris themselves were generally much discussed. They had arrived in the District direct from Arabi about eighteen months previously. At that time, the wife spoke only her native tongue and even though there was no 'Aberddu' way as such, it was obvious to the other residents of the Merchants Quarter that whichever way the Al Rahiris did things it was most definitely not the Aberddu way. It wasn't that people were openly hostile to them, they were in general very polite and helpful but it was clear that whilst they had come from a great range of Western nations that lived in the same climates and had the same kinds of clothing and diet, they were strangely uncomfortable in the presence of people of equal wealth and standing who were so very far from home.

The wife didn't wear a corset. In fact, both of them dressed in opulently dyed, loose-fitting silks. They had food specially imported for them. In the summer - at first at least- they had not worn shoes. Having arrived in August, when the sun beat down on the city and the buildings held the warmth well, they were comfortable. Some of the more ample matrons had suggested, not exactly unkindly, that when they were first met with the western winter they would return to Arabi on the first caravan going East. None of their husbands bothered listening to them, or they would have been forced to point out that getting a caravan back East would have been both easy and pointless as Mr Al Rahiri pretty much had the monopoly on East-West import into Aberddu and out across the sea to Aragon and Nortrol.

It was a strange kind of polite ignorance that kept the Al Rahiris at arm's length. No one knew what they ate or what kind of hours they kept. No one was even sure that they'd be able to get the wife to understand them. Whilst they were highly intrigued by the couple, they were not prepared to accept them into their homes with undue haste. More than anything they feared it may lead to nothing more than an uncomfortable and embarrassed silence.

It had taken six months for Aberddu City's in-crowd, which Mulligan had started to think of as 'the Metcalfe set', to invite them anywhere and it was Metcalfe herself that plucked up the courage to make the first invitation after running into Mrs Al Rahiri, whose name it turned out was Jali, at the Weavers and Dyers Guild perusing the same newly arrived batch of muslins and silks. After that, when Metcalfe had discovered that in fact Jali and her husband Kaseem drank tea, were prepared to keep local hours and ate 'normal' food, they were invited more freely to social events, although they were by no means part of the 'usual crowd' as Maurice Fortescue had swiftly become.

Tonight was much talked of because it was the first time that the Al Rahiris had opened their doors to so many people all at once. Until now, they had received company one or two at time and generally only as far as the drawing room - which was disappointingly western. Already tongues were wagging about the evening's entertainment as it was common knowledge that the Al Rahiri's had taken delivery of several exciting parcels. In addition to this, they had moved against local tradition and invited all the children as well.

Maurice Fortescue already had a reputation for arriving early, which is to say that Mulligan had a tendency to show up to gatherings at the given time and not later. It was testament to the impression the Fortescues had made amongst the Metcalfe set that this was seen as an endearing habit to be teased rather than an ignorant faux pas to be censured. As always, Maurice Fortescue was dressed and ready in good time, and little Tabby was bouncing at his side. He was sleek in a new frock coat that Angel had *acquired* a couple of weeks previously and he had been saving for a special occasion. Tabitha was neatly but plainly turned out in a simple clean shift that Clara had produced for the evening and two wispy little pigtails tied in green ribbon. The invitation had said seven o clock, so they waited in the drawing room until the evening bell rang the hour and then Luce, hair tucked up under her cap as always, brought the trap around.

It couldn't have taken them more than ten minutes at trotting speed to get to the Al Rahiri's opulent town house on the far side of the district. From the outside it looked like any other. It was well-positioned, with a clear view to the sea. On seeing it, Mulligan's first thought was that it must be bitterly cold when the winds blew off the Aragon Straits in February. Luce rolled the cart right up to the steps that lead up to the heavy oak door and halted the nag.

"I'll be here at midnight," she grumbled, as the Fortescues alighted, "and I'll not wait this time," but Mulligan and Min ignored her, they were already too taken up in the evening.

Much to Maurice's surprise, he was by no means the first person to arrive. It seemed that for a look at the Al Rahiri house, even Metcalfe herself would rouse herself to get ready on time. The Al Rahiris greeted them warmly at the door smiling widely and bowing low.

"Mr Fortescue, you are most welcome," said Mr Al Rahiri in a low, pleasant sing-song tone as a silent servant discretely took their cloaks. "I am Kaseem and this is my wife Jali. Come in and make yourself comfortable." Maurice smiled back. It was a genuine if slightly reserved smile, but his eyes gleamed in appreciation of the welcome. Tabitha, who had firm hold of his hand looked shyly back at them both and swayed from side to side.

"You are also most welcome young lady," said Mrs Al Rahiri, holding out her hand to the shy child. She had a sweet comfortable voice that seemed to fit her soft round face. Her eyes danced as she looked at the little girl and Tabitha, who had not held her mother's hand for over a year, reached out and took the soft hand offered to her. With contented compliance, Tabitha allowed Mrs Al Rahiri to lead her away into a back room, leaving Mr Al Rahiri alone with Mr Fortescue.

"Do go through," said the ebullient host gesturing flamboyantly with a widely spread arm, "Someone will offer you hospitality."

Maurice found himself being ushered into a large open room that was already full of people mulling with intrigue. Both the room and the crowd were interesting to Maurice. In a western household, this room would have been kept bland and empty of furniture as it had been designed as a ball room. The Al Rahiris, however, had decorated it lavishly with fine silk hangings and dozens of succulent looking plants in tall terracotta planters. Around the edge of the room were half a dozen or so low backless couches and a vast collection of floor cushions. The room was softly lit by flames burning in stoneware dishes a foot across supported by intricately carved dark wood stands that stood about the height of a twelve-year-old child. The flames burned high and bright and clear unlike the oil lamps normally used in Aberddu for lanterns and immediately Mulligan wondered what they used for fuel.

Perhaps the most striking thing about the room were the carpets. In spite of the cold weather prevalent on this half of the continent, floor coverings in the west had not really progressed far beyond straw, rushes and rag-rugs. In the orient things were different. They had spent hundreds of years studying silk and had made it into every kind of fabric they could think of, including these stunningly-coloured carpets, so beautiful that the westerners were nervous of standing on them. They were clustered in groups around the edge of the rugs and in spite of the surprisingly large number of people were making very little noise.

Maurice recognised pretty much all the faces as they whispered to one another and gazed about in awe. Moving among the crowd were two or three deferential young women dressed in bright orange silks and laden with trays of crystal cups filled with deep red liquid. Some variety of fruit and wine punch probably thought Maurice as they passed by and he took one. Tonight he would have to forego most of usual pleasures; he was working and drinking wouldn't help - but one glass wouldn't hurt. After all, if he turned down the hospitality all together that would be sure to draw suspicion.

Tabitha found herself in a different softly light room at the back of the house. About twenty-five small candle lanterns hanging high in the rafters, flickering gently and casting speckled shadows on the ceiling. There were about a dozen children already there playing hopscotch on a chalk court that had been marked on the floor. She had never seen a floor like it, rather than dirt, cobbles or flag-stones it was covered with red-brown tiles that made little noise under foot and was clearly warm - most of the children were bare foot as they skipped happily around the room. At the far end, there was a low table about a foot and a half from the floor. It was laden with dishes and trays that were covered in muslin Tabitha thought this was probably to keep the food a surprise. At one side of the room, there were two solid-looking women in respectable western clothing who watched over the happy throng. One of them hovered beside a small table with two large clay pitchers and a stack of earthenware beakers on it.

"Milk and juice," said Jali sweetly, pointing to the jugs, "enjoy yourself." She gave Tabitha a small smile and a gentle nudge and with that she floated away, leaving the scent of honey suckle blossoms in her wake. Tabitha smiled, fresh milk was becoming her favourite thing. She skipped off towards the woman with custody of the jugs.

Maurice paid careful attention to the crowd as it grew, making note of each new arrival, taking a silent inventory of the jewels and trinkets on display. It was not a sophisticated plan to be sure, but it was clever enough, he just needed to pay attention. Come eleven o clock, he would select a handful of targets who had drunk plenty and palm whatever he could reach. For now, he stood to the side and calmly observed. He was amused by how many of the crowd were here early, looking around at how the other half lived. He could hear them muttering words like 'Ka-leaf' and 'Ee-mir' and 'is that the same as a Duke or an Earl?' It seemed, that for all that the Al Rahiris went by the titles Mr and Mrs in town, they were in fact nobility - and more genuinely so than many in the room. There were more than a few noses that were slowly being pushed out of joint.

Metcalfe at least, was in fine fettle. She had had a new silk gown of distinctly oriental cut made especially for the evening. She was usually trussed up like a turkey for the spit - her ample figure needed all the corseting it could get. Perhaps, Maurice mused, she was enjoying the freedom. Apart from the loose silk gown, she was dressed in the usual manner - a delicious torrent of mahogany curls on her head and jewels dripping from everywhere she could get them to sit still. He couldn't see what she wore on her feet as she bounded over to Maurice with a gleam in her eye.

"Maurice!" she exclaimed as though they hadn't seen each other for months when in truth it had been five days ago at Lord Marriot's luncheon. "So good to see you."

"Metcalfe," he said taking her out-stretched hand and bestowing a delicate kiss on it with his now trademark coyness. "Good Evening."

"And Tabby?" she said jovially, "did you bring her with you?"

"Of course," said Maurice, well aware that Metcalfe found the doting father act highly charming. "She has a new dress and ribbons for the evening." A gentle smile that accompanied this revelation, delivering this calculated boast as though it were simple conversation. Mulligan, watching himself play the part of Maurice with confidence and, dare he say it, aplomb congratulated himself on the details of his performance.

Metcalfe drained her cup, leaned in close and whispered conspiratorially, "I have someone for you to meet."

"As you wish," said Maurice, well aware what was coming next and prepared to quietly indulge this woman's zealous need to play matchmaker for him.

"Come with me," she chuckled, guiding him by the elbow towards the far end of the room. "To meet a good friend of mine, tragically widowed in the summer of fire. She's normally too busy for socialising but tonight she's made an exception."

"Fascinating," said Maurice mildly, as Mulligan inwardly groaned - not another frumpy widow with a wobbling chin and very little sensible conversation. Metcalfe, clearly already well on her way to merriment, was guiding Maurice towards a solitary figure in the opposite corner. This figure was apparently more interested in the silk hangings than the hubbub of the guests, her back towards them. She too had thick curling hair although hers was auburn, longer than Metcalfe's and more simply styled with combs and pins so that the bulk of it cascaded down her back. She was wearing a black gown as Maurice would have expected of a widow, decorated with fine lace and silk ribbons. Unlike Metcalfe, she had clearly not forsaken her corsetry.

Cheekily, Metcalfe scampered over and tapped the woman on the shoulder and Maurice watched as she turned slowly and realised too late that he already knew to whom he was about to be introduced.

"Mr Maurice Fortescue," announced Metcalfe theatrically, "Allow me to present Lady Iona, Duchess of Pringle." Maurice made the small customary bow and Lady Iona held out her right hand, court-style, to be kissed. Nothing in her look gave away their acquaintance and neither would it, until Metcalfe had bustled off to meddle elsewhere.

"Charmed," murmured Maurice with a thin smile, as he took her hand and mimicked kissing it.

"Indeed," replied Lady Iona politely with a modest smile. "Are you having a pleasant evening?" It was an almost standard form of small talk. "These silks are very fine; you should have a look."

"Of course," returned Maurice blandly, desperately wishing Metcalfe would leave. "They really are exquisite. Tell me, have you travelled much?"

"Well," said Metcalfe, satisfied that she had kindled the conversation well enough to leave it burning, "I'll make myself scarce." With a discrete wink, she hurried off in the direction of the punch cups. The pair watched her go, waiting until she was definitely out of earshot before their conversation took a far less civil turn.

"Well, well," uttered Iona, her eyes firmly fixed on Metcalfe as she helped herself to another cup of punch and skipped away into the crowd. "Mr Maurice Fortescue is it now?"

Mulligan glared at her.

"And what of it?" he hissed.

"Just amused to see you here, Mulligan," she continued *sotto voce*, "done up like the Duke of Staynesbury and standing about like a fish out of the river,"

"Well, it takes one to know one," he retorted with a joyless grin. Mulligan was well aware that Iona Pringle was generally far too busy to hang about in ballrooms being introduced to eligible Albion widowers. She was more likely to be found in a tunic and hose on business for either the Adventurers Guild or the Guild Below - which is where she and Mulligan had first become acquainted. She was the last person he wanted to see after months of careful planning because she had the power to blow his cover with one simple sentence.

"Indeed it does," conceded Iona with a wry smile, "it would seem that we are playing at the same game."

"Are we now?" he snorted. "And what game would that be?"

"Well, Mr *Fortescue*," she said with a little more malice, "keep your secrets if you can but listen carefully," she narrowed her eyes to emphasize as she spoke, "These people are my friends. No, not them," she snapped waving at the chattering socialites behind Mulligan as he opened his mouth to contradict her, "the Al Rahiris." Mulligan shut his mouth again. He should have known better than to make assumptions with Iona. She carried on before he could get another word in, "Steal from them if you must, they have some beautiful things that I'm sure you'll be able to fence if you put your mind to it but don't you *dare* steal from their guests."

Mulligan was about to retort that Iona had no right to tell him what to do when he felt something sharp and cold press into his lower abdomen. Iona had produced, seemingly from nowhere, a slender silver blade, the tip of which was lightly resting on the flesh of his lower belly. She smiled at him sweetly as he processed the threat and nodded.

Angel wasn't going to like it, but it really couldn't be helped. She would have been even less impressed if he came home dead. At least he had the rest of the night to scout, but he would have to get word to Min somehow. Looking around, he spotted Mrs Al Rahiri standing pleasantly to one side as a group of Aberddu matrons fluttered about her talking a great deal but saying nothing much at all. He made his way discretely over to her, and with a polite cough interrupted their conversation.

Tabitha was having a lovely time, there were buns and fresh fruit pieces and strange little pastry sweets on the table - the muslin had been removed about half an hour previously - and the supplies of fresh milk and fruit juice seemed endless. Now they were playing *ratatatat;* a game that was becoming increasingly fashionable among the in-crowd girls.

Most of the children were sitting demurely in a circle chanting the rhyme, whilst two girls stood in the middle - one blindfolded the other turning her slowly.

"Ratatatat a knock on the door
Ratatatat who is it for?
Ratatatat come play at our game
Here's the voice, now what's the name?"

Then when the rhyme had finished all the children tapped out a 'ratatatat' rhythm on the floor, which was not such an impressive sound on these tiles as it was on the wooden floor boards of a nursery. Then one of the children in the circle spoke in a put-on voice and the blindfolded girl had three guesses to name the speaker. Tabitha loved it, because she had a surprising talent for making her voice different. Min supposed it was because she was very used to pretending to be somebody else. She was just about to take her turn when two people entered the room.

"Tabitha," called Mrs Al Rahiri gently and beckoned her over, "your father wants to speak you." Tabitha groaned and with a sulk on her lips came obediently to her father's side. He held out a hand which she took and he drew her to a corner, where he crouched down so that they were eye to eye before he began to talk. Mrs Al Rahiri wafted away and left them to it. It was a brief exchange after which Tabitha returned to the game having missed her turn, with a scowl on her face.

When midnight came around and the carriages started to arrive for the banqueters, Tabitha was wrapped in a shawl and dosing on a large cushion in the children's room like most of the other children. Many of the guests were indeed suitably drunk enough that they could have been easily robbed. It galled Mulligan to let them go with their jewels still intact but he did not dare cross Iona.

He had no idea why she was so against him stealing from these people and it was hardly important now. He just let them all go with a touch of sadness.

In order to not make the whole evening a waste of effort, he had throughout the evening, been helping himself to various items of silver and gold tableware which he had stowed in various places around his body. He was now moving very gingerly as he feared that he may clatter if he didn't take care. He had contemplated taking two or three of the crystal punch cups but he decided that that was beyond foolhardy given where he might have had to store them. Gently, he crouched done to shake Tabitha's shoulder gently - he would have scooped her up in his arms as some of the other fathers had done with their children but he thought this would probably end with one or the other, or possibly both of them being stabbed by one of the pickle forks in his doublet.

Chapter 9
The Morning After

The morning after was cold and drizzly. Min pulled the blanket back over her head when Clara tried to rouse her just after the morning seven bell. It was no skin off Clara's nose what time Min got up so she left her there and went downstairs. Mulligan wouldn't surface until midday at the earliest, which greatly angered Angel who was already sitting at the kitchen table looking sour when Clara went downstairs to light the fire. She was examining the previous night's takings, holding up each individual piece in the light of a single candle-lantern. She was in charge of taking the goods to whichever fence in the Guild Below would deal in this kind of thing. However, Clara and Luce had discussed it and had no intention of letting her go alone with quite so much. She was too tight-lipped these days, her temper slowly blooming like a livid crimson rose. It would be no large effort for her to take a second cut of the gold and stash it elsewhere before she came back to the house. *Swat I'd do*, thought Clara as she kicked the firewood towards the hearth, *so why wouldn't she?*

None of the three had been impressed by Mulligan's very small haul, feeling somewhat deflated as he let it tumble noisily on to the scrubbed wooden table top. They had been expecting gold and jewels not about a dozen items of silver flatware, a pewter cruet set and three fancy looking butter knives. Angel had been almost aggressively unsympathetic when Mulligan explained his lack of offering but Luce and Clara did own that it was probably better not to have crossed Iona Pringle if they wanted the rest of the enterprise to succeed. Clara was glad that Mulligan didn't pick a fight with Angel about it. She'd had the petulant look on her face that meant she was in the mood for a row, and she could be like a terrier with a rabbit in that mood. Clara, who spent more time with Angel than anyone else, was very glad – she didn't fancy hearing about it over and over again for the next three weeks.

Five silent minutes later, Luce came in from the yard wiping her hands on her tunic.

"Wha's for breakfast?" she asked pausing by the back door to take off her filthy boots. Without a word, Clara dumped a lardy loaf and some apples on the table and went back to cleaning out the grate.

"I was just rereading this ball invitation," said Angel looking up at Luce from where she had been laying the silver cutlery out in a line on a square of chamois. She was most disgruntled to discover that Min hadn't been invited to this ball because, unlike the Arabians, the Paravelians believed children should be confined to the nursery after dark.

"Oh?" said Luce as she reached for the knife to cut the lardy. She didn't like the sound of Angel's tone. She didn't want to find herself involved upfront in this escapade; she had high hopes of getting rich by looking after the horse. "Lardy, Clara?"

"Yeah," said Clara grumpily, speaking for the first time. She had become increasingly taciturn of late which Luce found odd, if not troubling, as Clara had been almost impossible to shut up before. "Stick it on the side."

"Anyway," snapped Angel as she rolled the silver tightly in the leather so that it made a neat sausage-shaped bundle, "This ball invitation," It was clear she didn't like being interrupted, "states that grooms and drivers will receive supper, ale and a pipe-full of smoking tobacco in the outer kitchen during the evening."

Luce just looked at her but Angel didn't notice. She was too busy fastening her chamois roll with a long leather thong. Luce, who had no idea what she was driving at, was forced to say,

"Yeah, and?" Surely, she hadn't just brought it up because it would mean free food.

"So," said Angel in a tone that suggested she was disappointed to have to spell it out. "You'll be in the kitchens, whilst Mulligan's upstairs at the ball. You can slip out and help him." Luce, who had been just about to take a bite out of her apple stopped dead and looked at Angel.

"Just like that?" she said after a moment, when it seemed that Angel wasn't kidding. This gained such contempt from Angel that Luce felt her palm twitch in response. She took a belligerent bite from the apple and chewed noisily. There were many retorts she could have made, but she just couldn't be bothered.

"Think about it," said Angel condescendingly as she stood up, picking up her bag from the floor beside her chair, "I'm off to market with our little harvest. I'll be back for lunch." She turned to push her chair in and found that suddenly Clara was standing behind her.

"It's okay, you don't 'ave to go alone," she said, removing her cloth cap, "Luce and I thought we'd come wiv' ya," Clara smiled. Angel was not fooled, there was no warmth in the gesture it was more a simple show of teeth than a display of friendship. Angel opened her mouth to argue, not at all intimidated when she felt movement behind her.

"Yeah," said Luce, now uncomfortably close, "We thought we'd all go. Together. Jus' like old times hey?" The girls had the weight advantage, but Angel was fast and if she'd really wanted to she could have made a break for it. Whether it ever crossed her mind to do so was something that only the Gods and she would ever know, as she capitulated with relative ease and waited by the back door for them both to change.

When Mulligan surfaced with the chime of the noon-time bells, he found the house eerily quiet. Staggering downstairs, he found an empty grate and the best part of a lardy loaf, a half-eaten apple and the invitation to the Marquis of Ventruvian's Ball lying on the table. The candle in the lantern on the table had long since dwindled away. He had no idea where any of the girls had gone but he also didn't really have time now to find out. It was the morning after the night before and he would be expected at Metcalfe's for tea and gossip at three o clock sharp. It was essential that he attend, because if the thefts had been noted he would no doubt hear about it there, and it would provide him with the perfect opportunity to be among the first to deplore them. Now all he had to do was remember how Maurice got dressed.

Unaided, it took Mulligan nearly the whole of the three intervening hours to sort himself out. Without the obliging Clara to provide him with warm water for his wash, he was forced to negotiate the laborious process single-handed and unsupervised. Simply drawing enough water to fill the pan made his back ache. Then he had to heft the buckets from the pump in the yard into the kitchen. Then he spent half an hour fighting with the fire in the grate to get it hot enough to warm the pan. At first it wouldn't catch, then it wouldn't spread and then it kept on blowing out. He was used to the rickety little iron range in his room which he fed mainly with charcoal and kept filled with long low-glowing embers most of the time. He rarely heated anything larger than a mug. Eventually, he lost his temper and pumped the bellows furiously until the pathetic embers he had managed to kindle roared in to life and he had enough flame to turn his back on for a few minutes. After all that, he couldn't be bothered to carry the pan upstairs so he washed himself in front of the kitchen fire, feeling smug with himself at his accomplishments until he was soapy and soaked, when he realised his drying cloths were in his room two floors up.

Irritably, he trailed through the house leaving a damp path behind him. The air in his bedroom was freezing cold on his wet torso and he shivered as he poked about looking for a clean linen cloth and some clothes to put on. After a few minutes he flopped down on the bed, cloth in hand and rubbed at his hair. He was worn out already, and he'd only just managed to get clean. Was he really that out of shape? He had only been in this life two months, if that - had he been so idle that his stamina had decreased this much? He found himself an outfit and put it on wearily. Next stop, he would find some food in the kitchen and then go out and tack up the horse and cart.

The afternoon two-hour was chiming as he went out to the yard, having made the best of the lardy that had been left on the table. The kitchen floor was awash, but he had no intention of drying it right now - he'd already got himself dressed to go out and wasn't about to get the knees of these knickerbockers grubby by scrabbling about on the flagstones. One of the girls could do it when they eventually reappeared. He had to admit that he was put out to the point of extreme annoyance by their sudden disappearance. In fact, the only thing that stopped him wondering if they'd done a bunk was the look of unquestionable greed in Angel's eyes the previous night, before he'd produced the cutlery. She wasn't going anywhere until they'd had a significant haul; she'd been gold-struck. If he was any judge, Angel wasn't going to give up until she found herself holding something so expensive that she couldn't conceive its price. The others he wasn't sure of, except that he doubted they'd leave her behind.

Out in the stable, he found that he was unfamiliar with things. Tacking up horses was part of life in the city, but finding his way around Luce's stable was not so easy. It was laid out the way she liked to do things and it took him longer than he would have liked to find the bridle, straps and reins he needed. Then, once he had located all the required leather items, he was forced to reason with the nag - who didn't know him from a common thief. Worn out it may have been, and beneath its magical veneer scrawny and scarred, but it was also spirited and had clearly decided that Luce as 'Jack the Stable Lad' was the only boy for it. It took more than a little persuasion to get the head strap and nose band on and then quite a lot of negotiation to get the cart attached. At last, though, everything was close enough to ready that Mulligan was happy and he tied the reins firmly to the tether ring by the gate. It was then that he looked down at his front idly, wondering what time it was, and found that he had a far more pressing concern. He was not used to being careful about staying clean, and hadn't noticed any of the straw or dirt that had found its way on to his person during his battle with the livery. Letting out an irritable groan, he stamped back into the house and upstairs to change, muttering darkly to himself as he did so. The girls were going to have a lot to answer for when they turned up later.

By the time he finally boarded the cart and cracked the reins he was done in, and not at all keen on visiting. Afternoon calling was a practice that had come to Aberddu from Albion and had been adopted wholesale by the rich, important and idle of the City State. It conveniently filled the dead afternoon hours which in Paravel would have been used for business and in Aragon and other Elven nations, who had longer life spans to negotiate, was mediation or solitary time. As Maurice Fortescue heaved himself out of the driver's seat of his cart and handed the reins to the Metcalfe's boy, he dearly wished that it had been the meditation that had caught on here instead.

Metcalfe, like ex-patriots of every stripe, tended to be very vigorous in her Albioness when it suited. Afternoon tea was the time when she was the most ferocious about it. She had a very fine collection of china cups and finely carved and inlaid tea caddies that supposedly contained a whole range of different teas from various regions of Jaffria, Kchon and even some from as far away as the Isles of Nippon. She paraded them about proudly on two custom-made, hand-carved rosewood trolleys and the women who drank the tea swooned over them constantly. Personally, although Maurice made the correct noises when handed cups to drink from and caddies to sniff, he couldn't tell the difference between one and the next. He just drank them all quietly and politely. Mulligan half-suspected that actually there was no difference and that Metcalfe's house-keeper was canny enough to fill all of them with the cheapest blends from the market and pocket the difference. It was what he'd have done.

Maurice sat down next to a spare, elderly woman with prominent neck sinews, who had her hands folded in her lap and kept sniffing. She was Count-ess Fandeaux, and in spite of her relatively plain mode of dress, she was actu-ally one of the wealthiest and most important people present. She was visiting the city, staying with her daughter Veronique, who had married the forth son of the Earl of Schroninghale and only afterwards discovered that, having re-fused to enter the Temple of Law as an acolyte, he had been disinherited of his not-massively-substantial fortune. The daughter was built like her mother, al-though the younger woman didn't wear her scrawniness nearly as well. Whilst the elder Countess looked stately and sparse, the younger one looked ill-feed, damp-eyed and sickly. Her husband, a porcine man who quite often fell asleep during tea parties, had long since given up doting on a wife who had never forgiven him for not being in the will. Maurice strove to be pleasant to all three of them as they were often left out of conversation, and more importantly were still active in the Royal Albion Court, unlike so many others. Mulligan watched contemptuously, and unkindly thought that the silly cow needed to get over it - fancy marrying that odious man-pig without checking on things first. That was just poor planning.

Mulligan through Maurice's eyes took that kind of social information very seriously. He had no idea why he thought he'd need it all but he wasn't about to pass it up. He took his tea cup very carefully from the tray with a pleasant smile, helped himself to a dainty from the silver tray and kept his ears open. Apart from cooing over the tea things, the conversation was largely revolving around the previous night - which Maurice was glad about. It seemed that there were many people with something to say about the evening and Maurice was content just to listen and drink his tea.

As he munched his way through several of the dainties, suddenly aware that he'd had nothing but lardy loaf since last night, he was largely relieved that the banquet food was considered to be the main scandal of the evening. He was waiting to see if the news about the missing cutlery had made it out of the household. Although, he doubted very much that the Al Rahiris would cause a fuss. Darkly, Mulligan wondered if they would even bother reporting the theft to the militia or if they would just extract their own justice from whichever serving girl broke down in tears first. He would probably never find out. It would definitely have trumped the disappointed wittering that currently dominated the conversation, over which Maurice was trying not to laugh.

The banquet itself had been superb. The table had been nearly the entire length of the room and each course had been served in style, with wine, mead and bread constantly available. However, it had not been the lavish exotic affair that the gathering had hoped for, with elegant dishes vibrantly coloured with unusual spices, trays of sweat-meats and imported fruits and the Gods only knew what else. Instead, the Al Rahiris had served a beautifully prepared western feast and as he had tucked in to it with gusto Maurice thought to himself that you would be hard put to find anything to better it even at the royal court.

It seemed that the Al Rahiris were as eager to show the locals that they had embraced Aberddu City life as the locals were to welcome the exotic. It was testament to the breeding of the guests that the Al Rahiris would never find out how disappointed they had been to find the nine standard courses with not an oriental spice in sight. Well, thought Maurice as he helped himself to yet another of the little buns from the tray, if that's all they can find to complain about then I'll call that a success. He was very glad when, clearly bored with the prattling too, one of the gentleman started talking about the upcoming horse fayres.

Clara slumped back against the dank tunnel wall, panting. A broad smile split her grime-splattered face. This was the life; crouching in an alcove, with one ear concentrating on what was happening just out of sight, around the bend. So much better than the endless rounds of housekeeping, and somewhat improved by her sturdy new boots. She couldn't honestly say that she missed the squishing feeling of cooling effluent between her toes. It felt, for the first time in a long while, as though she was back in her home, with her friends. The other two seemed to feel the same way, eyes twinkling as they kept themselves concealed and listened to the contretemps ahead.

The journey to the black market had been straight forward and almost silent. The three disparate girls had made excellent time from the Rich District to the spot under the North Wall slums where the market had come to rest. It was an easy route and needed minimal cooperation. However, it did have several downs that could not be easily 'upped'. This didn't concern the girls initially as they had an equally simple return route worked out. It was longer but didn't involve scrambling up any slurry-caked slopes or trying to wriggle through narrow gaps six feet above the floor.

The problem arose when they got to the market. Luckily, Johnny the Fence had mentioned it when he was counting out the coins for Angel after they had made their deal. It seemed that their chosen route home, which ran under the western half of the trade district, was currently extremely unsafe passage. It was a patch of territory that had been long-disputed by two rival cells of thieves from the Guild Below and in the last week or so it had suddenly become a battle ground - not an overt battle either, but the kind of sneaky underhanded attritional conflict that befitted two gangs of thieves. Many of the paths had been thoroughly and lethally trapped and gang members lay in wait for their rivals with garrottes, poison-covered stiletto spikes and all sorts of other pleasant things.

In the dark of the tunnels it was hard to tell who approached from even ten feet away and the gangs did not hang around to check. As Johnny was filling Angel with the gory details, the others saw two sombre-looking men trudging into the market from the tunnel they had been planning to leave by. They were carrying a body, limp and grubby, between them, which they dumped it unceremoniously off to one side beside a dark heap that, now Clara looked, had boots and hands poking out of it. Forewarned, and weighed down with more coin than they were expecting, spread evenly between them and safely concealed within their clothing, they started picking their way back by a far more circuitous route than they had intended.

They had ended up above ground after several false starts and had crossed the Brightling Bridge in the midday sunshine. Freed of duty through no real fault of their own and feeling flush, they were now in far better spirits and started to giggle and chatter as they had always done. Even the icy-faced Angel had started to melt as they scuttled down the wide streets of the Temple District looking for a down-hatch.

They were currently picking their way through the tunnels below the Docklands which were not familiar territory to them and it was taking significant skill not to get turned around and end up back where they'd started. The whole journey was taking far longer than they had initially intended but there was no point in worrying about it down here, out of earshot of the Temple bells. They couldn't get home safely any quicker in any case.

Min woke up still full and fuzzy from the night before. She didn't get up immediately; it was soft and warm in her little bed and she'd learnt to sleep through the sound of the others getting up - a full stomach could work wonders - so she was not surprised to find the room empty. She had no real notion of the time, although she was vaguely aware that she had rolled over and drifted back into a sweet peaceful sleep just as the morning nine hour chimed. At least she thought it was the nine hour, she only heard nine chimes but she may have slept through more. It was delicious to live this kind of life, where you had time for idleness and blankets enough to stay warm in bed. A life where you were not compelled to get up at the crack of dawn to take your chances with the world and see what you could scrape up to keep body and soul vaguely strung together. It was a life she could get used to. She smiled a thin self-satisfied smile, dangled her legs out of the covers, sat up and reached for her shawl.

There was no noise within the house as she padded downstairs. She'd changed into one of the old shifts which she now thought of as her house-dress. It was the one that one of the girls had made her one the day that Daddy-Mulligan had first opened up that suit-case. It smelled musty and the fabric was unpleasant. She could no more wear it out in company than she could her old tunic and hose.

It wasn't unusual for the drawing room to be empty, nor was it strange that fire wasn't lit. Firewood was saved strictly for cooking and company. If she was cold, she'd have to go downstairs to the kitchen range, but as it was a pleasant day and the sun was streaming in through the long windows she was happy enough in her dress and shawl. She curled herself up on the straw-padded couch they had come by on the black market and entertained herself with a small picture book she had acquired during one of the numerous and tedious nursery teas she'd attended a couple of weeks previously. She couldn't really read - although she was becoming very adept at pretending she could understand more than just a handful of words. This wasn't unusual, most of the girls of Albion stock couldn't really read either - the formal education of future idle wives being seen as a total waste of time and resources in the Royal Court, even though the young Queen herself had been well-schooled in three or four languages. Mind you, it wasn't as though she could be called idle, or indeed a wife. The girls of Paravelian and Aragonese backgrounds, and the daughters of the rich but common, tended to poke sly fun at the Albion girls for their illiteracy and the Albion girls poked it right back, particularly as none of them were forced to suffer a governess or even worse in case of the Paravelian girls lessons shared with not only any brothers but also the children of the servants - something that the Paravelian Barons considered a duty and obligation and the Albions, sniggering behind their hands, saw as nothing more than an embarrassment.

Luckily for Min, here in the melting pot of Aberddu City no-one questioned much about other people's arrangements, nor did they pay attention when the new girl Tabitha skipped over to the sparsely populated and dusty bookshelf and started leafing through 'Our Winged Friends - an illustrated guide to the bird life of Albion by Gilbert Horatio Halk'. The pictures were beautifully hand-coloured and it was clear that the book had barely been opened. Min knew no one would miss a treasure like this that had been ignored in a dingy corner, and at the end of the afternoon she had feigned a lost handkerchief, run back and pocketed the palm-sized volume. There was something to be said for these flouncy pinafores with giant pockets after all.

It was a good hour or so later when Min's stomach began to rumble and she realised she was thirsty. She had been far too absorbed in her book, examining every detail of each picture and had no notion of the time. She scampered downstairs to the see where the others were. They were usually down there these days, doing something or other. Luce was often in the stable and Angel out and about enjoying herself. Maybe Clara would have made a couple of new loaves and have the range going. Even though it was sunny, it was still cool enough inside to feel it when you'd been sitting around for a while.

"Clara," she called happily as she started down the stairs, "Clara, what's for supper?" There was no response, she probably had her head in the laundry or mending. At the bottom of the stairs, she pushed open the door and poked her head around it. The room was empty, and cold. Strange. Slightly disconcerted, Min picked her way across the kitchen trying not to disturb anything, not that there was really anything for her to disturb. She spotted the lardy bread, an apple core and an invitation on the table. There were great patches of water on the flag-stones and the fire in the range was nothing more than twitching embers. No wonder the room was cold, the back door stood wide open. Perhaps they were all out in the yard. The heavy stones were chilly beneath her feet as she tiptoed to the small vestibule by the back door trying to make as little contact with the floor as possible. There were no shoes or cloaks in the vestibule, which was not unexpected if they were all outside seeing to the horse or something, but it was also oddly quiet. Not that Min expected boisterous bantering any more, but there wasn't even the sound of people moving things about. All she could hear were voices in the street and the sound of the neighbour's groom being thrashed. Paravelians may believe in educating their servants but they also believed in beating them soundly if the spirit-merchant next door was anything to go by. The poor boy must be either extremely cheeky or totally incompetent, judging by the amount of time he spent at the wrong end of his master's birch, and also constantly black and blue with bruising. Having established that the back yard was empty, of everyone and everything including the horse and cart, she went back inside, the small coiling wisp of disgruntlement rising inside her.

Min was sitting at the kitchen table almost vibrating with rage an hour or so later when the back door burst open and the other three tumbled into the kitchen giggling and reeking of sewage. The familiar but unpleasant odour followed them into the room and Min to screw her face up into a tight little twist. She didn't say a word as the others started kicking off their filth-encrusted boots, chattering between themselves and ignoring her. None of them had actually looked much passed the vestibule yet to notice Min where she sat and the unintentional slight merely fuelled her anger. She pushed her half eaten lardy around the table in front of her, pointedly not eating it. This was a gesture she had copied from a particularly spoilt daughter of some Guild master or other who tended to throw herself in to the most appalling strops when she didn't get her own way. It didn't have quite the same effect on her three companions as it did on the spoilt girl's nanny because they didn't notice and wouldn't have been bothered by Min's sulking even if they had. 'Getting your own way' was not a concept they were particularly familiar with.

Luce raced grabbed a large shallow caste iron pan and scuttled outside to the pump. Clara, rubbing her hands together, scuttled over to the range, snatching an arm full of wood on the way passed. She opened the burner door, pushed the wood inside and fetched up the bellows. Within a minute or so, she had coaxed the dying embers back to life and the heat started to fill the kitchen.

"Alrigh' Min?" she said pleasantly as she turned and saw her still sitting at the table, glowering at the others her slice of lardy poked almost to bits.

"Where have you been?" hissed Min dangerously.

"Black market," replied Clara, either unaware of the accusation in Min's tone or choosing to ignore it. "We sold the cutlery din't we?"

With that, Clara reached under her top, pulled out her money pouch and dropped it on the table with a clatter. The pouch was her own contraption: a long tube of fabric a little wider than a guilder coin, tied at each end with a piece of string. The tube could then be wrapped around the chest and tied securely with the string making it near invisible from outside the clothing and the contents impossible to pick. Clara was proud of the design and had made one for all of them. Luce was wrestling with hers at that moment, having dumped the pan of water on top of the range to warm. Angel, still taking her boots off, was far more schooled in nuance than either Luce or Clara. She eyed Min carefully.

"How much did you get?" snapped Min grabbing Luce's pouch as she dropped on the table and grabbing at the knot at one end.

"Sixty-five," replied Clara triumphantly.

"Sixty-five what?" spat Min as she gave up with the knot and tossed the pouch back onto the table.

"Silver," said Angel coming over from the door. She was far less ebullient than the other two. Naturally unimpressed and taciturn, and freer to come and go, she had not been so elated by their lengthy trek. She was also well aware that Min was spoiling for a fight.

"Got a problem with that?" She said, with the implication that if the answer was yes then there was going to be some violence to follow. Min scowled. Luce and Clara, who had been practically bouncing when they had come in both visibly shrank and shifted close to the fire and out of the firing line.

"How do I know it's all there?" was Min's reply. Not exactly a 'yes' but escalating things nonetheless. Angel, whose white face was almost translucent with anger leaned forward over the table nastily and snapped

"You don't. How do I know if all the goods were handed over in the first place? I notice you didn't put anything on the table last night?"

Min's eyes sprang wide open and wounded. Clearly she wanted to retaliate but she was also sensible of the fact that she could never beat Angel if it came to actual blows. Instead, copying another gesture she had learnt from the nursery tea circuit, she flung herself back in her chair causing it to scrape on the floor with maximum volume, stood up and flounced out of the kitchen.

Min's tantrum had precisely no effect on the progress of daily life in the household. No one had bothered to chase after her when she stormed out, nor had they changed their plans or behaviour. They didn't really understand what had happened, tantrums being one of the many luxuries not afforded to street brat sneak-thieves. The other three just set about the chores they'd left undone before the trip to the market and by late afternoon it was all but forgotten, by everyone except Min. In fact, the performance was totally overshadowed when Mulligan arrived home from the Metcalfe Tea Party and announced that he had a date for the Paravelian Ball.

It was not a necessity by Paravelian etiquette to attend the ball accompanied, Paravel being one of the few nations that didn't really care who you arrived with and cared even less who you went home with. In fact, in Paravel it was perfectly acceptable to arrive with one person and leave with another. It was also the only place on the civilised continent where it was acceptable for two gentlemen to dance together in polite company. Hence why the expression 'he's been to Paravel' had become a discrete if not kind way of alleging that a gentleman was homosexual. It was that kind of flagrant decadence and freedom that would never have been allowed in the Aragonese or Albion Courts - where it was perfectly acceptable to betroth girls of as young as twelve to full-grown men, just so long as the girl's father agreed.

Aberddu, being a melting pot of all these cultures and still in its infancy, was fighting its way haphazardly through these cultural restrictions - based mainly on what the resident aristocracy had liked and not liked of their home nations. Thus, because Metcalfe thought it unconscionable for anyone to go to the ball alone, Maurice-Mulligan had found himself unable to avoid being coupled to a drippy-eyed, constantly sniffing war-widow from somewhere south of Port Selliar who had been making doe-eyes at him for the last few weeks. Her husband had been some military no-account who had bought it during the Siege of Aberddu and as far as Maurice-Mulligan could tell was about his height, weight and general colouring. Maurice-Mulligan had no intention of being a made-to-measure replacement, however much money Metcalfe insinuated this woman might have. Escorting her to the ball on the other hand, Maurice-Mulligan decided, might get Metcalfe off his back for a while.

The three girls - Min had not reappeared from her strop - listened to Mulligan detail the whole thing with rapt attention, exchanging the occasional look. Courting had not been part of the initial plan, it had never even occurred to them that it might. That made a whole new level of complication and scrutiny. For a start, they would have to get Luce a proper livery - she couldn't very well drive this woman to the Ball in her usual scruffy dark tunic and hose.

It was apparent from Angel's eyes that she was playing it all out in her head - to what she considered the likely conclusion. Her lips thinned as she was thinking, the she said,

"You can't bring her here," in a low voice.

"Relax," said Mulligan calmly, with a look of mild disgust on his face. "I wasn't planning on it. It's just a ball."

Clara and Luce nodded and smiled, reassured. Angel however did not. She was not so easily persuaded of anyone's innocence and, constantly suspicious, she continued glowering at Mulligan with her face scrunched into ugly folds of displeasure. Mulligan and the other girls ignored her.

"Anyway," said Mulligan languidly as he stood up by way of punctuating the discussion, "I must go and change out of these clothes, don't need to make Clara any more laundry! Besides, I need to pick out my outfit."

Clara and Luce did not stay to watch him leave, they just leapt up and returned to their work. Angel remained at the table for a moment longer with a poisonous glare fixed on Mulligan's back until he vanished through the door.

"Pick out his outfit," she spat contemptuously under her breath. "Who does he think he his? The Queen of bloody Albion?"

Chapter 10
Going to Paravel

Mulligan had never seen anything quite like it neither had Luce or Clara, who had been smartly liveried for the occasion. Even the Bard's Guild did not produce things like this. Evidently you could take Lord Raimund Ingst of Lendlslaus out of Paravel but you couldn't take Paravel out of Lord Ingst. The front garden of his town house was not the vast park he had left in Lendlslaus but it was a fair size for the city and someone, presumably the resident magician, had filled the shrubbery with small orbs of ice-white swirling light. It was breathtaking and enchanting. Luce and Clara, sitting in the front of the cart gaped at the spectacle freely. Behind them, Ms Hortensia Frink was smitten.

"Oh, how charming," she breathed, staring with fascination into the shadowy bushes as they waited to park the carriage. Beside her, Maurice Fortescue remained the soul of staid sophistication, producing nothing more than a genteel smile in response to it all.

The Ball to Celebrate the Emperor's Passing was quite the occasion in Aberddu - even though, as far as anyone could recall, the Emperor of Paravel had never been to Aberddu either before or after his passing. Lord Raimund Bendik Ingst, Baron of Lendlslaus, Marquis of Ventruvian styled himself as a 'from home' Baron, and was the richest, oldest and most aggressively Paravelian of all the aristocracy who were no longer welcome in Paravel. He had been exiled to Aberddu since long before independence and had by far and away one of the largest houses. Unlike most of the other posh-knobs in the city he had enough ground and stabling to accommodate three or four dozen carriages. This meant that not only could he invite anybody who was anybody, and a fair few people who weren't, he could allow the favoured few the privilege of having their drivers and page boys wait in the kitchen for them. Somehow, probably due to his acceptance in the Metcalfe set, Maurice Fortescue had been granted this privilege.

As nameless-pageboy Clara helped Ms Frink 'please call me Horti' down from the carriage, Maurice was having trouble containing his awe. The massive wooden front door stood open and it was just possible to see the shimmering chandeliers in the ballroom and hear the exquisite music. A wigged and frock-coated footman who could barely see passed his upturned nose directed Luce and Clara to the parking area where a far less well-dress and much less arrogant man took the reins of the horse and pointed them in the direction of the outer kitchen, where the visiting servants were gathering to be fed. Maurice Fortescue didn't even glance after them as he offered a stiff elbow to Ms Frink and escorted her in through the door.

Even the entrance hall was grandiose beyond anything Maurice had imagined; lit by dozens of ensconced candles reflected in ten or twelve floor to ceiling mirrors. The ceiling itself was vaulted, plastered and painted with a variety of classical scenes concerning mostly naked young men, completely naked young ladies and a rather worrying amount of fruit. The floor was some variety of shiny white stone that Maurice thought might be marble although this was more idle conjecture than actual knowledge. The air was thick with floral smells, heady and fantastical.

They joined the couples who were waiting to be announced by the Holder of the Roll. There were long trellis tables draped with golden velvet either side of them. One side had a display of fruits and dainties for the waiting guest to pick at and the other had several free standing mirrors and porcelain bottles containing various scents. Quite a few of the ladies, and more than one or two of the gentlemen were making use of these facilities. Maurice helped himself to a small bunch of grapes and tried to take it all in. It really was true what they said about the opulent decadence of the Paravelians, no wonder the Frisians and Albions despised them so very much - they were clearly just very, very jealous.

It was obvious that Ms Frink, former wife of an Albion Captain, was just as awed as he was. She stood gazing about with very little restraint, like a child at a fairground. As the queue moved on, more of the ballroom became visible. The chandeliers that had caught Maurice's eye were far more spectacular than he had first realised. They were suspended about ten feet from the ceiling purely by magic and moved gracefully in an intricate pattern, casting shadows over the dancers below. The ceiling in here was even more lavishly decorated with quite a quantity of gold leaf and mirrors, in addition to naked youths and fruit. As well as these soft white chandeliers, the room was lit from the sides by thirty foot-high flickering flames, burning in shallow stone dishes, each balanced on top of a unique, intricately moulded nine-foot cast iron frame. Even Maurice, who was largely uneducated when it came to magic could tell it was magical rather than natural fire - for one thing it was changing colour in time with the music. Interspersing these torches were various works of art and sculpture, the most captivating of which was a small fountain that shot plumes of water high into the air so that they caught the magical light. The music, which seemed to be blending with the pervasive flowery scent adding to the intoxication of it all, was coming from a group of about fifteen minstrels who had been carefully seated on a suspended balcony about ten feet above the floor, so that they didn't take up any valuable dance floor space. There was no sign of the banquet table but Maurice surmised it was probably behind one of the heavy velvet curtains at the far end of the ballroom that presumably covered doorways to other rooms.

However, as enthralling as this display was, the thing that amazed Maurice the most was the people. By now, he was used to the Aberddu socialites with their ever changing fashions, hems and neck lines that yo-yoed with the seasons, pastel silks and three years out of date knickerbockers, nothing there to surprise him, but the local glitterati were not the only ones here. A significant number of the real Paravelian Aristocracy had portalled in for the occasion and were being announced at another door by an almost identical Holder of the Roll. Even if Mulligan had never set eyes on the Aberddu in-crowd he would have been able to tell that these people were not them.

Chapter 11
When in Paravel...

In a society like Paravel where death was not the end and undeath was considered the ultimate in social climbing, something as ephemeral as fashion was both vital and superfluous. Amongst about half of the idle rich, whose main occupation was hanging about waiting for their fathers to give up on the mortal plane - in some cases for a hundred years or more - keeping up with the minute changes of style and frippery was essential to fill the long tedious days. Attention to detail was the key, and everyone must be absolutely 'a la mode' or be shunned. This season it was towering wigs, white faces with black beauty spots and dark silk knickerbockers buckled *just* below the knee. For the other half, it seemed fashion had long since passed them by, more the concern of the still living - to the extent that it was actually possible to tell when someone had 'died' by what they were wearing. It was like looking at a moving exhibit of fashion through the ages.

Two further things struck Mulligan as he took another step closer to the door. The first was that there were very probably several outfits in that room that were twice as old as he was. The second was that it was very apparent that whilst colours, fabric, necklines, buckle lines, fastenings, hems and cuts had changed a lot over the years, frills had never been out of style in Paravel. Ever.

They were attached to everything - collars, cuffs, hems, shoes and handkerchiefs - so many different colours of handkerchief being wafted and flapped and dabbed all over the place. Maurice was so enthralled that he didn't hear the Holder of the Roll announce them.

"Mr Maurice Fortescue and Ms Hortensia Frink."

He didn't move on cue, he just kept gaping at this amazing sight of amazing people who didn't seem to be in anyway amazed by any of it. Hortensia was forced to shake him by the elbow and the Holder of the Roll sniffed and tutted before he re-announced them with a flat edge of irritation in his voice. No one even looked up as he did so, and they descended the staircase into the softly lit sparkling hubbub.

Mulligan, hovering behind Maurice's wide-open gaze was delirious with excitement; such a vast jewelled harvest twinkling away before him, ripe for the picking. He smiled greedily, all he had to do was off-load this drippy widow and he would be away.

Down in the kitchen, Luce and Clara were having an equally eye-opening time. The people down here were far more what they were used to - the other drivers and pages were barely less common than the girls were. They swore and spat, they just looked a little better fed and had fewer unsightly skin conditions.

However, in spite of the familiar people, they had never been in a room the size of the outer kitchen nevermind the rest of the 'below stairs' area. There were at least five separate ranges and cooking fires, two in the outer kitchen alone. One of them had a spit so long it could comfortably have held Luce if it hadn't already been occupied by what she guessed were two whole sheep. It was being rotated by two sweating, grimy looking lads who, judging by the state of their footwear, usually worked in the stable yard. The room was crawling with people, all striding about with great purpose and piles of food. There was a vast harassed-looking cook standing in the doorway between the outer and inner kitchens bellowing orders indiscriminately so that her chins and bosom shook wildly.

It was overwhelming. Clara and Luce had no idea what to do with themselves, they just stood beside the spit-roast and gaped. They weren't idle long, a panting red-faced lad in a grubby leather tunic and hose waved a dismissive hand first Clara and Luce and then at the lamb spit and snapped,

"You two turn that, Jack, Deryn with me." Jack and Deryn abandoned sheep-turning duties immediately, shook their arms and followed gratefully after him. Dumbstruck, Luce and Clara had no option but to grab the spit handles and start turning.

Apart from being strenuous work, it turned out to be to their advantage to be occupied so close to the door. They saw people come in and out, babbling instructions and harrying each other. They got a sense of who was who, and who was in charge of what. Apart from the immense perspiring cook, there was a spindly, tight-lipped butler by the name of Mr O'Hanan and two under-butlers one of which had a large ring of cellar keys clanking from his belt. The head stabler and his team flew in and out trailing straw and oats much to the annoyance of an almost silent, slender woman in well-made plain brown gown with a worn but gleaming silver chatelaine hanging from her girdle. Her dark hair was pulled so fiercely back into a bun that she looked constantly surprised. It was clear from the way she comported herself that she was of significant authority, sliding through the chaos like a carp through a shoal of minnows. She quietly countermanded the cook's frantic shrieks and directed people with calm points and whispers. Luce eyed the chatelaine greedily and decided that it was probably a bad idea, too hard to obtain and too easily missed - unless by some crazy miracle the woman took it off.

Clara was more intrigued by the jangling under-butler who she had last seen heading out of the far door holding one of the larger cast iron keys and followed by a flock of willing looking lads. Her guess was that they were headed to a wine cellar. There was probably some very expensive wine down there, just sitting about. Doubtless most of what would reach tonight's guests would be the cheap, sour red sold in large leather skins and decanted into pitchers before being topped up with water, but there were bound to be more than a couple of casks of Paravelian Brandy as well as flasks and amphorae of the more expensive vintages that the Baron was saving for an actual special occasion.

Clara thought that that particular key might be quite easy to get hold of, as would a couple of innocent willing bodies ready to help them drag their prizes up the cellar steps. It was more than apparent to anyone paying close enough attention that at least half the people rushing back and forth in this kitchen were from other households and had no idea who belonged where or ought to be giving them orders. She paused for a moment to wipe her forehead on her tunic and was repaid by a tirade from the cook about burning the lamb. Glowering, she went back to turning the handle as the cook redirected her wrath on an unfortunate scullery maid who was struggling under a silver salver piled high with poached pears. Clara could feel blisters forming on her palms. She would be less than happy if she ended up turning this spit for the rest of the night. She had no intention of going away empty handed but it was very difficult to help yourself to anything, even the passing delicacies, when you were under the cook's beady gaze.

Upstairs, Mulligan was having a little more luck. He had handed Hortensia off, for now at least, to another war-widow and had left them merrily trying to out-tragic each other. Maurice had walked away, ostensibly to get drinks but actually so that he didn't laugh. He sensed that laughing at the two competing widows whose gruesome back and forth was conducted with grief-stricken po-faces and saccharin sympathy might be considered insensitive and cause affront. It was the opportunity he had been looking for to survey the pickings - which were undoubtedly far beyond what had been available at the Al Rahiri dinner.

Mulligan had been just as fascinated as Maurice when he had first laid eyes on the room, but for entirely different reasons. Whilst Maurice's innocent wonder had taken in the sights, sounds and smells of his first taste of Paravelian hospitality, at the back of his mind Mulligan had been calculating the cash value of everything he laid his gaze upon. Among his many talents as a thief, Mulligan had a particular flair for appraising items. He could spot a fake or a forgery from a dozen paces and was highly amused that this room contained such a large quantity of cut glass and paste. However, all was not lost, for the out of town Paravelian guests would never stoop so low. Virtually every single one of them dripped with gems and precious metals - the gentlemen as much as the ladies. It seemed fine jewellery in Paravel was not a gender concern, they all wore rings, chains, fobs and lavish drop earrings that glittered as they caught the candle light. The other thing Mulligan had delightedly spied were the jewel-encrusted toe buckles. They were apparently quite 'the thing' this season, and whilst most of them were low-grade rhinestones and coloured glass there were a significant number that were worth in excess of twenty guilders a clasp. Ideal. Toe buckles were small, easy to conceal and not likely missed if they were light enough. Like most jewellery, their disappearance would likely be chalked up to misfortune, particularly if Mulligan were canny enough not to steal both from a pair. It was a question of timing. Judging by the way they were putting away the frankly awful red wine, by midnight most of them would be what was colloquially referred to in the less salubrious parts of town as 'too pissed to puke' - a term that Mulligan had never understood because it was usually a total lie. Not that he was much bothered. As long as they didn't choose to puke on his head whilst he was hiding under their chairs trying to steal the buckles from their shoes, he couldn't care.

Clara was beginning to think they were never going to get the opportunity to make a profit. They had spent the last few hours running about the kitchens and scullery at the beck and call of the gargantuan sweating cook who had a fast tongue and an even quicker strap hand when displeased. Clara had first-hand experience of that. Hiding in the larder, she nursed a blossoming bruise on the back of her calf as she poked through the contents of the shelves. There were some expensive spices in here, but she doubted there was more than a couple of guilders worth all together. It was better than nothing she thought as she tried to decide how to conceal them about her person. She hadn't actually managed to lift anything when she was joined in the larder by Luce holding a large ring of keys.

"Come on," she hissed grabbing Clara by the sleeve, "We've got twenty minutes the staff are eating."

Luce explained the plan. Apparently the banquet had been served and nothing more needed to be done below stairs for a while, except the cleaning up. At this point, the butler was upstairs with his fleet of footmen and the cook, the under-butlers and the hawk-faced woman in the brown dress would have a twenty-minute supper break in the inner kitchen. The drivers, pages and assorted staff from other households that had been running around lifting and carrying were also allowed dinner, which was to be served in the outer kitchen and eaten wherever there was space, under the supervision of the Head Stabler. Clara didn't inquire how Luce had come by the cellar keys but she could see what she was thinking of.

"Bu'," started Clara, "How'z we supposed slip outta supper?"

"Simple," grinned Luce.

Luce sank her bowl of vegetable soup with frightening speed and excused herself to the privy. Clara, who was sitting on the opposite side of the room kept eating but with her ears pricked. Luce's plan was ingenious in its simplicity. Even a house of this size would have to pack beasts and carts in pretty tight to accommodate everyone who had arrived tonight. The head stabler, who was currently ladling soup into a small bowl for timid looking girl with lank hair, would have had to work some kind of miracle to fit them all in without harm, and if he was any cop as a horseman he wouldn't relax until the horses were all safely returned to their correct carriages and out of his yard. Instead of heading directly for the privy Luce veered off towards the stables, picking her way carefully through the maze of carriages.

A few minutes later, Clara heard the sound she'd been expecting – one horse objecting loudly to something in such a way that all the horses around it started objecting too. The head stabler dropped the ladle into the copper pan with a clang and raced out of the scullery door without looking back. Luce reappeared with a broad grin a few moments later. Taking advantage of the chattering surge of servants heading for windows and doorways to get a look at what was going on in the yard, they threaded their way towards the back of the outer kitchen and the cellar.

For two girls who had basically grown up in the sewers, it was the work of barely five minutes to trot down the cellar steps, retrieve four bottles of expensive looking liquors and spirits and resurface locking the door behind them. Luckily, whatever Luce had started in the stables had escalated and most of the visiting drivers were now out in the yard trying to calm their own horses as the rest looked on listlessly from the back door step. Without any delay, Luce and Clara went straight to the grain bins in the outer kitchen and dropped a bottle into each one - pausing only to scoop a thin layer of the real content over their takings before replacing the lids and joining the gathering outside.

"The beauty of this plan," thought Mulligan with an unbecoming degree of self-congratulation, "is that by the time most of these frilly nit-wits miss their toe buckles they'll be safe and sound back in Paravel and they'll just send out for new ones in this week's fashionable styles."

He smiled blandly at Hortensia who he had been obliged to re-join, she really was the most uninteresting woman. She had made a bee-line for Metcalfe and the women had taken up residence on a large opulently padded couch beside the fire in the banqueting hall. Maurice, by virtue of the fact that he had some pretence at etiquette, found himself sitting to one side, trying to appear interested. The man that he had taken to thinking of as Mr Metcalfe, even though he was technically Lord Metcalfe San Clear, was attacking a large pewter plateful with gusto and had no intention of stopping for a chat. Maurice didn't mind, he just smiled effetely and fingered his wine goblet.

It took him the best part of the rest of the evening to offload Hortensia again. He'd been forced to dance with her which he did with good grace and no rhythm whatsoever, so that when another gentleman asked for her hand and she looked over with some enthusiasm for his consent he was able to nod with magnanimous reluctance. The band had barely finished the first bars of the rondo before Maurice slipped back into the banqueting room in search of a specific implement.

After that, he managed to avoid company altogether, picking his way through the exquisite food as he waited for the debauchery to reach a crescendo. This really was quite a sight to see - no wondered everyone else tried to pretend to be disgusted by the excesses of aristocratic Paravel. From what Maurice-Mulligan could see they were simply jealous that they lacked the skills to enjoy themselves quite so thoroughly. It was a shame, Mulligan reflected, that it was a work night or he would have dived in to just about everything on offer. As it was, he was reduced to scanning the fruit stands in search of something he had just realised would come in very handy. When he found it, he snatched it up and took himself off to lie in wait.

The third room that had been given over to the evening was actually a portion of the banqueting hall. A heavy screen had been pulled across to create a dark, warm room populated with fur rugs, cushions, stools and several low couches. The air was thick with a cloyingly sweet smoke that was a mixture of incense from low brass burners and opium from pipes. What light there was came predominantly from the large roaring fire that made the room excessively warm, although there were a handful of oil lanterns casting pools of shadow at various intervals. The music was muted in here, and there were four smug looking footmen specifically to attend to the needs of guests that ventured into the room.

In Paravel, this would have been a separate room known as the 'Salon' but this was a house originally of Albion construction so a banquet hall and a ballroom had been considered sufficient. The purpose of the Salon was to provide a quiet corner for intimate conversation and such like. Since this was not Paravel, the room had accumulated a more than usually large number of people who were not so much interested in the pursuit of acquaintance or hedonism as finding somewhere quiet and warm to doze off after a good meal. Mulligan smirked to himself as he wondered over to one of the darker corners. If he sat still long enough, then with a bit of luck the smug footmen would forget he was there. On the floor beside a stool he folded himself as small as possible and, trying not to breathe too deeply, let time pass.

He was rewarded for his patience sooner than expected. Barely fifteen minutes later, a portly Paravelian in an ageing velvet frock coat and thread bare pastel silk knickerbockers lowered himself onto the stool right beside Mulligan. Apparently, pleasantries were not required in the Salon, as the man flopped down without a word. He paused for a moment to see if there was going to be a sudden acknowledgement of his presence. There wasn't. In fact, the man simple shifted himself in his seat causing the seams in his knickerbockers to strain worryingly and then he flopped back against the wall, his eyes closed. His wig had tilted forward over his brow and his chins had gathered up on his chest. It was a most unbecoming sight, not that Mulligan really cared - he was preoccupied trying to work out what to do. The rattling snore that issued from the man seconds later decided for him. Fate was smiling on him, for now at least. He drew the small silver pear knife he had appropriated from the banquet table (which in itself was a valuable item) and leaned slightly to the side. One deft slice and the soft shoe leather relinquished its gem encrusted buckle straight into his hand. He didn't even need to look, allowing him to keep his eyes on the footmen as they attended to other guests. Without even the delay of looking at his prize he transferred it to an inside pocket that Clara had specially sewn into his jacket and tucked the knife away up his sleeve.

In Albion, if you were still at a social event during the midnight rush etiquette dictated you should make the correct noises, send for your cloak and your carriage and leave. In Paravel, things were different. In for a penny, as they liked to say. If you were out for the night, you were out for the whole night. These affairs tended to last until dawn and sometimes beyond. It wasn't unheard of for the hosts to swap minstrels or keep a couple of rooms closed until the early hours to give the guests variation. There was also a whole separate menu saved for just after midnight. *Après-le-retour* cuisine was very much in vogue these days, and good 'post-rush' chefs were much sought after.

This being Aberddu, the Butler and the hawk-nose housekeeper had anticipated the confusion come midnight. A compact but varied '*Après-le-retour*' spread had been devised and prepared by the normal cook and her browbeaten kitchen maids. It would be served with ceremony once the Albion guests, and anyone else without the stomach or stamina for any more debauchery had departed. It was something to see, as the whole fleet of liveried footmen paraded through the ballroom to dispatch the departing guests and clear the banquet table

Mulligan had to admit that this corner was really quite comfortable. He was loath to get up but he supposed he better. He could hear that the music from the minstrels had ended, leaving only the soft eerie melodies in his head. It had been a lucrative endeavour at the start. He had two poacher-pockets sagging with buckles to prove it. However, he had been forced to stop because the room was talking to him. He gave up fighting it and let it. Now, though, his head was starting to clear like the water of a mountain stream gurgling over stones as it coiled down towards the majestic flood plains. He could almost taste the fresh, crisp air. With a contented smile curling his lips, he pulled himself to standing and made his way slowly into the ballroom. The floor beneath his feet was deliciously viscous. He blinked furiously as he stepped into the twinkling lights of the ballroom. He could hear Metcalfe before he saw any of them.

"Maurice," she exclaimed in her shrill, overexcited end-of-the-evening voice. "There you are,"

"Yes," mumbled Maurice-Mulligan with a serene smile, "here I am." He giggled. "Here I am indeed." He wove his way across the floor towards Metcalfe and her companions. He was more than a little amused by it all. There he was, just as Metcalfe said, standing in this fancy pants ballroom wearing a fine suit - albeit full of hot shoe buckles - and topped to the eyeballs full of fine food, cheap wine and passive opium. For a kid who grew up in the muck on the docks, it was funny as hell. He burst out laughing, much to Metcalfe's confusion. Maurice tried to pull Mulligan back into role again as he fought against the comfortable blue envelope around him to take control of the situation again. Through the haze he plucked the name Hortensia and scanned the faces surrounding Metcalfe. None of them seemed to fit. Metcalfe stepped in to help him out before he had to frame the question.

"Horti went home," said Metcalfe gently, as though she was trying to be kind. "With Adam." She paused to see how Maurice would react and when all he did was stare at her curiously she added, "Adam Fitzgerald? Weavers and dyers? Tall, big nose, black curly hair, very long legs?".

Maurice had no idea, he made a strange rolling gesture with his head that was a combination of a nod and a shake.

"Fair enough," he said mildly trying to focus his eyes. He was largely unbothered by this, as it meant he wouldn't have to go half way around the quarter to take the tedious woman home. Gerald, or whatever his name was, was welcome to her, much to his amusement he felt that the long streak of piss would do very well with the drip. Evidently, her Albion propriety didn't stretch that far after all. "Well, you know what they say," he added as an ill-advised afterthought, "When in Paravel…" and winked.

Metcalfe snorted, looked him up and down, thoroughly amused, and then reach over to smooth down his lapels. All she said in response was

"Apparently so."

It wouldn't be until later that Maurice had enough sense to realise that he should probably have appeared more crestfallen that he had been ditched for the secretary of the Weavers and Dyers Guild, but at that moment he was too intoxicated to feel anything other than relief at being spared.

Fumbling through the poppy-haze, he decided it was time to go home. He hung around in the ballroom looking dazed as the Metcalfe set streamed out towards their waiting carriages. He would give them time to get clear away before he followed suit. He wasn't entirely sure but he thought he might be swaying. Slowly he turned around, stumbled over to a chair and sat down clumsily. A familiar voice said,

"Fancy seeing you here Mulligan." He turned to look and found himself face to face with Lady Iona, Duchess of Pringle, complete with a ludicrous feathered head-dress and ample décolletage. Apparently, even though she was technically Albion nobility, Iona Pringle preferred the Paravelian fashions.

"Iona," he said, with an intoxicated leer, not even attempting to talk to her face, "as always a pleasure."

"The pleasure is entirely yours," returned Iona wryly with a feline smirk as Maurice continued to gaze freely at her cleavage, "and if you keep staring at my tits like that I may be forced to send you a bill." Not as embarrassed as he should have been, he managed to force himself to look away.

"Can I help you at all *Madam*?" he hissed, adding the 'madam' with malicious relish.

"I don't know what you're up to *Maurice Fortescue*," she said with amused emphasis on the name, "and I don't really care, but I think you dropped this." She held out a square inch of gem-encrusted silver. Mulligan just stared at it, he was having trouble coordinating his brain and hands. "I'd put it away quickly if I was you," said Iona pushing it into his hand "before the Comte de Claudeaux notices you've got a bit of his shoe." Mulligan nodded slowly and slipped it back into his brimming poachers pocket. "And I'd go home now if I were you, before I embarrass myself any further or drop anything else. If I'm any judge, you'll be chasing dragons for another few hours yet." Quasi-stupefied and unsure of the direction of the ceiling; Mulligan did at least have enough sense left to nod in agreement.

"Don't worry," said Iona with a patronising grin, "the footmen are used to it. They'll put you straight in your carriage." Then, without another warning she put her fingers in her mouth and very inelegantly whistled to attract attention of a nearby liveried flunky who was at that moment crossing the ballroom, baring a large silver platter and heading for the banquet hall.

"Madam?" he said stooping to present them with the platter. Iona helped herself to two or three of the small red-brown squares that smelled vaguely of salt fish and said,

"This gentleman is ready to leave."

"Of course Madam," he said in a pompous nasal drone, snapped his fingers and beckoned a colleague. Then he disappeared into the banquet hall without another word.

"I just love *après –la-retour*," mumbled Iona smugly, popping two of the squares into her mouth at the same time as she stood up.

"See you around," she said through a mouthful, winked playfully, clapped Mulligan companionably on the back and followed the footman and his tray.

Being relatively junior, Mr Fortescue had to wait his turn until more important people drove away and left enough space for Luce to steer the cart carefully out of the yard. After ten minutes of Luce and Clara trying not to giggle as Maurice Fortescue hummed and whistled and eventually started to sing his way through the great street-corner classics such as 'You Can Tell She's a Lady by What She Charges', Sir Charelton Reynolds and his wife Lady Rebecca finally pulled away, leaving their path clear and they were free to go. Luce rolled the cart slowly on to the main thoroughfare that was surprisingly busy given the hour and started to clatter forward with a fair lick of speed. They turned the corner into a narrow side street. Luce had worked out that it was just about feasible as a somewhat undignified short cut. As they rattled rapidly over the uneven ground, Mulligan stopped singing and suddenly vomited. At this point, Clara scuttled up the cart and joined Luce out of the splattered range. They both stopped trying not to laugh.

It was late the following morning when the five of them reconvened in the kitchen. Mulligan, whose first opium experience had not agreed with him, had spent much of the night on the back step clutching a pail and groaning. This elicited no sympathy from the girls whatsoever. Angel, who'd fallen asleep on the hearth waiting for them to return, said it served him right for over-indulgence and her sour face was only softened when Clara produced a handful of sweetmeats which she had purloined for her from an unattended dish in the kitchens just before they left.

Clara and Luce were so exhausted from their evening of non-stop kitchen work and larceny that they fell asleep almost as soon as they sat down on the range rug. Min was nowhere to be seen. She had moved herself into one of the empty bedrooms on the day she had flounced out of the kitchen and now she spent most of her time in there, generally only venturing out for food or when she needed something. None of the others much cared, you couldn't afford to be soft in their business and if she wanted to get over it then she could. They were all too busy to really worry, as long as she didn't start expecting them to run around after her more than they already did.

That morning, she appeared almost on the dot of the morning eight hour looking curious and much less hostile than she had in previous days. The other girls, who'd slept curled up together on the hearth, had been up since dawn taking affectionate pot-shots at the dry-heaving and white-faced Mulligan, who was still on the back step in dashing distance of the privy and holding his nose to block out the smell of cooking.

Breakfast was thick oatmeal porridge. Min, who was now experiencing better food regularly poked hers with a spoon, a look of disdain on her face. Angel watched her with a bitter sneer on her face, as Luce and Clara, still full of the night before, rattled away about what they had seen, done and eaten. Mulligan had managed to wriggle himself around so that he was mostly inside the boot-hole and could join the conversation.

"So," said Min, after five minutes of picking over her oatmeal. "What did you actually steal?" She was totally uninterested by the stories of their escapades and just wanted to get to the point. Clara put down her spoon and leapt to her feet to fetch the bottles. None of the girls could claim expertise when it came to expensive liquor but these bottles certainly looked the part. Luce and Clara had had very little time to select what they stole and used only two criteria - they put their hands on the first four bottles that had both a fully intact wax seal on the cork and a thick layer of dust. It didn't help that only Angel could read, and even she wasn't able to decipher any unfamiliar words on the hand-written labels. Mulligan on the other hand was very impressed. They had lifted two bottles of fifty-year old claret, a flask of the famous Paravon turquoise gin and a bottle of a clear and viscous-looking fluid that Mulligan hazarded as being something in the realms of vodka. Angel snorted at that, and pointed out with a bitter chuckle that Mrs D's grime-remover was also something in the realms of vodka. For the first time in a while they all laughed, if only for a moment.

Min nudged the bottles curiously.

"What're they worth?" she asked pensively, gently rubbing the caked dust from the label of the flask.

"Oh," said Mulligan, as all eyes turned to him, "well it depends on getting a good fence but I'd imagine we'd get a fair whack, maybe as much as five, ten guilders a bottle." Min acknowledged this with a subtle nod, pleased but not excited by it. Five to ten guilders was apparently no longer big money in her eyes. Luce, Clara and Angel were more impressed but they stayed quiet

"What else did you get?" she said, rubbing the dust from her fingers. Mulligan groaned,

"In my jacket," he said waving a hand up the stairs. "Luce?"

"Hang on," said Luce, leaping up. Clara had taken the jacket off him on the way home to save on laundry and Luce had stashed its contents safely in her boots when she had got in to the kitchen. She grabbed them from beside the range where she'd kicked them off. The irony of storing these finely crafted, gem-encrusted buckles stolen from soft leather slip on shoes inside a pair of stinking hobnail boots was lost on Luce as she tipped the haul on to the kitchen table. This seemed to please Min far more, she smiled down as the pile twinkled up at her. Mulligan had become quite adept at slicing the buckles free and pocketing them before he'd become too addled to continue. There must have been more than a dozen and a half there, several of which were clearly extremely high quality. They drew the eye, and all five of them were staring at the hoard mesmerized and reluctant to touch.

"Now these are worth a pretty penny," said Mulligan redundantly.

"We're going to need a higher class of fence," said Angel in a whisper, which was the closest she was going to get to sounding excited. Min was the first to lose interest,

"What else?" she said, looking around greedily.

"What do you mean what else?" said Mulligan crossly, surely that was enough.

"Well, is that all you got?" she was starting to look sulky again.

"Yes," snapped Mulligan. He was content with the night's work, his head was pounding and now an urchin was being snotty at him.

"Oh," said Min, with poorly conceal scorn, "okay then."

"It took bloody long enough; I tell ya"' said Clara wrinkling her nose in annoyance. "I've still got flippin' bran in my 'air." and Luce just grunted. Strangely, Angel - who hadn't had an active role in the night's thievery - seemed to take the most affront at this comment.

"And just exactly what have you lifted this week?" she demanded of Min coldly. Min returned her venomous look and matched her tone as she said,

"More than you," but did not elaborate on the point.

"We're playing too small," she continued before anyone else could chuck their pennyworth into the slowly blossoming argument. "We need to seriously up our game if we're going to make any real money." Clara just looked askance at her, to her a couple of guilders was real money and she remembered not that long ago when Min would have considered it was a fortune.

"Well, it's not you has to do the actual lifting is it?" retorted Mulligan, clearly burned by this disparagement. "It takes time to plan you know. You can't just waltz in and start helping yourself to things. People notice. It's not as though any of you have the option to do it is it?"

Min just snorted scornfully.

"Why on earth did you bother with this crazy façade if all you were going to do was lift a few jewels? Why go to all the trouble of having us around if you're not going to use us?"

"Well," hissed Mulligan, "what exactly do you suggest?"

They sat and listened and by the end of Min's careful explanation they had to admit - albeit grudgingly - that she did in fact have a point. There were several ways to skin a cat after all, and apparently even more to help yourselves to rich people's stuff.

"Okay," said Angel, who was more than happy to be nice to Min now that she was actually contributing something more to the scheme than snarky comments and piles of dirty laundry. "When's the next do, and who's the first target?"

Chapter 12
The Use of Tabitha Fortescue

Tabitha Fortescue, although a relatively recent arrival, had already established a reputation. She was, as one of the more forgiving mothers styled it, a sweet-natured free-spirited child desperately in want of a mother. Behind closed doors, the governesses and nurses of the Metcalfe set, who were forced to deal with Tabitha on a daily basis, were far less polite. They called her ill-disciplined, contrary-wise and in desperate want of a large dose of fish-oil and liver salts. Even further behind those tightly shut doors, one of them had gone so far as to call her an 'absolute pain in the arse' and such was the level of agreement that none of the others tutted at the use of that appallingly vulgar colloquialism. The mothers, who were in a position to be far more charitable as they did not have to do anything for the child apart from smile indulgently at her, had discussed the matter of Tabitha in depth.

It was common knowledge that Mr Maurice Fortescue had been very recently widowed and had moved to Aberddu for an undisclosed reason - which the women had decided was very likely that he was trying to escape the painful memories of his wife and start afresh with his daughter. It was also well-known that Tabitha had no nurse and, apart from the suspect-looking maid and the stable boy, was alone with a grieving father. They had therefore decided to take her discretely under their wings, inviting her to join their own children almost every day, so that could benefit from company, structure and their genteel feminine influences.

Min had spent a significant amount of time painting this portrait of Tabitha Fortescue. She had initially considered sinking in to the background, but she was well aware that she was never going to be able to catch up with six years of life as a child of the Albion gentry and she was at great risk of somehow not quite fitting in. Instead, she had elevated the concept of hiding in plain sight to a whole new level: far better to hide her little uncertainties amongst a whole festival of whimsical oddity than have to make excuses for them at every turn.

It had the added bonus of making life easier for her when it came to moving around the houses she visited. Everyone else would be in the solar playing a game and Tabitha would be in the garden with her nose in the flowers, sunny afternoons that saw everyone else out on the grass playing with hoops and balls saw Tabitha in the shade of a tree leafing through a large, dusty book. Whenever she was corrected or brought back in line, albeit briefly, by an exasperated nurse or governess, she was all big-eyed contrition and dismay, but she never seemed to learn. One notoriously uptight nurse asked her to return to the table eleven times during a single nursery tea, only to be met with the same vague "oh okay, sorry," followed by a non-quite-apologetic half smile every single time. The governess later confessed that whilst she didn't mind children who were 'away with the fairies', in the case of Tabitha Fortescue she'd very much prefer it if the fairies kept her.

It was in this Nurse's domain the following week that Tabitha went to the privy during dance practice and did not return for the best part of half an hour. Saddled with the responsibility of half a dozen offspring whilst her mistress took a leisurely tea with their mothers in the garden, she didn't really have the wherewithal to find out where the wretched girl had got to this time, nor did she really care. If she had wondered off below stairs the cook would no doubt put her to work unless the housekeeper laid hands on her first and dragged her back upstairs by the nose. If she broke anything expensive or important the nurse would probably get off extremely lightly - a mild scolding at best - because no one else could get Tabitha Fortescue to do anything either.

Tabitha may well have been mooning about gazing at objects of interest, but Min was not. She was taking the opportunity to very carefully case as much of the house as she could. She was making a mental note of every door and window that could be utilized. She was trying to guess where staff might be whilst the family were out. The household were Aragonese in descent, although they had been on the mainland for long enough that both their younger daughters had been born here. Only their arrogant son and his impetuous older sister remembered the 'Homeland' and its stark social hierarchy. Luckily, they were both too busy rebelling against the liberalism of Aberddu to bother with their sisters' friends.

Even though the rest of family had tried to adapt to mainland living, first in Albion and then - once the new order had been imposed - Aberddu, their home was still very much in the Aragonese style. Children were confined to the top of the house, two flights up where they were neither seen nor heard by anyone but the steel-willed and hirsute nurse. The family's private rooms were on the first floor, including a generous solar that Tabitha had wondered into and been removed from gently but firmly by a stern footman who had been polishing the silverware. She had noticed that there was a strongbox in there, which had been open and invitingly full at the time. Guests were supposed to be restricted to the ground floor, which was split into two to form a dining hall and a 'ladies withdrawing parlour' where the refined ears of the Aragonese ladies could withdraw peacefully from the ribald talk of their menfolk, or more accurately have a good bitch without being interrupted or patronised. Kitchens and utility areas were out the back of the house in a separate low building not far from the back access of the dining room – another Aragonese idea. It performed a two-fold function. Predominantly, it reduced the risk of the kitchen fires burning the whole house down but it also had the handy side-effect of that the aroma of the cooking obscured the less pleasant odours from the stable and privies beyond.

Min hazarded a guess that even in Aragonese households the kitchen wenches slept in the kitchen, the stable boys in the hayloft and everybody else too lowly to have a bedroom probably slept by the hearth in the dining hall where the banked fire would keep them warm. She doubted that anyone slept in the Ladies' parlour. What they needed was a path to the solar and the family chambers on the first floor that avoided the main hall and the back of the house. Luckily the stairs, unusually, were not in either the main hall or in the welcoming chamber by the front door. They were tucked in a small vestibule behind the ladies' parlour. If they could find a way to get to them then the thick stone walls should make it easy to climb them without disturbing anybody. This was her fifth or sixth trip to this household, she had lost count. She had no idea why she had been so solicitously invited here, unless it was because the youngest daughter Marina-Julienne found it hilariously funny to watch her play up the nurse. Min didn't care, whatever the reason it was very convenient.

Under the stair case was a slatted wooden door that wasn't locked. Min opened it cautiously and squinted to examine the floor. It seemed to be there, so she tapped a cautious toe into the darkness and was relieved to find solid boards beneath her feet. She slipped into the dark and found herself in a strange smelling little room. She was surrounded by cloaks, hoods and boots that had been hung on various hooks and rails. The smell was damp and must, but there was also the faint hint of salt-sea air. In fact, there was a breeze.

Min dropped to her knees and followed her nose. It took moments to find the wicker covered vent behind a damp and grubby cloak hem. It was quite tight weave and wasn't letting in much light but Min guessed it would still be easy to break. Running her hands around the edge of the frame, she found the pegs that held it in place and with some effort managed to pull three of them loose. That gave the screen enough play for her to be able to squeeze a hand out. She left it at that, in case some diligent household worker spotted that the screen was detaching and went to put it right. With a gleeful smirk she crawled backwards out of the dark space. Then, she straightened up, brushed down her pinafore and skipped back up to the nursery as though it was perfectly natural to take over half an hour in the privy.

The host of the evening's entertainment was a proper Aberddu-born parvenu. Once known as 'Knock-out Jack', he was now Sir John Taylor, Guildmaster of the Weavers and Dyers' Guild. According to Metcalfe, he really had worked his way up from the gutters of the North Wall slums by a combination of hard slog, sheer cheek and a wife with exquisite taste. The wife, Lady Darnia Taylor, who had started out as a docklands' runner was also credited by the Metcalfe set for making sure that her upcoming husband comported himself in a clean, civilised manner befitting to their growing social stature. He might still have a voice like 'sludge in a down-spout', to quote Metcalfe, but at least he could sit at table and chew with his mouth closed which was something you couldn't always count on from the aristocracy, especially those brought up in Paravel. The other feature of note that Metcalfe had mentioned about Sir John's house was that they had the most sophisticated garderobe she'd ever seen, not least because it was actually inside the main building. That was all that Maurice Fortescue knew about Sir John Taylor and his lovely wife, except that they had kindly extended an invitation for an 'informal late spring soiree' to him and a companion of his choosing. It wasn't to be the same kind of grandiose affair as the Marquis of Ventruvian's Ball and he'd had to seek a little subtle advice.

According to Metcalfe informal and casual were not the same thing. Soiree implied cold supper, snippets of entertainment such as minstrels and jugglers, lots of gossiping and probably a brief spate of communal dancing. Apparently, informal still meant normal evening attire, it simply implied that they were excused wigs, feathers, ribbons, powder, lace, stockings and excessive jewellery. Maurice just nodded politely to this, as he wasn't entirely sure what that all meant and until the last few weeks would have assumed that that was the kind of sentence that only applied to women. He didn't question it, he just helped himself to another fruit bun, sat back and let Metcalfe rattle away.

The four girls were far too busy organising their own evening's entertainment to have any interest in the soiree at all. Mulligan appeared in the kitchen just after the evening five hour with the intention of getting Clara to sort out some hot water for a bath and to mend a small tear in the shirt he was planning on wearing, only to find that all four girls were at the kitchen table with looks of concentration on their faces. Min had used a piece of chalk to sketch a floor plan of the target house on the kitchen table and they were currently moving egg cups around it as though they were playing some kind of surreal pub game.
"Er, Clara," said Mulligan loftily, flapping his shirt in front of him, "When you've got a moment." Clara looked up from the table but before she could open her mouth to respond, Angel beat him to it.
"Get your own bath water and mend your own shirt" she sneered, "Clara's busy. And for god sake, sort out your hair." Mulligan shut his gaping mouth, even though he was somewhat put out by the tone in her voice. Clara wasn't actually the maid and they did have better things to do. He knew she was right, but he didn't like being told. As he took the pails out to the pump, he thought ruefully to himself that he would sooner be in their shoes tonight - for one thing their shoes almost certainly didn't pinch. In three trips, he'd filled the large iron pan on the range, pumped the bellows enthusiastically. Then he went over to the table to put his oar in. After all, he was the master thief here.
"Are you sure that's wise?" he interjected after he had badgered Min into repeating her explanation of how they would be gaining access to the house. "That's quite a distance by rope." His sentence ran out of steam before he could finish the word rope because Angel and Min were both glaring at him. He managed to hold his tongue for about another thirty seconds as Min continued her second run through of the plan, purely for his benefit.

"How do you plan on opening the strongbox?" was his next question, a tone of amused condescension edging its way in. This was met with another icy stare from Angel. Min said simply,

"Clara," and scrunched her brow with scorn as though this was beyond obvious. He let her continue, and when she was just about to explain the exit strategy - Angel, Luce and Clara were going to drop down the rope with the haul leaving Min to untie it and let it drop. Min would then slip back into the house, after closing the strongbox and the solar door behind her – and exit through the wicker panel. He opened his mouth to interrupt again, thought better of it and closed it. Angel saw. She smiled in a dangerous feline way and said in a hushed, threatening voice,

"I realise you could easily have picked up a couple of kids from the Temple, but you didn't. We may be sewer-brats but we're also professionals. What do you think we were doing before?" It was an ice-cold challenge that Mulligan almost choked with shock at, "It's our job, so back off okay? Just go get dressed and for gods' sake do your hair." She turned back to the plan, ignoring Mulligan who just stared at her with his mouth open for a full thirty seconds afterwards.

Mulligan was inexplicably irritated by the total lack of interest the girls had shown in either his opinion about their plan or what he intended to wear to the soiree. He was still in a taciturn sulk when Luce pulled the cart around to take him to the do. None of the girls could have cared less; they were in the kitchen kitting up so that they could leave the moment Luce got back. It had been a long time since all four of them had looked and felt like themselves. Min had put on her trousers for the first time in months and they'd decided they would all go barefoot for the occasion.

It was only a twenty-minute drive to Sir John's town house which had a glorious view of over the docks out across the Aragon straits. Luce took the most direct route home, cutting down side-streets and narrow lanes that all the drivers of the small carts used when they had no passengers and made it home in just over ten minutes to find Clara with the range open and a piece of charcoal in her hand. Unusually clean, they had realised that soot would be needed so that their pale skin didn't shine in the moonlight they were ready. Clara turned down the oil lamp in the scullery window and the four of them slipped out of the back door and into the shadows of the soft summer night.

They found the house easily enough, and were relieved to see the first two floors in darkness. Only the nursery floor had any light at all - a small flickering candle lantern in the window Min knew belonged /to the older of the two girls and an oil lamp glowing in the nurse's chamber. It being dark, the stable hands and most of the rest of the staff would be in bed, only the lady's chambermaid would be waiting up for the family's return. If she had any sense she would be in the main hall with the rest, toasting her toes by the fire. It wasn't a cold night as such, but after a cloudless sunny day the sea air always brought a chill after the sun had set.

As planned, Luce Clara and Angel tucked themselves into the bushes around the front door and waited, like a set of horrifying garden gnomes. Min slipped off into the gloom to pick her way carefully towards the wicker grill. This was the first risk point in the plan. As far as they could calculate, the grill let out on to a small patch of ground within plain sight of one of the kitchen windows. If there was anyone still about in the kitchens it would take all of Min's not inconsiderable skills to sneak past undetected. She paused in a puddle of darkness and waited for a moment. The lights in the kitchen seemed to be out. She was pretty certain that it was only the glow of the banked down range that left any trace of colour at all, but she wanted to be certain. She could smell the scent of the herbs from the beds by the kitchen windows. The aromas thyme, lovage, rosemary and sage coiled up on the tails of the warm summer air.

After a few minutes, when she was certain that she was safe, she slipped out of her cover and trotted around to where she hoped to find the wicker grill. There it was. Exhaling with relief, she dropped to her knees and pulled the grill, which was still loose. Making a gap, she pushed her scrawny arm through so that she could pop free the remaining pegs. Carefully, she collected them up and pushed them in to a corner for safe keeping. The gap was more than ample for someone as slight as Min to crawl through, even with a large coil of rope around her and she managed to get herself comfortably inside in a matter of seconds. Conscientiously, she pulled the grill back across the gap and slipped a couple of pegs into place to keep it still.

With the same steady caution she made her way to the cupboard door. She clicked the latch and pushed it open so that she could smell the fresher air of the passageway. There was a small candle lantern hanging from a bracket on the wall opposite the door, just enough light that she could be sure the corridor was empty as she slipped out. The flagstones were damp and cold beneath her bare feet, she grimaced but didn't utter a sound. Without pausing, she made her way straight up to the first floor. She knew that the solid oak staircase wouldn't squeak under her meagre weight but she was a little warier of the landing. She tiptoed towards the door to the solar, ready for the heavy wood and creaking iron hinges. Just in case, she moved carefully past the sleeping chamber that was directly at the top of the stairs and padded to the end of the passageway. She reached out in front of her in the dim light groping about for the heavy velvet curtain that covered the door to the solar. She found it easily enough, and stretched her fingers out to find the door. Nothing. She stepped forward until she was up to her shoulder and still hadn't put her hand on solid wood. Her heart started pounding. Had she made a mistake, was this not the solar door? Was she waving her hand into someone's bed chamber? Was there someone watching her flailing hand, about to grab the wrist, yank her off her feet and trot her straight down to the militia building? She took a deep breath, and tugged the curtain slightly to one side. To her amazed relief she found herself looking directly in to the solar; the door was open.

She headed straight for the large rag-rug that covered the centre of the floor so that it would cushion any noises she might make. Then, she deftly un-loaded the kit she had been carrying – the rope, a bundle of lock-picks rolled in chamois and four sacks that had been wrapped around her middle. They always worked light; a habit born of necessity due to not having a vast deal of equipment in the first place.

This was the second big risk point: she had to open a window. She was al-most certain that they would open as they appeared to, but she had no idea if they needed a special technique or even worse opened with a dream-shattering screech that would bring the whole household running. With trepidation, she moved a small stool under the largest window and lifted the latch. She gave it a gentle nudge and, to her relieved delight, watched it swing out from the wooden frame without so much as a squeak. Clearly the housekeeping staff took pride in every little thing. Kneeling up on the stool, she let down the knotted rope. The end was tied around her waist and as long as Angel came up the rope first, she was enough weight to act as an anchor. Once everything was ready she leaned forward a little gave a short shrill whistle and hopped off the stool so that she was standing solidly on the wood of the floor.

The girls had climbed into far more complex places than this. There were no unsavoury patches of slime, unusual fungus or concealed traps to avoid on the way up, the window was ample space and they were dropping barely three feet to a nice, clean solid surface that definitely was not covered by any kind of effluvia.

First Angel, who scaled the rope so deftly it would have put Min in mind of a monkey had she any idea what a monkey was. Then, when both of them were tied on to the end, Clara and Luce followed. Luce, the last up, hauled the rope up after her and gently pulled the window closed. There was no point in provoking suspicion for the sake of a few seconds attention to detail. Clara had already found her way to the strongbox. Having trained underground, she worked mostly by feel and often with her eyes closed when it came to this kind of thing. It was a large but unsophisticated lock, set into the solid wood of the iron-bound chest. The chest had then been bolted to the floor joists and the wall as though the owners thought that Aberddu was full of marauders that would burst into their house, rampage upstairs into their private rooms, snatch all the valuables, even the trunk and run for it. Perhaps that was how they carried on in Aragon, but Aberddu was not that kind of city. In Aberddu, it was far more likely that someone would sneak in to your house in the depth of the night, pick the locks, rob you blind of anything that could be carried, cover their tracks and vanish. In these circumstances, a large locked chest just made it easier for them to locate everything you considered to be worth stealing and saved them the trouble of trying to work it out for themselves. It took Clara less than a minute to pop the lock and check for any sort of spring mounted booby-trapping, which was sadly lacking. Then with the utmost care, Luce and Angel lifted the heavy lid and the four girls stared down at their treasure.

The chest was full. There were pieces of silverware, small pouches containing items of gold, jewellery and coins and one or two objects that probably contained magic. At the bottom a shallow, flat wooden box. The girls filled their sacks carefully, aware that clattering and clanking would disturb the sleeping household. As soon as she was able, Clara eased this second box out and placed it carefully on the rug. The lock on this was finer and far better made. Well worth a look thought Clara, as she replaced the large pick in her chamois and selecting the fine but sturdy wires instead. This lock took significantly longer. In fact, she was still nudging and fiddling, eyes closed and tongue poking out in concentration, when the others had emptied the rest of the chest. None of them had spoken a word the entire time, and even though they were anxious to leave they didn't want to break the silence.

Suddenly, Clara grinned and the lid of the box popped. She lifted it up and looked down, expecting to see more jewellery but she was disappointed. There was nothing there but a load of old parchment. Some of the bits were tightly scrolled and tied with ribbon, the rest were just lying there. The girls looked sullenly between the papers and each other, totally underwhelmed. Clara pulled a few out; they were all exactly the same. What could possibly be the value of identical bits of parchment? Wondering if they were some kind of spell scroll she'd not encountered, Angel ran her hands over them but failed to detect any traces of magic. She tried to read the words but she didn't understand the language. Clara put the paper back in the box and let out an exasperated breath. She looked around at the others, they were all looking nonplussed. Taking this as general consent, she shut and locked the box and shoved it back where she had found it. Then she closed the strong box and replaced the lock.

With breathless poise, the girls picked up the sacks and headed towards the window. Much practice had taught them the most effective ways of moving heavy sacks up and down ropes. Luce shimmied down first, unburdened. Then, once she was on the ground Angel went next and stopped just out of Luce's reach, coiling her arm and ankle into the rope to anchor herself. Usually Clara would have gone, but as Min wasn't strong enough to anchor two of them, she stayed on the ledge. With confident dexterity, they passed the sacks from hand to hand, out of the window and down the rope, until they reached Luce with the minimum of clanking so she could stash them under a nearby bush. That done, there was a fair amount of swapping about so that Clara could climb down the rope and then Angel, leaving Min inside.

Wary of the noise a heavy rope might make thudding to the ground, she pulled it back up and departed the solar swiftly. Her route out was the same as her route in. Pausing only to reattach the wicker grill as best she could in the dark, she scuttled back around the side of the building to the meeting point in an alleyway about fifty yards from the house. She slumped against the wall and they all breathed out. They had left no signs of the break in and as far as they were aware hadn't disturbed anyone, so with luck it would be a while before the theft was discovered. Sticking to alleyways and shadow-pools in the lee of the buildings, they picked their way across the quarter and back home without exchanging a single word.

The whole operation took less than an hour and a half. The girls flopped down exhausted on the hearth, their bags of treasure beside them. Stoically

Angel pumped the bellows, then Clara yawned theatrically and the tense silence was broken. They all started talking at once, uttering their relief that everything had gone to plan. Luce heaved herself up and fetched a flask of cider and a large loaf of lardy bread from the pantry. They passed the food and drink between them, lounging against their sacks. Slowly, they fell into silence, although it was now contented and companionable, all of them feeling like themselves for now.

Min, who'd had by far the most strenuous part in the plan fell asleep cuddled up against Luce's leg. For a while they forgot that things weren't the way they had been before. They lost track of time. The midnight chime broke in to their contentment and Luce let out a strangled yelp that woke Min. Shoving her dazed friend to one side, Luce snatched up her cap from the kitchen table and raced out to the yard.

The soiree invitation had specified 'carriages at midnight'. She was late. She coupled up the horse as fast as he would let her and zoomed through the back streets arriving as the last carriage was rolling away. Maurice was standing in the doorway with a sour look of irritation on his face. A large, unrefined but well-dressed man, that Luce took to be Sir John himself, was standing placidly beside him with a pipe in his mouth. He was rosy with drink and clearly enjoyed an abundant lifestyle. The hand that wasn't guiding his pipe was softly caressing his ample belly. Luce rolled up in front of the steps panting just in time to hear Sir John grumble,

"Damn good thrashing, I would," before clearing his throat and jamming his pipe back in his mouth. Maurice just nodded in response and with a tight smile thanked Sir John for his hospitality. He climbed into the cart without a word to Luce and stamped when he was ready to go. Luce cracked the reins and started to drive.

She took him the long, dignified way home, pulling in to the yard twenty minutes later. He had not said a word, and when she turned to him as she dismounted she was shocked to see that he was actually red with fury.

"What?" she said with no intention of pretending servility in their own yard.

"You were late," he spat, "do you know how embarrassing that was?"

"Oh, get over it, I was only ten minutes or so late,"

"I was the last one there," he hissed.

"Well, you could have walked," she returned as she started to groom the horse.

"Walked?" spat Maurice, "Walked?"

"Yes, you know that thing that real people do," growled Luce as she heaved the stable door open. Maurice didn't respond to that immediately, but after a few moments, having recovered his upper-crust composure he said levelly,

"Perhaps I should thrash you."

Luce dropped the hay she was shifting and just stared at him,

"Or I could slit your throat in your sleep," she said with a dark, dangerous glint in her eyes. She took a threatening step towards him, and without another word he turned on the spot and stalked in to the house with his nose in the air.

Luce slammed about the stable as she finished off dealing with the now some-what disgruntled horse and stamped across the yard towards the kitchen, ready to go for another round with Mulligan. However, when she got there she found the others all sitting around the table with the night's takings spread out in front of them and Mulligan gaping at the hoard with same gleeful greed as the other three.

Chapter 13
Barrels and Fences

Two things became apparent over the day or so that followed. First of all, they were going to need to get the stolen goods off the premises as soon as possible for which they were going to need a much more sophisticated fence than Johnny Wossname down at the Black Market and a more reliable way of transporting the goods than humping them across the city via the tunnel network.

The second thing was that if it began to look like a crime spree, then even the Aberddu militia would start to notice. In order to avoid drawing too much attention to their crimes and thus provoking a militia lock-down or curfew followed by an uncomfortable fortnight and a potential trip down One Way Walk to Hangman's Hill, they needed to be cautious.

As Angel wisely put it, it was a 'less is more' situation. Yes, they could do a job every night for a week and then at the end of that week they could well be the richest heads spiked on the city wall. It was all very well making jokes about how stupid the militia were but they suddenly weren't funny when you had rope around your neck. That thought silenced them all for a second or so and Luce turned quite pale. Playing it safe was relatively easy, all they had to do was stick to pick pocketing for a few weeks, until an opportunity presented itself that they just could not resist.

The new fence was a far more complex and pressing issue than strategically doing nothing. Johnny Wossname was the best the girls had been able to get, a lot of the black market fences didn't deal with children and most of the ones that did were not nice people, even by black market standards.

Mulligan, on the other hand, was left pondering. He put on his own clothes for the first time in weeks for his trip into the one of the grubbier bits of the city. Taking Maurice Fortescue with him was a bad idea, just in case he was recognised or worse robbed. Besides, it was Mulligan who had business there, not Maurice; he would just be faintly discomforted by the smell and the greater prevalence of rats.

Iona Pringle only played at being a Lady, most of the time hanging around in powder and lace just irritated her. She enjoyed the finer things without a doubt, but she tended to treat her role as a rich Albion Dowager like an extravagant hobby. Generally, she lived and worked in the New Quarter – a quarter she had built up from the ruins of the Summer of Fire, using the fortune left by her late husband - the alleged Duke of Pringle – who, by all accounts, had been even less gentrified than his widow. She took her duties as a prominent citizen seriously but that didn't stop her dabbling in almost everything. She did a bit of this and a lot of that, most of which was blown out of all proportion in the retelling. She was an active member of the Guild of Adventurers and had vested interests in many place including the Temple of Kesoth. She was even a ranking member of the Guild Below – although this was not public knowledge. But for all that, there was only one place that Mulligan would bother looking for her.

Knocking Shops were to Aberddu what High Tea was to Albion, Frills were to Paravel and exotic dancing girls were to Jaffria - only all at once and charged by the hour. In a bustling port city, full of freshly paid sailors and traders that were travelling to B, having left their wife at A and possibly their mistress at C, discrete personal entertainment was a lucrative market. Aberddu prided itself on having the best services on the continent. There were probably a hundred knocking shops of all different sorts spread throughout the city state, and a lonely gentleman - or lady, for they were open to everyone - could find him or herself some company for a price to suit just about every pocket.

The Duchess' Pleasure was one of the finest establishments in the City. In the New Quarter, well away from the poxed-up dockland doxies that would raise their skirts in an alley for a groat and a mug of ale, it offered a wide range of personalised entertainments as well as excellent beers, wines, spirits, and ablutions. Valued clients were treated to a vast array of opportunities, and even better were offered a two-guilder surcharge that guarantee absolute discretion. It was rumoured that the great and the good, as well as the bad and twisted, bought their fun at the Duchess's Pleasure and Iona Pringle was the Duchess in question.

Even though Iona had the knack of appearing at home wherever she was, whether that was a Paravelian Ball or the back room of a docklands bar, for all her ease and poise the one role in which she seemed truly happy was as the Madam of the Duchess' Pleasure. If anyone would know where to find her, it was the staff there.

As luck would have it, Iona was actually in the Duchess' Pleasure when he came to call - although she made him wait in the bar for quite some time and when she finally did appear she arrived highly made up and in her 'working clothes'. Mulligan wouldn't have been surprised to discover that she had kept him hanging about just so that she could change out of something more respectable. She smiled at him, and he forced himself to meet her gaze, although his rebellious eyes took a meandering route upwards from her waist as she sat down on the stool beside him.

"I'm a busy woman," she said without making any pleasantries, exposing her garter as she sat down on a stool. "What can I do for you?" She punctuated this with a wryly raised eye brow and a half smile that cause a dimple to flicker across her cheek for a moment. It said clearly there might be plenty to choose from but it would be better not to assume you can afford any of it.

"I need a contact," said Mulligan flatly, refusing to fall for Iona's games.

"I thought you might," she said with a vulpine grin. "Do come down to my office." She got up, and when Mulligan hesitated, she added, "don't worry I don't charge for that. Well, not much anyway." Then she winked and strode away, trailing silk-satin and wafting scent of rose-water behind her. Mulligan scowled, finished his drink in a single gulp and followed her. A little humiliation would be worth it he told himself as he removed his hat to step through the low door. Just keep it cool.

When Mulligan returned home tired but triumphant, he announced to the girls that they had a new fence. He did not elucidate as to how he had come by the contact or who had helped him and he was very glad that none of them asked. They just stood and looked at him in stoic silence.

"Repack the stuff in the sacks," he ordered, flinging one of the empty potato sacks at Luce and another at Clara. "It'll be collected at dawn." Obediently Clara and Luce started to refill the sacks, making a neater job than had been possible on the night of the actual robbery. Min just looked on and chewed her lip wistfully until Luce kicked a third sack at her irritably and she joined in. Angel, who had been watching the whole thing with her arms folded and a look of sour irritation wiped across her face turned to Mulligan and said,

"And how do we know we're getting a good price?" She fixed him with a gaze so icy that he actually shivered. He had been dreading her reaction the most, because he was not about to explain himself and she wasn't going to like what he was about to say. Gulping and trying to keep a tight rein on his voice, so that he did not appear intimidated by a child, Mulligan said,

"You'll just have to trust me." He knew as the words rolled out of his mouth that it wasn't going to cut it but it was all he had. Angel's whole countenance became unpleasantly sharp. She didn't say a word; she didn't need to - the implied threat was by far and away enough. Mulligan forced himself to meet her gaze and smile at her until she snapped her head away and started to help Luce with her sack. As her back turned, Mulligan gulped again, let out a long-held breath and rubbed a wary hand around his scrawny throat. He had better be telling the truth.

The re-sacked valuables were lumped over and stored overnight in the unused fireplace in the drying room by the back door. Mulligan had offered to take care of the dawn call on his own but he had never really expected the girls to let him and was unsurprised when they didn't. When the morning six hour came and the Law Temple bell tolled out across the whispering hush of the early city morning, all four of them were up, dressed and waiting for him at the bottom of the main stairs.

A few minutes later, they heard the sound of steady hooves clopping up the road. If Luce had had to guess she'd have said it was a team of two sturdy ponies pulling a very well laden dray. When she opened the kitchen door in answer to the cheery clang of the bell moments later, she found that she was right.

A serious-looking Dwarven gentleman in a tough leather apron and gloves was standing on the doorstep with a business-like expression on his face. His colleague, the driver of said dray, was making himself either useful or scarce at the back of the cart.

"Good Morning," said the gentleman, "Delivery for Mr Parks?" Luce looked confused and turned to look back in to the kitchen to find Mulligan already stepping forward to take over. The dwarf didn't smile, he just nodded acknowledgement of the man who was clearly Mr Parks and said,

"Three barrels as requested sir, we'll bring them in now and take your empties afterwards."

"Thank you," said Mulligan, "Do you need a hand?" This was obviously the wrong thing to say, given the expression on the dwarf's face which changed from solemn to haughty.

"Thank you, no," he said tartly. "We'll bring them in now."

And so they did, hefting the large oak casks between them and staggering towards the back steps. Mulligan, aware that this 'delivery' was actually of empty barrels was impressed with the acting until he tried to nudge one of them sideways.

"Er," he said tentatively, not really keen on engaging the terse dwarves more than necessary, "excuse me?"

"Yes?" said the dray driver as he straightened up from depositing the second barrel.

"These barrels are empty aren't they?" asked Mulligan carefully. The dwarf fixed him with a contemptuous look and said,

"Of course sir."

When the third barrel was inside and the lids were popped open, Mulligan discovered that they were indeed completely empty.

"Now," said the first dwarf turning to Mulligan, "if your ... helpers... would be so good as to assist my colleague Kelyn by loading the barrels, you and I can sort out the payment."

It took a few minutes. Although each sack was a pretty neat fit for one barrel, Kelyn insisted on examining everything as it passed through his hands. It was clear from the expression on his face that he was impressed by the quality of the goods particularly some of the buckles, but he didn't utter a word. At last, he popped the lids back on to and with a considerable effort closed a metal ratchet clip on each side of the rim.

"Ninety guilders, I reckon," he said speaking for the first time in a gruff rumble.

"That's what I was told too," said the dwarf at the table with Mulligan, nodding stoically with grim satisfaction. "That's a deal then." He shook Mulligan's hand, signed his parchment with a flourish and folded it into thirds so that he could put his seal on it. Promissory notes were standard in this kind of transaction, lighter and easier to store than coin. This note was made out in the name of 'The Auld Clarensi United Treasuries' – the 'bank' that issued notes for the Guild Below.

Whilst his companion fastidiously unpacked his wax and seal, Kelyn started to load the goods in to the wagon. Much to Mulligan's amazement he picked up one of the barrels and almost flung it on to his shoulder, striding away with it as though it weighed no more than a small wayward child. Too curious to stop himself, Mulligan nudged the barrel he had nudged before and found it moved easily under his hand. He turned to the money dwarf, who was carefully dripping hot green wax on to the folded edge of the note and before he could open his mouth to ask, the dwarf said,

"It's the clips." He hadn't even looked up. "Those metal ratchet clips are enchanted to make full barrels lighter - the barrels themselves are lead lined. They weigh a bleeding ton unless the clip is closed." Mulligan shut his mouth again and watched with careful satisfaction as the dwarf pressed a seal into the soft wax and the puddle of green spread and solidified.

Once the dwarves had gone on their way, with Kelyn whistling merrily as they clattered through the misty dawn light, all five of them gathered around the promissory note. A folded piece of parchment that fitted neatly onto the palm of Mulligan's hand seemed so completely innocuous. One strong breeze and it could just flutter into the embers in the range. Clearly, Mulligan had that thought as he closed his hand around it just quick enough that Clara and Angel who were examining the crest on the seal weren't quite able to make out the all the devices. They had seen clearly enough that it was a seal from the Guild Below - which was quite distinctive in the way that it suggested at first glance that it might be any one of a half a dozen more reputable seals. However, it was necessary to take a far more prolonged look to ascertain exactly which seal-holding officer of the Guild had given their crest to this enterprise. It wasn't one that Angel had seen before, and Clara couldn't place it.

"Right, let's put this somewhere safe," said Mulligan, making to pocket it. Before he could, Min's bony hand darted out, grabbed his wrist with surprising strength and announced,

"I've got the perfect place! Come along Daddy dearest." Min pulled Mulligan by the wrist towards the stairs and the others followed them up to the drawing room. The remnants of the last fire were still littering the grate but Min didn't pause, she tiptoes deftly into the ashes and half-disappeared up the chimney.

She reappeared in a matter of seconds with a smut on her nose and a small round tin in her hand. She held out her other hand to Mulligan, who handed over the promissory note to her without question. She rolled it up and popped it in the tin and shot back up the chimney before anyone else could blink. As far as the girls were concerned it was a perfectly sensible hiding place, Mulligan who was neither small nor nimble enough to climb up the chimney was a little more dubious but was also aware that he was outnumbered, so said nothing. Having seen it safely stowed, the five of them separated and went about their day's business without a thought of it. None of them had thought to question Min as to why she had a tin stashed up the chimney in the first place.

Chapter 14
The Quiet Life

Living the 'quiet life' was easy for the first few days. Mulligan threw himself in to his social duties and Min was kept ever more occupied with tea parties, dance practises, learning clubs and whatnot. Angel went back to doing whatever it was Angel did when she was 'elsewhere' and Clara and Luce found themselves back to the household grindstone.

It had been agreed that the next big pull would be during the celebrations of Gaiahiak Haia - which was either the Elven name for The Alendrian National Freedom Day or the sound of someone trying to breathe through custard. Unaware of global politics, none of the girls were as amused as Mulligan about the idea of Alendrian National Freedom Day. Alendria was a large, Elven nation high in the moutains between Arabi in the east and Hasselt on the coast of the Sea of Stars. It was famous for majestic mountains, opulent citadels and a particularly vicious feudal system, in which humans featured below even the most criminal of Elven blood. Gaiahiak Haia was the day every year when the Alendrian Court pretended that the humans that lived there had equal social status with the nation's Elven population and celebrated by holding a vast banquet to which they invited about half a dozen of them. As far as anyone could tell, the irony was completely lost on the court.

It was being celebrated in Aberddu, like most national days from other 'civilised' cultures, by some imported posh-knob pointies - as Luce so eloquently put it - who were hosting a hoity-toity fourteen course banquet to which Mulligan and the rest of the in-crowd had been invited. It was three weeks away, and the girls were in the process of pinpointing a target from the invite list.

Min had made a hand-drawn floor plan of every single house she'd been to, thanks to Tabitha was exercising her whimsy and trying the patience of every governess in the district. The top two contenders were the Guild Master of the Merchants Guild, who was so paranoid that he had at least three well-filled, trapped and enchanted strong boxes about the house - any one of which would be a worthwhile target, and a peculiar character who style himself 'Principia Scarla'. He was a mincing chinless twit who claimed to be the first-born heir from a mineral-rich tin pot province somewhere in the region known as The Middle Kingdoms. General consensus was that he was a total fraud, although he was clearly stinking rich and ebulliently generous, if somewhat shrill and mercurial. Mulligan suspected he claimed to be from the Middle Kingdoms because the area was so volatile that not even the itinerant peasants could keep up with where they lived and who was in charge of them between land-grabs and sieges.

The Principia was very much unmarried and had no children of his own. Some of the gruffer men of the Metcalfe set raised their eyes at his flamboyance and muttered about him having been to Paravel. He liked to invite the women for afternoon tea and gossip, so the girl-children were dragged along too - including Tabitha if she happened to be about. They were expected to play at being grown-ups for half an hour or so, sitting in the drawing room taking tea and dainties, and then they were let loose to get under the feet of the household's staff so that the grown-ups could talk about things that may provoke awkward questions later. The Principia, like many people who don't have children, both had a fascinating collection of breakables on display and no concept of how much havoc unsupervised children could wreak. Most of his horde was mostly Kchonese porcelain and Jaffria jewel-work, harder to steal but far more valuable than simple silver. He also had what he thought was a well-concealed compartment in the wall, behind a painting in one of the back corridors. He didn't know Min had watched his butler open it and fill a coin purse from it one day.

The other thing he had was a particularly eccentric lift system. Tabitha had drifted about the house, chewing her braids and wafting her skirt, humming dreamily under her breath whilst Min counted up and came to the conclusion that there was at least one room on the top floor that would only be accessible by the lift. However, she had never seen a servant use the lift, and whilst she was there the Principia himself usually remained with his guests in the drawing room. It was turning Min inside out with curiosity. She simply had to find a way to get in to that room.

Throwing caution to the wind, she opened the gilded door slowly and took a step inside. It swayed slightly as she transferred her weight into the small car and looked about. It was like a giant canary cage hanging precariously on a thick cable. She could feel the tingle of magic on the soles of her feet. She had never been particularly adept at sensing enchantments but this one was so strong it was unmissable. The cage smelled vaguely of jasmine and lavender, reminding her of Mrs Al Rahiri. She looked around for clues as to how to power it and found only a small handle attached to a thicker bar at the back of the cage. She gave the handle a turn and the cage shuddered in to life, lurching downwards. Emboldened, she cranked it the other way and gave it two thorough turns. The lift shot upwards and then jolted to a halt. She turned again more slowly and kept going. The lift had moved up into a shaft above her and plunged her into a brief darkness. After a few more turns, a sliver of light started to appear at the top of the cage and she found herself rising up into this mysterious room.

With one final turn, the lift clunked to a halt and hung there, level with the polished wooden floor. Min looked out at the room she had been desperate to see and was not disappointed. She had never seen anything quite like it, she couldn't even have dreamed of it. She had no idea what she thought she might find up there, a sordid little part of her had expected something unpleasant or illegal but now she had found her way up here, she never wanted to leave. It seemed that the Principia was some kind of wizardly scholar on the quiet. The room - which must have occupied the same floor space as the ample dining room below - was full of instruments and devises that spun and oscillated. The light from the large glass panels in the roof reflected from myriad mirrors, making the room sparkle as the soft afternoon sunshine flooded in. Min, who had rarely left the sewers until the Fortescue escapade, knew very little of the world of the higher guilds and even less about what she had only ever heard referred to as *'book learning'*, but if this was it then it was beautiful - and more importantly worth an absolutely fortune. She was sold. This was the next hit. She let herself down again in the life a little faster than was wise and arrived with a jolt moments before a maid appeared to chivvy her back in to the drawing room for the tedious round of fare-welling. The other young ladies were already there, sitting primly together and gave her a unanimous look of snooty exasperation as she ambled in twiddling her hair. Min wasn't remotely bothered that Tabitha didn't really have any friends, she was still up in the glorious room above.

It was a harder sell than she'd anticipated. Angel and Mulligan were both far keener on robbing the Guild Master of the Merchants Guild - Min suspected that Mulligan had a score to settle if nothing else. However, Clara and Luce were as intrigued by the mysterious room as Min had been in the first place.

"It's the lift," declared Angel, "I don't like mechanisms, they have a tendency to let you down. What if its trapped or it sticks or something?"

"Well it was fine when I went up in it," protested Min a little more petulantly than she'd intended as she was hit with the sudden realisation that she hadn't even thought to check.

"What is the stuff up there anyway?" demanded Angel, not at all placated. "And how do we know we can take it apart without it exploding?" Min opened her mouth and shut it again. She genuinely had no idea.

Mulligan just snorted.

"Stuff exploding's alchemy," he said with almost silk-smooth derision. "What Min described sounded more like pattern magic or possibly portalmancy."

The girls stared at him, Clara's mouth dropped open. "The worst that's likely to happen is a sudden change in temperature or something. I doubt it would be anything loud or violent." Clara managed to shut her mouth. Still dumbstruck, Min didn't react, it was Angel once again who shrieked,

"since *when* did you become an authority on book-learned magic?"

Mulligan looked at her down his suddenly very aquiline nose and said haughtily,

"Maurice Fortescue knows more than you think." and then added in his more normal manner, "And that boring old bastard Sir Ranulf talks about nothing, and I really mean *nothing, else.* And of course, being the new boy who has to sit next to him?"

Luce chuckled, clapped him on the back and said

"Well, at least it wasn't for nothing. If Min can find us a safe route in, I think we should do it."

The following laughter broke the tension. It took Min less than five minutes to explain the best three ways of getting in to the house after dark and her preferred exit strategy and it was agreed that the Merchants' Guild Master could wait. On the night of the banquet the Principia Scarla was going to lose his instruments.

Chapter 15
The Big Night

"Try not to eat too much," said Clara tersely handing Mulligan his freshly laundered and mended knickerbockers. "The seams won't stand it." Mulligan didn't say anything he just grunted and took them, along with the rest of his banqueting clothes, up to his bedchamber. He had nearly suggested that Luce or Clara should help him dress as he was the only person attending the banquet who was likely to be responsible for their own hard to reach buttons, but he hadn't quite had the gall to get the words out. The Alendrians, not being quite as indulgent or progressive as either the Paravelians or the Arabians had specified no minors, which by the local definition was anyone under the age of eighteen. This had annoyed a few teenage daughters who were on the constant trail of that elusive beast: the rich, handsome, generous and deaf-as-a-post husband, but it pleased Min because it saved Tabitha from a nasty case of a highly contagious imaginary rash.

When Mulligan appeared in the kitchen twenty minutes later, so that the girls could check he'd been tucked in properly, he found a hive of activity that had no interest in how well the stripes on his cravat matched the silk of his waistcoat. In fact, he had to wait some minutes and cough loftily before he got any attention at all. The girls were far too busy putting their kit together and trying to work out exactly how much rope they could hang from Clara before she over-balanced.

There were advantages and disadvantages to performing cat-burglary in the height of summer. Whilst it was true that you have to wait a lot longer for the cover of darkness, it was also true that if the weather was right then there was a significant chance of finding an open window somewhere. There is a certain temperature at which people stop caring about these things and start making stupid statements like 'I don't care if we get robbed, that window stays open'. In the case of the unfortunate under-butler who had retired to bed and left the large pantry window ajar, because it was the only way to get any breeze at all, it would turn out much later that he should have cared a great deal and that life would probably have been better if he'd just lay awake and sweated through his linens.

Min had to admit that she was actually, on some level, disappointed to find the open larder window around the back of the Principia's Villa. She had gone around the back of the building to find a suitable entry point and break in. She had a belt full of tools and a substantial length of rope and had been looking forward to puzzling out the best way to gain access. She didn't really know where the servants slept but she had a fair idea where they wouldn't be and a couple ingenious plans she had been hoping to try out.

In the event, the rope and tools were actually a hindrance. She was forced to take them off and pass them through the window before she could climb in. Nimbly, she leapt from the sill over a neat row of stoneware crocks and landed silently, barefoot on the flagstones. She picked up her equipment and started to make her way cautiously into the dark corridor.

Whilst she had spent a significant amount of time wondering around the Principia's Villa, she had only been down this corridor once - having retreated the moment she had spotted the butler filling his money purse from the safe. She looked with interest through the open doors as she passed them, recognising a grain store and a laundry in the navy blue darkness. At the third door, she paused and looked on longingly at the delectable moonlit sight before her. She had found the stills room. Paradise lay before her. Rows and rows of jars and bottles filled the shelves in the tiny space, at least three quarters of them seemed to be jams. She would definitely be popping in on the way back out to purloin three or four of the jars. Given what else was going to be taken, she doubted they would really be missed.

She lingered longer than she ought, losing focus for a moment and as she pulled herself away and back to the job at hand she smacked her cold toes hard against the door frame. A shooting pain jolted up her leg, and before she could clamp her mouth shut a sudden yelp slipped out. She rubbed her injured foot for a minute before she realised her yelp may have given away her presence.

Panicked, she ducked into the stills room and pressed herself against the door wall, ears pricked for any sounds of movement within the house. Adrenaline washed over her, dulling the pain and sending blood pumping around her body so fast she felt like she was visibly fluttering. She had no idea how long she stood there, wondering if anyone from the household would suddenly appear with a lamp and a cudgel to deal with the jam thief. It was impossible to tell how long she waited, time seemed to stretch out of proportion, but at last she convinced herself that it was safe, and that if anyone was going to come they would have appeared by now. With somewhat less confidence than before, she crept out on to the long dark corridor that lead to the posh part of the building and started to make her way to the drawing room.

Outside the front of the building, the other three were crouched in a large ornamental shrub. The large flowers were releasing a heady oriental aroma into the damp night air. Angel was fighting against the urge to sneeze. She pinched her nose hard between her finger and thumb and let the sneeze convulse her whole body.

"Where the hell's Min?" she hissed, cringing with the aftershock.

"Shh!" replied Clara, her eyes fixed on the front of the house waiting for a pale hand to appear in the darkness, beckoning them forward. Luce, whose feet were slowly going to sleep, didn't respond at all. She was trying to stay focused. This was always the hardest part of any job for her, the waiting. She never knew what to think about. Running over and over the details of the plan only made her twitchy and inclined to make nervous mistakes but trying to distract herself was even worse because she started to worry after a while that she would forget what she was doing. She was just circling back around this quandary yet again when she spied what she had been waiting for. A small movement in the shadows around one of the vast windows followed by an almost translucent white hand waving at them.

Although the inside of the Principia's Villa was labyrinthine in comparison to the simpler Albion and Paravelian style abodes it was still no trouble for a sewer-brat like Min. She had found her way to the drawing room without further incident and managed to heave open one of the leaded glass windows with only slightly more force that she had hoped. It took less than two minutes to get everyone inside and close the window behind them, although Min was very careful to latch it so that it would open more easily on the way out.

Although there was no actual need for her to go back out the way she had come in, she fully intended to make the best of the open still room door and she didn't want the others to accidentally break the glass in their haste to get out with their full sacks.

Min lead them to the lift, which appeared to be a simple double-doored cupboard halfway down a passage not far from the drawing room. The next part was carefully planned out to play to the girls' individual strengths. Angel and Clara were to go up in the lift, because Angel would be able to identify the magical properties of just about anything she found and Clara had the kind of eye for profit that the Merchant's Guild would have killed - or more likely paid an awful lot - for.

With a delicate flick of her wrists, Min rolled back the flimsy wooden panels that concealed the front of the lift cage. The other girls stood for a moment in open-mouthed awe at the sight before them. The bars of the cage were covered in gold leaf and seemed to glow in the faint traces of moonlight that had found their way into the corridor. It was the most opulent thing Clara had ever seen close up. She reached out a hand to touch it, evidently struggling to believe her eyes. If she could have thought of a way of doing it, she would have suggested they take the lift cage and bugger the rest, even though she had no idea how you fenced an object that looked like it had once housed a vast gem-encrusted canary. However, this was not an option. Min, amused by the reactions of the other three, held the cage open for Clara and Angel.

"Turn the handle," she whispered, pointing to a small silver hand fitted on a bar at the back of the lift, as she shut them in and stepped back. Angel, not one to take a back seat, fell upon the handle and started to turn it furiously. The lift jolted suddenly into a life and started to rise rapidly out of sight leaving a gap where it had been. Luce and Min watched it go, and then having nothing better to do in the gloomy corridor sat down back to back to keep a tentative watch.

Clara had no idea what to expect. She had been told that they were going to steal highly valuable magical instruments but having no idea at all about book-learned magic she didn't know what that meant. The best she had been able to conjure up in her mind's eye was a roomful of enchanted concertinas and jewelled ukuleles playing folk music all by themselves. She just hoped they'd all be playing the same tune or else the noise would be excruciating.

She held her breath as they began to emerge into the secret room. A sliver of lighter darkness appeared at the top of the cage, growing with every turn of the crank. It took barely twenty seconds to expand the gap enough for Clara to lay eyes on the room and its contents and for the second time that evening she was totally dumbstruck. The room was chock-a-block with all sorts of gold and silver constructions, whirling spindles, quivering springs, fly-wheels and oscillating armatures. Anything that didn't move and about half of the stuff that did was embellished with semi-precious stones and fine engraving. Moonlight flooded into the room through glass roof panels that formed the shape of a heavily-stylised sun. The light played on the moving instruments making the whole room shimmer.

Clara had no worldly notion what any of this stuff did but she did know it was worth a fortune just as scrap. Angel, on the other hand, had had the privilege of more learning in this area. She could read the magical traces on just about anything and had experienced equally lavish surroundings previously. She was not fighting against her sense of awe, more the habitual sense of revulsion she felt whenever she was presented with this kind of wealth. She held out her hands in front of her before she even stepped out of the lift, closed her eyes and focused. Suddenly, she knew what was bothering her. Something didn't feel right, and she had just figured out what it was.

Down in the corridor, Luce and Min were struggling to stay awake, let alone alert. Luce could feel Min's warm little body sagging back into her. If she's had to guess she would have said that Min had drawn her knees up under her chin and was resting her head on them. It was yet another long wait in which Luce's mind circled round and round her usual quandary She had almost lulled herself into a stupor when something in front of her caught her eye.

Wakeful, thanks to the clammy night air, the under-butler had decided that he had better shut the pantry window after all. Clad in a sweat-stained night shirt and shawl and carrying his candlestick, he padded down the stairs from his chambers at the top of the house grumbling to himself under his breath. He paused a couple of times to wipe his face on the linen of his nightshirt. He was half tempted to go out into the stable yard and stick his head into the horse trough, except that he would be furious if any of his underlings if they did that, so he decided best not. Having closed the window, he decided to take the long route back to the stairs just to check the place was still all quiet. He had no idea why his guts were telling him to check.

There was no sign of anyone who shouldn't be here, but he would get no peace until he looked. He crossed the entrance hall holding his candle before him, casting flickering orange light into the shadows. He opened the drawing room door, nothing out of place. This was ridiculous he knew, random thieves don't just creepy around the back of big houses, slip through open pantry windows and start poking about the house. He gave in and headed back towards the stairs.

Luce started the moment she saw the light levels change at the end of the corridor. Then she heard the footfalls through the silence of the night. She tensed and the change in her posture alerted Min. There was someone approaching, carrying a lantern or something. They were both up and on their feet instantly. They dived for the shadows, pressing themselves hard against the walls in the darker end of the passageway. There was no time to slide open the door at the bottom of the shaft and conceal themselves there. They dare not breathe, except that whoever was coming seemed to be taking an age to get here. The light grew closer and closer, and still they waited clinging to the shadows. The footsteps grew louder and then at last the shape of a man appeared at the end of the corridor.

Judging by the silhouette, because that was all they could see of him, he was a rotund man of middle-years, with an authoritative baring and slightly bandy legs. His bright white legs, poking out of the bottom of his nightshirt, glowed strangely in the candlelight making him looked faintly comedic - although neither Luce nor Min felt much like laughing at that moment. He lifted his candle to cast the light further down the corridor, momentarily lighting a grizzled face with wiry grey hair and sharp dark eyes that seemed to take in every detail the light touched, even maybe a little from the darkness beyond. Min held her breath - one step forward and she would be in that range. Luce, across the passage from her, had one hand on her dagger already. She was ready to cut and run should it come to it. Min held her nerve, counting her breaths as she waited for the man to take that fateful step, but he didn't. He just let out a discontented grunt, turned on his heels and stamped off again. Min didn't dare breathe out loudly in fear that the sound would bring him running, but she did unclench her fists and slacken her stance. She looked over at Luce who was returning her gaze, wide-eyed and buzzing from the adrenaline. They didn't sit back down, they didn't dare.

In the secret room above, Clara and Angel were having a dilemma of their own. Angel had put her finger on what had been troubling her but there was nothing she could do to tell Clara. A room full of moving instruments should have an audible background hum, but this room was completely silent. Silent because it was blanketed by a powerful muting enchantment. Angel opened her mouth to explain to Clara and found herself forced to swallow the words she was trying to form. The magic was so powerful that it stopped the air vibrating to form sounds, making it difficult to breath and impossible to speak.

Clara, who had little by way of magical skill was somewhat more upset by the uncomfortable feeling of trying to breathe the sluggish air. She stood stupidly by the lift door, one hand clutching her throat. Angel had already moved on undeterred to the first piece of apparatus. After a minute or so, she looked around, spotted Clara and rolled her eyes, then she made a sharp gesture to indicate that she should just get on with the job at hand. Clara did as she was bid by Angel, and went over to examine the objects, although struggling for breath in the sluggish air she couldn't really concentrate to value anything with more accuracy than 'bloody hell that's worth a fortune'. After a few moments she gave up trying, shrugged and nodded at Angel.

The plan had always been to steal a single lift-full. Hence why Angel and Clara had been dispatched to make the selection. If they were going to restrict themselves to a sack each they needed to be filled with the most valuable items they could lay their hands on.

Min was smart enough to realise that she had no idea how valuable anything in that room was, it certainly looked impressive but she knew that meant nothing. In the corridor, she waited in agonising silence for the lift to spring into downward motion. Standing close to the lift shaft she could feel the subtle changes in the air flow that told her the cage was moving ever so slightly - probably being loaded. The appearance of the man with the candlestick had shaken her more than she was happy to admit and she found herself wishing she hadn't made such a fuss about getting the best quality items because at this moment she would have been more than happy for them to have simply filled the sacks with the first shiny things they could lay their grubby hands on and come back down.

Angel and Clara had done a far less thorough job than they could have on the magical apparatus, the weird-air-silence situation having robbed them of the opportunity. They had selected a fair collection of objects that were definitely of great value and more importantly easy and safe to dismantle. It had taken them mere minutes to fill the sacks and they were just in the process of stacking them in the lift. Angel had ended up having to sit on the pile as there was only space for one of them to stand by the crank handle. From her vantage point she wriggled carefully to pull the cage door closed, which took a considerable amount of athletic skill. Once they were secured, she signalled Clara who put both hands firmly on the handle and shoved. Nothing. Confused she tried the opposite direction, pulling on the crank handle with all her might. It wouldn't budge. She repeated both actions, giving as much force as she could. The cage shook but didn't drop at all. She looked up to Angel, who was sitting atop the piled sacks giving her a look of pure scorn. She snorted noiselessly, shook her head pityingly and gestured to Clara to change places. It was no small acrobatic pantomime, negotiating the teetering pile of sacks and the minimal space to trade positions, but after a minute or so of careful crawling and sliding they managed it. Clara sat and watched Angel, certain that she would be able to get it moving, and braced for the descent. Angel flung herself at the crank handle and managed to force it clockwise - but only barely. The whole cage juddered and dropped slightly. She threw herself at it again and produced similar effects. By now she was sweating and red in the face. Clara would have been smugly enjoying Angel's irritated exertions had she not been so busy panicking about how they were going to get down.

It was Luce who noticed the shuddering above them first of all. They have both been standing in the open doorway to the lift shaft since Mr Bandy Legs Candlestick had gone and for the last minute or so had been concentrating on subtle differences in airflow as the cage shifted under the weight being loaded into it. Luce, who was by far the most confident and competent when it came to mechanisms such as locks, traps and indeed lifts, had been puzzling for a while how this contraption worked at all - the hand-crank seemed a very odd choice but then who was she to question a posh foreigner with a secret room full of magical stuff.

She had concluded as she stood waiting in the darkness of the lift shaft that it must involve some sort of counterweight and possibly an array of book-learned magic she wouldn't understand even if she could read. She had been looking up the shaft for clues when she spotted the shuddering cage. It was different from the swaying that had occurred previously, that they had taken as the girls loading the sacks. This was more violent, coming in short swift bursts that caused the faintest creaking sound, which Luce assumed was from coming from the lift cable.

"What's up?" she called up the shaft in a stage whisper, letting the space amplify her words. There was no response except another painful shudder. "You stuck?" This met with a response, or at least Luce assumed it was a response, because someone deliberately banged the bottom of the cage three times very clearly. "Hang on," she replied hoping that her hoarse messages were finding their way to the girls and not to the rest of the Principia's household.

Carefully, she leaned back into the corridor and tapped gently on the wall to the right of the doorway. Then, reaching over Min's head she tapped the left and paused. She repeated the process and frowned in concentration. Min just watched, she had no idea what Luce was up to but she was well aware that now was not the time to ask.

Luce stuck her head back into the darkness and craned her neck to examine the walls. It took no more than ten seconds for her to exhale in satisfaction. She had spotted a rectangular patch about six feet up that was darker than the rest. Years of picking her way through sewer tunnels told her that this was in all likelihood a gap, and if her calculations were correct it would lead to the cavity that contained the counterweight.

She beckoned to Min.

"The lift's stuck," she said making barely any sound, "Need you to fix it."

Min was about to open her mouth to protest when Luce held up her hand and carried on explaining. "Big weight," she whispered pointing furiously at the wall on the right hand side of the door. "Climb over, hang on to it and tap."

Min took in every precious word, nodded and was facing the wall feeling for gripping points before Luce could blink. Min scuttled up the wall like a lizard and disappeared through the dark gap like a self-posting parcel. There was a slight thud and an ignominious grunt, followed a few seconds later by a faint but distinct knocking sound. Luce sucked in a deep breath and tried to avoid praying, as she called

"Try the handle now," up the shaft as softly as she could. She was rewarded by a startling jolt as the cage sprang into action and made a swift and relatively smooth descent. She ducked out the shaft just in time, and found herself confronted suddenly by the golden cage, almost completely full of potato sacks, with a white-faced Clara sitting in the foot and a half between the top of the pile and the cage roof like an eccentric and irritated cake-topper. Luce was about to ask where Angel was when she heard a faint rustling sound from behind the stack of sacks.

Luce and Clara had unloaded all but one of the sacks to let Angel free when at last Clara mouthed the words,

"Where's Min?" to Luce.

Luce made a flapping pointy gesture to indicate that she was somewhere behind the wall. Clara opened her mouth to question it and shut it again; this was not the time or place for curiosity. Angel shoved the final sack out of the lift in front of her. She was red-faced and sweating.

"How are we going to get Min out?" she demanded through her teeth.

Mr Bandy Legs Candlestick had been lying in his bed sweating and worrying. He'd shut the window and had a brief look around but somehow he didn't feel quite right. He had two choices, he could either lie here staring at the ceiling and make a damp spot on the linen sheet or he could get up and check again. He heaved himself out of bed and stamped down the stairs to the ground floor again. This time he'd bothered to light his lantern which cast a much larger pool of light than the candle he had taken before. He was intent on making the full rounds this time, it was the only way he was likely to get any sleep at all. The thick summer night hung damply around the house. It was truly unpleasant in the way it clung to everything. The Master wasn't back yet and everyone else was tucked up in bed. It was so still and quiet that the slightest sound would travel a long way. But by now he didn't trust his ears, the only thing he could do would be to check everywhere. He shone his light into the salon and let it dance over the cut glass adorning the massive chandelier. There it was again another sound. He hurried on to the lift corridor.

Luce and Angel were just about to start the pantomime of moving the lift cage to release Min from her temporary confinement when they both started. There was a sound like a door closing, breaking the heavy silence of the sleeping household. Without pausing for a second thought, they began to shove the sacks back into the lift.

It had been enough of a squeeze with two girls and the sacks. With an extra Luce, who was easily the largest of the four girls, it was an almost impossible fit. Angel was the last one in, tucking herself into a very slender gap as she slid the outer screens across the gap. Luckily, there was no need to close the actual cage, the screens were enough and it bought an inch or so of extra space for which Angel was extremely grateful.

Mr Bandy Legs Candlestick held his lantern high to spill the light as far down the corridor as possible. He could have sworn he'd seen a movement about half way down the passageway, around about the lift doors. His plodding footfalls sounded loud on the flagstones as he did what he should have done previously and walked the whole length of the corridor. The girls dared not breathe as they listened to the approaching steps, the light of the lamp visible as the merest sliver along the top of the door. Angel could actually smell the sweat of the man as he came closer and paused to examine the lift doors. As the only one that wasn't trapped, Angel was the only one in a position to make any attempts at evasion and escape.

Judging by the smell of him and the sound of his footfalls, he wasn't a small man. She was pretty sure she could duck away from his grip and hot-foot it to a window somewhere. She bit her lip as he prodded at the door, tensed and ready for action the moment it became necessary. The man lingered a long while outside the door, judging by the way the light moved he was scanning the lantern over it. Eventually, having spotted nothing of interest in the soft light, he let out a grunt of dissatisfaction and stumped off down the corridor. The girls did not let their breath out just yet. Angel leaned forward and with great caution and a remarkably steady hand she slid the screen doors apart just a fraction. It was enough to let her know that the corridor was dark again, she opened the gap wider so that she could poke her head out and listened. She could still just about hear the muffled footfalls but they were fading fast. She decided to take her chances and slipped through the gap before carefully rolling the screens back.

The girls re-piled everything with more caution than last time, very aware that a single clank could be curtains for all of them. Terrified out of her wits by the second of two extremely close shaves, Luce was almost rigid with fear as she tried to move sacks full of metal instruments without making a noise. By the time they were finished, Min was getting restless - having no idea what was happening except what she could piece together from the very faint noises coming through the wall.

The next part was probably the riskiest of all with Mr Bandy Legs Candlestick was on the prowl, because once they'd started they wouldn't be able to stop. Clara hopped back in the lift and cranked it up just above the slot in the wall. Then, with feline agility, Angel scurried up Luce, balanced on her shoulders and posted the knotted end of the rope threw the gap. Then, she let the slack fall and sprung back down, landing barefoot and silent on the flagstones. Luce, already tied to the other end of the rope braced herself to act as the anchor point and Min started to scramble up the sheer wall. In a matter of moments, Min was wriggling out of the slot.

All that remained was to signal Clara to come back down in the lift. Then they could clear out. The retreat was an extremely wary one, with Angel on point to check the coast was clear of Mr. Bandy Legs Candlestick at every turn. They were just in the process of passing the sacks carefully through the window when the silence of the night, and their intense focus, was shattered by the chiming of the Law Temple bell marking the evening eleven hour. Luce started.

The whole escapade had taken far longer than they'd planned, she was supposed to be back at the house by now readying the carriage so she could collect Maurice at half past the hour. Clara, who was standing beside her on the lawn, noticed her sudden expression of panic and mouthed the word

"Go," at her urgently. Luce didn't wait to argue, after the last time she had been late to collect Mr Fortescue she had no intention of doing it again. She just very carefully made her way through the shadows of the Villa's garden and on to the main road, where she broke into a sprint. Clara didn't bother explaining where Luce had gone, she just picked up Luce's share and slung it over her shoulder before hefting her own in the other hand.

The three girls heard the unmistakable sound of Luce racing the trap down the main street as they headed through the back alleys with their prize. They had hoped not to be still on the streets at this time of the evening, when people were returning from social functions and some of the more pious religious types, rich enough to not have to be up at the crack of dawn and too boring to be invited to the banquet, would be just heading out to the Temple District for Midnight devotions.

However, Mr Bandy Legs Candlestick had thrown out their schedule and robbed them of their guide – Luce being the one who had the encyclopaedic knowledge of the quarter's back routes and alleyways. With not inconsiderable skill, they managed to make it home unchallenged and collapsed panting on the kitchen hearth, even though the embers were also on their last legs.

Adrenaline subsided and with it the tension. Clara threw a handful of kindling into the burner and pumped the bellows until a small curl of fire danced up, spilling warm orange light over her. Angel wondered out of the kitchen into the house and returned rapidly with a heavy stone flask that apparently contained a faintly blue liquid masquerading as gin. Min was just about to take a swallow of it when all of a sudden she let out a pathetic wail.

"What?" demanded Angel, so startled she nearly emptied her cup on to Min's head.

"I completely forgot to get the jam."

"Min," said Clara, draining her cup and holding it out for a refill, "With what's in them sacks, you can prob'bly buy all the jam in the city." Relief amplified the humour, and they roared with laughter until they were red-cheeked, teary-eyed and gasping. Then with bread, apples and the not-gin, they celebrated their glorious larceny. They didn't say anything more; there wasn't really anything to say right now. When Luce and Mulligan got in, accompanied by the chimes of the Midnight bells, they found them all sleeping peacefully on the full sacks, Angel cradling the stone flask like a rag-doll.

Chapter 16
A Country Seat

Summer had peaked. Days became cooler and shorter, clammy days and sweaty nights were replaced with patchy sunshine and the fresh bluster of autumn rolling in across the Aragonese strait, carrying the chilly air east. The 'Scarla theft' was still being discussed *sotto voce* in the better homes and gardens – although less so the gardens now, more the conservatories. This was largely due to the fact that try as they might, no one could find out exactly what had been stolen. There was naturally a vast deal of speculation, made even more interesting by the fact that the Principia had withdrawn of the social scene the morning after the Alendrian Freedom Day Banquet and had not been seen or heard of since. Most of the flabby, thin-haired socialites that did the backbone of the gossiping were enjoying themselves no end, worrying at what little they did know of the crime trying to tease the meagre detail into ever more complicated and sordid scenarios. Maurice Fortescue, the soul of discretion and decorum, simply smiled politely during these conversations and said nothing.

Min, or rather Tabitha Fortescue, was getting her money's worth out of the turning season too. With the change in the weather, life had withdrawn indoors again and she was able to spend a couple of hour or so every day totally exasperating one nurse or another. Sometimes, she even remembered to case the joint whilst she was doing it. There was no rush she figured. They couldn't very well attempt anything on the same scale as the 'Scarla Theft' for a while - at least until some other scandal had become the talk of the town. Not one to pass up an opportunity though, she was making quite a fair side profit lifting trinkets and jewellery that would lay virtually flat in her pinafore pockets. That was the glory of rich people - a treasured ring goes missing and they'd sooner blame the faithful maid who'd served them well for twenty years and never so much as swilled their wine than ever contemplate that it might be one of their own class. She had also managed to get her hands on three jars of jam.

It was going to be difficult to plan the next big target in any case. The social calendar of the city was getting fuzzy as autumn approached. With the summer over, many of the Guilds were returning to trade and the start of a new business year. This was the lull between the glamours of summer and the excess of the winter feasting. Functions were far less formal, there were 'at homes', table suppers and minstrel nights but nothing that required one to 'dress'. Clara pointed out that this was just as well because Mulligan really needed to lose some weight before his dress knickerbockers would be seemly and she was buggered if she was letting them out any more.

Much to Clara's irritation, children were welcome at these less sophisticated occasion - which meant twice the laundry. She complained bitterly about the sticky stains on Min's pinafore until Min handed her a small stoneware jar of jam - and she suddenly understood why Min kept putting it in her pockets. Angel was less easily placated, and took every opportunity to remind Min that she had a job to do that extended beyond playing Ratatatat and purloining preserves. She needled Min so often that Min had taken to scowling every time Angel approached. Angel either didn't notice or didn't care but Clara did.

It was early September when they received a slightly unexpected invitation. Metcalfe was having 'a few chums' over to her 'divine little country house' for the whole weekend. Apparently, Maurice and darling little Tabby were two of those chums - no doubt because one of the other chums was some dreary spinster or wet-eyed widow that Metcalfe was trying to marry off. The invite had been very casual, Metcalfe had bagged Maurice after supper one night and sprung it on him then. Mulligan had done his best not to look shocked or frightened. She'd given him all the particulars then and there - or at least what she'd thought were the particulars. Mulligan would have done anything for a translation dictionary. She'd said something about 'informal luncheon', riding, archery and a few other things Mulligan knew of only in theory. She'd also said, as though it were an afterthought,

'Do bring your boy'

Mulligan went home and told the girls. Min was almost giddy with delight until Angel snorted something unkind about the fact she was just excited about the food.

"You're just jealous," spat Min and vanished from the kitchen, sniffling.

"So what if I am," snapped Angel as she went, "*I* haven't forgotten what it's like to be hungry."

To an extent this was true. Whilst they had stolen nearly a thousand guilders, the majority was now tied up in Guild promissory notes. The cash they did have had to stretch a lot of ways and the girls tended to scrimp on the food out of habit. Whilst none of them had rumbling stomachs any more, they still subsisted on the same diet of pease pottage, oatmeal, and the better quality scraps from the local food waste. The way they saw it, most of what was thrown out in the Merchant's District was fresher and more easily identified than what they'd find in the poor-quarter markets. They just had to be careful not to get spotted whilst scavenging.

Clara, who agreed with Angel but whose common sense prevented her from actually saying so, just turned the talk back on to the problem in hand.

"Okay guvn'r," she said, taking a breath, "wha's the plan?"

"Well," said Mulligan, "We're going weekend after next, so I guess I need to learn to shoot and ride by then, oh and acquired some country clothes or something. And a trunk to put them in. And we'll need to horse topped up because we're to provide our own transport and Metcalfe said to bring 'my boy' - which I assume means Luce." Clara was just looking at him, that wasn't what she had meant at all.

"Acut'lly," she said with a controlled tone, before Angel could wade in, "I mean' what're we gonna steal while your away?"

"Oh," mumbled Mulligan, totally stunned. It was clear that he hadn't even considered that question. "Well, er…nothing."

"What?" screeched Angel, "You, and Min and Luce are going to swan off to the country for the weekend and leave us here to steal *nothing*?"

Maurice recoiled. He still found Angel in a rage difficult to handle, and you could see him reminding himself that he was the grown up here and the mastermind behind this whole venture.

"Nothing," he repeated with ice cold calm, "Nothing at all, it's too risky."

"Risky?" snarled Angel. "Risky?"

"It aint you doin' the stealin' Mulligan," added Clara, stepping in because she was apparently the only person who was able to keep her temper these days. Looking around to see if she could get some solid, reasonable backing from Luce, she found that her friend must have slipped out into the yard during the argument. It was a habit she had started to develop whenever discussions became heated. Clara didn't blame her.

"Listen," hissed Mulligan, starting to colour in the cheeks, "You don't understand. This isn't a big, public event - it's just a 'few chums'" Angel snorted derisively at the word chums, Mulligan ignored her, "it's not common knowledge. If you hit someone whilst we're away it'll be far too easy to point the finger at an informant." Clara nodded reluctantly, she could see sense in what Mulligan was saying even though she could tell Angel didn't. "Besides," continued Mulligan, starting to sound a little pleading, "I don't know who else is going, so I can't give you a target."

"What about Metcalfe?" retorted Angel disdainfully. "We know she'll definitely be going." Mulligan looked stricken.

"No," he screeched, somewhat louder than he had intended. "No, not Metcalfe. You can't do that."

"Why not?" demanded Angel with a malicious delight.

"Because," he stammered, "because you can't. It's a really stupid idea, it's just not a good plan." Angel looked at him with ice cold disdain as he continued to stutter his objections. Angel just waited for him to run himself to a stop, almost willing him to utter the words 'but she's my friend' – but he didn't. When he finally did shut up, they just glowered at each other, it was clear that neither had any intention of backing down and Angel had a look in her eyes that reminded Clara of a cat with a cornered shrew.

"Okay," said Clara after a moment of uncomfortable silence, "Well let's get everythin' ready anyway and we can iron out the details la'er."

The bulk of the preparations fell to Clara, unsurprisingly. Luce had said she would 'handle the horse and cart' but both Min and Angel were so touchy that Clara couldn't be bothered to argue with either of them. Apart from the housekeeping tasks that needed to be performed, there was the matter of the riding and shooting. Mulligan was a crack shot with a crossbow, as you would expect from a thief of his calibre, he was proficient with just about every compact weapon going. However, in he had never laid his hand on an Albion long-bow in his life. When Clara handed him a narrow yew stave that was about an inch taller than he was and a crumpled ball of hemp string he was somewhat bemused. It took Mulligan, Luce and Clara to get it strung.

Mulligan, whose profession demanded flexibility and dexterity but not necessarily brute strength, struggled to draw. Sweat beaded on his brow as he tugged furiously but he just couldn't get the string to his jaw. After an hour he still hadn't managed to do anything other than damage half a dozen fletches and snap an arrow by standing on it. The straw boss that Luce and Clara had set up across the back yard was still untouched. Angel, who had mysteriously vanished the previous day strolled through the back gate just in time to see Mulligan lose his temper with his bow and fling it at a somewhat disgruntled Luce. She didn't say anything, she just paused by the kitchen door and let out a derisive snort. Mulligan ignored her. Clara, who bitterly wanted to know where Angel had swanned off to overnight, bit her lip.

Over the following weeks of preparation, for the trip that would benefit her not a jot, Clara started to develop the kind of resentment that it was difficult to articulate. When it came to the profits, it was supposed to be a straight split five ways, but really Clara thought she should have an extra cut for doing all the jobs that nobody else bothered with. She threw herself into the work because it was the only way that it was going to get done and it stopped her plunging into a towering fury.

The blisters on her feet were stinging, the skin on her hands was dry and split from the lye she had been elbow deep in for hours trying to whiten Maurice's linen. She had burned her thumb on the pressing iron. She was hungry and exhausted. This had been a normal state of affairs for years, but previously she had not been forced to spend time around other people who were neither. Min, who was certainly on the chubby side these days, hadn't been seen downstairs in forty-eight hours. She couldn't possibly be expected to crack her hands in the lye - young Albion ladies didn't do their own linens. Luce, who did at least work for her living, had made an art form out of taking care of one bony old nag and spent as much time doing that as Clara did looking after the house. Whilst Clara was the first to admit she knew nothing about horses, she was pretty sure they didn't need that much time spending on them. As for Angel, she had made no excuse for her constant absence and barely lifted a finger. Mulligan spent pretty much most daylight hours, when he wasn't forced to be out and about being Maurice, practising his archery. His bow arm was covered in swollen bruises and raw scrapes and the fingers of his drawing hand were riddled with sores and calluses, but he was undeterred. He just bound his arm and hand with leather strapping and carried on relentlessly. This tough determination would have impressed Clara, had she not been too busy to really notice.

Had Clara had time to really think on it, the person she would have been most put out by was Angel - she had become preoccupied to the point of surliness and secretive with it. She point blank refused to help out with menial tasks, which might have been okay if Clara had any idea what she was doing instead. As it happened Clara didn't really have time to wonder she was far too busy doing everything that no one else was.

She was more than relieved when the morning of the trip arrived and she shoved two fully-packed trunks towards Min and Mulligan. She didn't stick around to watch Luce load the cart, she was too tired. She was actually quite looking forward to it - a couple of days to slack off and enjoy herself with no one generating laundry in the immediate vicinity.

Luce was far less delighted. She was going to be forced to pretend to be Jack the likely lad that drove the Fortescue Trap. She - or rather he - would probably be expected to work eighteen hour days below stairs in this pile of Metcalfe's, shining the bolts on the privy door or some other such pointless rubbish. Until now, apart from the few hours that she and Clara had been at the dim kitchens below Paravelian banquet, Luce hadn't been under any kind of scrutiny. She wasn't particularly happy about it. She had been forced to cut and wash her hair and find herself a more convincing livery. She had also had to have the spell on the nag topped up by Truvalle, who was starting to get snotty about making house calls in the rich district with no explanation. She sighed as Clara dumped the luggage on the back step and disappeared back into the kitchen.

Even though the cart was being loaded out of view, in the back yard, Min and Mulligan - or more accurately Tabitha and Maurice stood back and let Luce do the heavy lifting. She heaved and grunted more than necessary as she shoved the two trunks into the under-slung luggage rack of the wagon, but the other two ignored her theatrics. They couldn't risk their clothes or their soft, clean skin actually doing anything like work – particularly as it had cost Mulligan more than he was prepared to admit to have Truvalle fix his archery scars.

Min had one thumb planted firmly in her mouth and a rag doll under her arm. Strictly speaking, Tabitha was a little old for that kind of behaviour but a girl without a mother was excused and indulged by the socialite mummies. In fact, Min had high hopes that she might be spoilt rotten this weekend, even though she didn't know who was going to be there she knew that at least Metcalfe had a soft spot for her. She didn't know which, if any, of the other girls - she didn't think of them as her friends because she knew they didn't like Tabitha - were going to be there. There was a possibility she would be the only one, in which case she was likely to be indulged silly.

The carriage ride to Metcalfe's country seat San Clear Lodge Hall would have been far more pleasant in a carriage that had even wheels or any padding on the seat. Whilst the Fortescue trap looked the part - due to a lick of paint and a little help from Truvalle, it was basically still an adapted corn-merchants cart. It didn't help that even Truvalle's magic couldn't make the horse any younger so the journey took significantly longer than it would have otherwise.

Luce didn't speak to the other two as she drove, she was finding it increasingly difficult to know what to say. They didn't seem to notice, they just sat in silence and watched the Albion country side pass them by. The Metcalfe San Clears were old Albion money who had been in Aberddu since it had been the Royal Port of Albion. Independence had not daunted them, Aberddu was still a bustling port city vital to international trade so they had stayed put. Metcalfe, in her irrepressible way, had opened her arms to all the incoming would-be aristos, scooped them up and drawn them to her ample bosom. Having the seniority of establishment, she was able to the play the Queen bee and ensure things were done very much in her way.

''The Lodge' as Metcalfe called it, was in fact a vast sprawling manor house in the middle of acres thriving farm land. The courtyard was full of activity as Luce steered the trap in through the open gates. Apart from arriving guests and the attending stable-hands and baggage flunkies, there were also workers about their normal business, a cart of full apple boxes was being unloaded into a barn on the far side of the stables by a gang of sweaty labourers. None of them so much as looked up at the trap as Luce pulled up and a stable lad caught hold of the bridle.

Min and Mulligan, or rather Tabitha and Maurice as Luce had started to think of them, alighted from the back with the aid of a liveried footman and were ushered off in to the house through the front door without a backward glance. Luce got down and received nothing more than a

"Baggage around the back," from the stable lad who was now stroking the nag's muzzle obviously eager to get on with the stabling.

Metcalfe was in full flow when Maurice and Tabitha were shown into the drawing room. Country Metcalfe was surprisingly utilitarian, much to Tabitha's confusion and amusement. There were no silks or lace, and no jewels save her wedding ring. Her hair was up, apparently held fast by a single tortoise-shell comb, no doubt aided by four dozen invisible grips and pins. On her feet she was wearing sturdy brown boots with a small bronze buckle on each ankle. Most surprising of all however was her gown. It was plain green wool, cut beautifully and fitted perfectly to her. There was no question that a very expensive seamstress had been commissioned to produce this garment and had gone to great lengths to make it appear authentically homespun. It was certainly impressive. None of this however seemed to make any difference to Metcalfe.

She paused mid anecdote to welcome them warmly with clasped hands and a kiss on the cheek. Then she introduced them to the gathered company. When she had said to Maurice it would be a select few, she hadn't been kidding. Apparently the Fortescues were the last to arrive, making a total of nine people in the drawing room. Maurice and Tabitha hung back until Metcalfe had done the obligatory introductions. Everyone was coupled up, except for Maurice and a radiant-looking youngish woman, sitting guardedly on the edge of a two seat settee. She was giving Maurice a coy glance, as though she was trying to decide if she dare smile. It was very clear that the seating arrangements had been carefully contrived so that Maurice would have to sit next to her. This was clearly Metcalfe's scheme for the weekend - she was determined to marry Maurice off to somebody, the Summer of Fire having produced among many other undesirably things a surfeit of young widows. Usually Maurice was charming and blandly attentive to the widows that were put in front of him, until he could find an ever so polite way of leaving. However, this time was different. Tabitha looked first at the woman, who had decided to brave a small sweet smile that made her deep crystal clear blue eyes twinkle like fine-set sapphires, and then back at Maurice. She was horrified to see that he was smiling back, not with his usual superficial grace but with the same shy intensity. Tabitha looked over at Metcalfe; given the gleaming gloat on her face she had noticed the look and was busy congratulating herself. She spied Tabitha and gave her a conspiratorial wink meant to convey a shared excitement that Tabitha didn't feel.

"Do sit down," fluted Metcalfe after a longer than necessary pause, spreading her arms hospitably, "please." Tabitha did the only thing she could think of by way of damage control: she took a seat. She took the one right next to the lady with the sapphire eyes, ignoring Metcalfe's less than subtle attempts to direct her to a cushioned settle by the window. It was only when Tabitha, as ever oblivious, sat down and smiled politely at the Lady, whose name was Lady Arabella something or other, duchess of somewhere, that Min actually bothered to look at her properly. With chilling horror, Min realised that she had seen this beautiful face before nd felt her guts clench themselves into a very tight ball. The last time she had looked on Lady Arabella she had been the bait in a very cruel trap, and she had made off with her corset and pearls. Apparently, Lady Arabella didn't recognise her because she simply smiled at her and said,

"Hello Tabitha, call me Bella. How are you?"

Tabitha was left with no choice but to brazen it out, relying on the fact that she was so far out of her original context that Lady Arabella wouldn't even think to make the connection. She just continued to be charmingly oblique and slightly supercilious in a way that only Miss Tabitha Fortescue could manage. Lady Arabella seemed completed enchanted by it.

Back in the city, charm in no way came into it. Angel had returned home after her final piece of business down in the Black Market to find the house empty and unlocked. Whilst Clara's disappearance wasn't exactly pleasing to her, the fact that any chancer could just waltz in and help themselves was far worse. After all the efforts they had made to accrue other people's fortunes she was damned if she was going to let some back-street opportunist get rich in one easy swipe.

Clara had left no indication where she had gone but Angel could take a fairly educated guess. She didn't have an exact location but she had a few in mind. She was so certain that Clara was in an alehouse somewhere drunk as a skunk and carousing that she would have gambled a sizeable part of their newly accrued fortune on it – if anyone else would take the bet.

The Startling Toad was well known as a Goblin bar - and with a name like The Startling Toad it would be stupid to expect otherwise. The innkeeper, Charlie, was human as far as it was possible for the observer to tell and Aberddu born and bred, having grown up here when the city was actually just the Royal Port of Albion. He had mostly kept his head down during independence and the Summer of Fire and emerged into the newly born City-state with wide eyes and a nose that could sniff out profit at a thousand yards. In fairness, given that his profit came from getting goblins drunk the whole city could have smelt it at a thousand yards.

In a place like this a low-born stable hand could get rich if he was smart, and Charlie and was very smart. He'd spotted a gap in the market and with a bit of borrowed cash and a lot of cheek he managed to fill it. Goblins get everywhere, like a peculiar constantly-talking rash. In a major trading port like Aberddu they were it abundant supply; ships liked to use them as skivvies because they preferred to work for barter, considered maggots a treat and didn't mind the smell of the bilge in the hull. The only problem with them was that they most of them enjoyed being keel-hauled, which meant they were difficult to punish unless you were more inventive. Goblins, like all sailors of calibre, would swarm off ship when they made port and drink everything in sight until they ran out of pay - and this is where Charlie's genius came in. Goblins are a unique experience, and not to everybody's taste. Also, because they preferred barter to coin often found themselves out of luck when it came drinking their wages in most regular inns. However, Charlie would take just about anything as payment - he had a very inventive fence - and didn't mind the random noises or smells that his little green friends produced. He opened the Startling Toad with in staggering distance of the docks and the Ddu and within three years had made himself a small fortune and an interesting reputation. He had also had seventeen cases of scrofula, twenty-one bouts of something similar to ringworm, five different types of parasite and a lingering dose of white-powdered mildew. Charlie didn't care apart from when he couldn't stand the itching, he was raking it in and having a blast to boot.

Clara liked The Startling Toad, apart from the fact that you could pay for beer with barter, she found the goblins easy to talk to and totally unbothered by her youthful appearance. Besides, the singing was hilarious. On this particular visit, Clara was relieved to discover that whilst Charlie was happy to accept virtually anything of a not-too-perishable nature as payment he also accepted coins. She had filched two silver florins from the coffers and headed straight for the Toad the moment she'd been left unsupervised. If Charlie hadn't accepted the money, she would have probably gone to the market and bought him a couple of brace of rabbits instead. As it happened, Charlie was so confused by the unsolicited offer of two silver coins that he was rendered speechless and forced to check their validity. Once satisfied that they were genuine, he put them 'behind the bar' handed her a full tankard and told her to come back when it was empty.

That had been sometime around the morning eleven hour. It was now approaching dusk and Clara had taken full advantage for her bottomless tankard. She was lying on the floor under a table, giggling merrily to herself as she listened to recitation of the 'old goblin favourite' *Pushing Round De Shiny Moon* by an extraordinary goblin she had met a couple of hours previously and had taken and instant shine to. Pudding The Goblin - full name 'Bread and Butter Pudding with Custard' - was a goblin bard because only goblins could consider what she did to be bardic. She was small, round and bawdy and dressed in what can only be described as a festival of brightly-coloured poor taste, topped by a cloth covered bowler hat that boasted at least seven different religious symbols.

Clara had been listening to her 'repertoire' for nearly two hours now and both of them were so drunk that they hadn't noticed Pudding only knew seven pieces at least three of which contained an awful lot of 'tum-it-tum…something or other'. It was lucky for the pair of them that the pub was relatively empty and that what clientèle there was had consumed as much ale as they had.

Clara was just joining in yet another rousing chorus of 'She Likes It Like a Well-Boiled Ham, Pink and Firm and Juicy' when she found herself unceremoniously dragged out from under the table by her ankles. With bemused irritation she opened her mouth to abuse whoever had hold of her and found herself staring at the furious face of Angel.

"What do you think you're doing?" she snapped, hauling Clara to standing by the shoulders of her tunic.

"I'm singin'," slurred Clara, "or at least I though' I was. Am I not?" She then dissolved into a hopeless, helpless tittering mess. Angel, who didn't find the present situation remotely amusing, snatched hold of Clara's ear. Pinching so hard that Clara's normally pinkish ear turned white under her thumb, Angel started dragging her towards the door.

"Your drunk," she growled,

"Well spo'ed," chuckled Clara, not about to let Angel's anger affect her bonhomie,

"We've got work to do," Angel continued in a sour whisper, with her mouth close to the pinched ear.

"Shit," exclaimed Clara with a look of genuine terror, "Is it Sunday already?" Angel didn't dignify that with a response, she just snorted.

At this point Pudding stepped up, clearly aggrieved. She cleared her throat, swayed slightly and in a hilariously fake Royal Albion accent said,

"Hexcuse me my good woman! Would you care to explain this rumpus?" Angel just stared at her, she had no idea how to respond. Pudding, sensing the need for more authority drew herself up to her completely insubstantial height, an act that only served to emphasis her terrifying striped bosom, grabbed hold of her braces in an effort to hold herself upright and said, "Madam would you kindly let go of my hassociate" She slurred the word *hassociate* so badly it had nearly twice the syllables it needed. It was very obvious from the sight of her holding tight to her braces that she was so drunk that her eyeballs may well have been floating. She clearly didn't dare let go of her suspenders in case she fell over. At this point, if Angel had had any kind of sense of the ridiculous she would have started laughing. Instead, with a completely deadpan face, she looked Pudding straight in the swimming eyes and said,

"Who the hell are you?"

"Madam, I am Bread and Pudding Butter with Goblin the Custard!" declared the goblin with all due pomposity, wobbling dangerously as she tipped her hat. "And I am a highly renowned bard and prestidigitator of the finest calibre." The word prestidigitator took two run ups, but she managed the whole thing with a perfectly straight face. "And the young lady you have so forcefully by the ear is my 'ssociate Crara Clopper." As a final punctuation, she pinged her braces hard and instantly regretted it. The forces of the suspenders snapping at her shoulders sent her off her very delicate balance. She went into an uncontrollable sway and Angel, who was still not smiling, simply leaned forward and with one hand gave her an almost imperceptible nudge. It was a cruel, calculated and accurate gesture, proving to be just enough to cause the goblin to topple over completely. She hit the floor with a dull thwack and her feet flew up over her head in a flash of glorious technicolour. Angel didn't pause to help her up, she just dragged a protesting Clara out of the door.

"So long fair Clara," declaimed Pudding, waving theatrically from her prone position. "See you on the other side." Clara didn't reply, she didn't have the chance. She was preoccupied by Angel who had her by the scruff and was about to dump her in the horse trough.

Angel dragged Clara from her chilly, algae-filled bath and led her, grumbling and sodden, across the city. Conscious not to make a spectacle, Clara waited until they reached the kitchen before she rounded on Angel and at the top of her now painfully sober lungs shrieked,

"What in hell do you fink you're doin?"

"What in hell do I think I'm doing?" echoed Angel scornfully accentuating the correct pronunciation.

"Yeah," demanded Clara who was shivering as she vigorously pumped the bellows on the range.

"Our job. That's what I'm doing," spat Angel.

"What do you mean our job? There aint nuffin' to do 'til Sunday. Mulligan said no robbin'."

"Use your brain Clara," continued Angel, "Mulligan is full of it. He's using us so he can prance around playing Lord of the Manor. Of course he doesn't want us stealing whilst he's away. He doesn't trust us. How much do you think he's creaming off as we speak? Stuffing his belly with rich food whilst we slave away." Clara, who had managed to raise a small flame in the range, looked up for a moment. She had to admit that what Angel was saying struck a nerve with her but some of that was at the implication that Angel did as much work as she did.

"But Mulligan's right, apar' from Metcalfe we dunno who else is away," she protested but with scant conviction, more squeamish than Angel when it came to overturning the status quo. "There aint nobody to rob."

"What do you mean nobody?" snorted Angel almost amused by Clara's apparent naivety. "You just said it yourself. Metcalfe."

Clara didn't say anything. She knew that was going to be the answer before she'd even asked the question. "Tomorrow night," continued Angel, "We're going to get ourselves a little compensation for drawing the short straws in all of this." With that, she went out of the kitchen leaving Clara to ring the water out of her hair and wonder exactly what it was that Angel did that she felt she needed compensating for.

Luce was definitely earning her share this weekend. She had been forced to hide herself away in the stable-block outhouse. It smelled revolting but it was better than her other option, which was sitting in the outer kitchen or around the brazier in the feed barn with the other grooms and stable hands. Most of the drivers that had brought their toffs for this weekend jaunt were considerably older than Luce. A group of gruff, weathered men that were hale and upright and lost somewhere in that indefinable period of age between late twenties and mid-forties. They had been doing this job for years and were used to each other's company. Well aware that they were at leisure until Sunday, they felt free to drink, smoke and gamble as much as they liked. The humour was extremely ribald and the conversation could just about be politely described as 'manly'. The young lads - Luce was not the only one, some of the households had sent stablers as well as drivers - were included aggressively, with much amused winking and nudging as the older men laughed at their confusion and blushes. The other lads lapped it up, along with the cider the old men pressed on them, but Luce couldn't bare it. Even after her years in the Guild Below, Luce found it beyond what she could stomach. Hiding was the only thing she could do. She had a vague inkling that Tabitha and Maurice were having a better time than she was. It was difficult to tell, because Metcalfe had everything arranged so that the visiting servants weren't needed and therefore spent all their time hanging about in the outbuildings, looking after their respective horses.

Tabitha was enjoying a long, luxurious bath. This was one in a long range of delights arranged for her by Bella. She was sitting in a deep enamelled tub that had little cast iron feet, covered to the elbows in hot water and a liberal scoop of herbs and oils. She had to admit it smelt divine, even if she did feel like an oversized casserole. Beside her on a stool, Bella was sitting wrapped in a fine Kchonese silk robe. She was readying herself with a small perfumed bottle that apparently contained something called 'hair tonic'. Min, who washed her hair with the goose-grease and potash soap when she bothered to wash it at all, was curious to discover what would happen when it was poured on to her wet hair. Carefully, Bella poured the tonic into her palm and another heady aroma filled the air. It was cold as it hit Tabitha's scalp and made it tingle. It was strange but in a good way. She sagged a little backwards into Bella's hands as she massaged the oil into her hair.

This was the end of an absolutely delightful day. From the early morning 'trot out' through the picnic lunch all the way to this luxurious bath Tabitha had been the apple of Bella's eye. It was blatantly obviously that Bella was yet another in the long line of single women that Metcalfe thought Maurice might marry. She was another young war widow, although unlike the others she showed virtually no interest in Maurice at all. She was pleasant and charming to him in company but her attention was focused completely on Tabitha. Much to Tabitha's amusement she could see that, in spite of what he would claim if challenged, this was starting to really vex Maurice.

It had started the previous evening after supper when Bella offered to take Tabitha up to bed. She had settled her in the neat little room that Metcalfe had sorted out for the child and had sat with her and read to her for a long while. Min was intrigued. Lady Arabella was supposed to be an Albion lady, but she had clearly been educated. She read with fluency and grace and encouraged Tabitha to read passages for herself out loud. Albion ladies were usually taught their recitations by rote – being able to read freely was considered unrefined. Either Arabella was a fraud or a social reformer. Either way, Min wanted to know more. She was now completely confident that she hadn't been and wouldn't be recognised as the urchin that had suckered her off her horse.

It seemed that Lady Arabella was a woman of hidden depth, and Tabitha adored her. She was spell-bound the moment Bella had reached down from the fine grey jennet on which she was mounted to lift Tabitha up into the saddle with her. She had even let Tabitha hold the reins for a while. After that, there was the picnic and then they had been for a walk and collected some wildflowers for Metcalfe, - who had cooed all over them and smiled widely over Tabitha's head toward Maurice. The bath was the cherry on the cake. Bella had told Tabitha that she would dress her up like a 'real lady' for dinner, with jewellery and everything. Min was excited about that, but for a completely different reason to Tabitha and Tabitha had to keep reminding her that she must keep her hands to herself and give it all back intact because to pocket it and run would be fatal. Besides, Bella was intriguing and lovely and even the harsh voice of Min in the back of Tabitha's head had to admit that she didn't want to rob her again.

While Tabitha was lounging about being perfumed and pampered, Clara and Angel were sitting in a damp shadow outside Metcalfe's house. Clara couldn't pretend that any of their previous thefts had been the most elegant or ingenious crimes but they hadn't been the crude acts of vengeance that Angel hungered for. She had been terrified by the look in Angel's eyes when they started planning this job. She had been hell-bent on vandalism and arson, not simply content with filling her pockets she wanted to cause as much damage as she could in the process. Clara had managed to talk her out of most of it, by pointing out it would attract too much attention but she had been forced to concede that it might be necessary to break a window to get in. Angel seem accepting if not satisfied with that, although Clara had wished she didn't look so excited about the prospect of forcing entry by causing damage.

This was the trouble with the others being away. Without Min's reconnaissance and Luce's calming influence they were left with a seat-of-the-pants scheme based on exactly no concrete information at all. It was pure guesswork that Metcalfe would keep her jewellery in her bedchamber and they didn't actually know where her bedchamber was. The whole thing was giving Clara an uncomfortable sinking feeling.

Metcalfe's house was in the middle of the most fashionable part of the District. At this time of night, the lamps flickered in the unshuttered windows of the houses around them. Even Metcalfe's house showed some signs of light, most of the household had stayed in town. Finding an access point was going to be the first challenge. The front of the house was mostly in darkness, the staff quarters being around the back, but Metcalfe's house didn't have much by way of a garden which made it easy to see any activity from the street. Clara and Angel crept through the shadows darting from dark puddle to dark puddle, senses alert. They made their way around the back of the building without mishap but found themselves crouched in the shade of a low wall and faced with an unhelpful scene.

Lord Metcalfe was a 'horse man' and had an extensive stable block with a fleet of a dozen or so grooms and hands, most of whom were apparently gathered around a brazier in the yard three sheets to the proverbial wind. There were also numerous utility buildings - a laundry, an store and so on, which had lights in the windows. Either the staff were working late or saw fit to keep whatever hours they chose whilst the Lord and Lady were away, and to burn the lamp oil and tallow candles with careless abandon. There were patches of warm light scattered all over the outbuildings and the fire in the kitchens - a low building tacked on to the back of the main house - was still burning judging by the flickering around the edge of the shutters. There was no way they would be able to break in here, even if all the stable hands were too pissed to puke.

Back around the front, things looked a little more promising, provided of course there were no nosy neighbours or strolling militia patrols. Angel found a convenient ground floor window, Clara kept tentative watch on the empty street and reflected that glass was a very silly thing to put in a window. Something so fragile covering an access point did not seem practical to Clara. She had one ear on Angel, as with a practised deftness she covered the small pane with a chamois and tapped it with a small mallet. The trick was to crack the glass without shattering it immediately. It may have been more time-consuming but it also caused far less disturbance. Clara turned her full attention back to the road, wondering idly what Angel would do if she just took to her heels right now and ran off in to the night. She had serious misgivings about this, and worse she was ashamed of herself that she had not been strong enough to stand up to Angel. She was still pondering this when Angel hissed at her to get her attention. She had made a very neat job of the breaking and was waiting by a wide open window for Clara to join her in the entering.

They found themselves standing in a dimly moonlit room that was probably the drawing room, with no real notion where the bed chambers, the stairs or even the doors might be. Angel was undeterred, she grabbed Clara's wrist and dragged her in the direction of the middle of the house. After several minutes of cautious shuffling they found themselves at the foot of an impressive stair case that swept up to a wide landing. It was the logical location of the bed-chambers, so up the stairs the girls scampered, not wanting to hang around. Once up there, they were none the wiser. They found themselves looking at four closed doors, none of which had any distinguishing features. There wasn't even a sliver of light coming under any of them. Angel waved at Clara indicating that they should split up and take a door each and, before Clara had time to respond, had pressed her ear up against the door directly in front of them. Clara did the same to the next one. The wood was cold against her cheek and smelled oddly astringent. It was a heavy door, not likely to give away the gentle breath of sleeping householders. She had no choice, she reached down to the handle and turned. Luckily, it was a high-quality well-maintained mechanism and it opened without a sound allowing her to push the door open an inch or so. The moonlight streaming into the room was much brighter. She could clearly see that this was indeed a bed chamber, unoccupied and with the curtains open. It occurred to her as she stepped inside that she would need to move below window level as her silhouette would be easily visible to the drunks in the back yard. She dropped down and scuttled forwards. She couldn't immediately see anything that looked like it might contain valuables, just a few nondescript mounds in the darkness and something that looked like the bottom of a cupboard door. That seemed promising. She was pretty sure that she could probably pick the lock in this gloom even without Luce to help her.

She looked down and found a pair of wide rheumy eyes looking back at her. She didn't scream, in fact, given that the wide rheumy eyes were not that far above a set of gleaming white fangs, she didn't dare to breath. The dog -

she was pretty certain it was a dog at any rate - let out a sour snort of breath and pulled its upper lip back ready to either bark or bite (at this point Clara would have preferred bark but it was close). It gave the impression that the beast was smiling, maybe even chuckling cruelly to itself. With lightning speed Clara recovered herself; before anything more than a timorous whimper could escape the dog's lips she babbled a spell and put the animal to sleep. It took a moment or so for her to embed the enchantment enough that she could walk away. With luck, that little parlour trick had bought them quarter of an hour or so. She hurried across to the cupboard, tried the handle and with relief found it was unlocked. It was unlocked because it contained nothing of any value, unless you were a very specialist linen and blanket thief, which Clara was not. She glanced about, apart from the bed, the sleeping mutt and a couple of floor cushions there was little else in here. She took her chances and dashed past the window, back out to the hallway, realising a moment too late that she had abandoned the necessary caution. Luckily, there was no one about except Angel who was just pulling her door closed, her bag bulging and a grin on her face.

"Come on," she hissed without pausing to ask what Clara had found. Clara thought it best to keep quiet, with a bit of luck they would be out of the door by the time the dog woke up and it was probably best not to waste time trying to explain. They went to the next door together, pushing it gently so that it swung open. Clara stood in the doorway as the room was revealed before her and her mouth dropped.

This was not a bedchamber, which was just as well as Clara severely doubted anyone would be able to sleep in here with all those eyes staring. She shuddered. It must have been Lord Metcalfe San Clear's personal study, where he kept all the things his wife wouldn't allow him in the rest of the house: most notably a vast and terrifying collection of taxidermy animals. It was clear that he had shot, trapped, snared or otherwise murdered the majority himself, and judging by the state of some of them had possibly also stuffed them. Clara didn't know what was worst: the slightly boss-eyed badger with half an ear missing or the extremely militant looking weasel that had been posed in such a way that he looked as though he was missing a miniature broadsword and a helmet. She didn't dare look at any of the fish.

Angel, who had spent more time than she cared to remember in the homes of the stinking rich, simply ignored all the trophies and started to look around at the other detritus that covered every surface of Lord San Clear's furniture. She lifted a solid gold candle snuffer, an engraved silver ink well - tipping the ink careless into a puddle on the desk - and a pewter snuff box before she realised that Clara hadn't moved. She didn't say anything she just cleared her throat angrily breaking Clara's horrified trance, and stabbed an aggressive finger at the bookcase against the far wall. Clara didn't argue, she was still aware that time was of the essence. She took a deep breath and scurried past an entomology display, keeping her eyes fixed on a huge beetle with a shining blue carapace and a horn just in case it started to move.

The bookcase proved fruitful. It seemed Lord Metcalfe had an eye for fine things and, having travelled extensively, had brought many rare and wonderful things back with him. Clara, who had an eye for what would sell, left a rather run of the mill pewter dish in favour of an exquisite jade figurine depicting the four faces of the Goddess of Life and a collection of Jaffrian enamelled icons. They would be tricky to fence, and the Lord would miss them sorely, but if she was any judge at all that small handful was worth the best part of two hundred guilders alone. She paused for a moment and cast about.

It would probably be as well to wrap the items. Shoving the statue in with the enamel willy-nilly would not be a good idea if she wanted them to remain in pristine condition. She was aware of Angel behind her glaring daggers at her perceived faffing about, but she didn't bother to react. If Angel wanted to weigh herself down with a bag full of mediocre Albion silverware then Clara wasn't going to argue, not whilst they were at the mercy of an enchanted sleeping dog. She planned to wait until they were home and belittler her selection then.

Whilst she was looking for something to wrap her finds in, she pocketed a few other less interesting trinkets before her gaze fell upon a small square of soft, pure white fur. Clara, who was born and bred in the roughest bit of the poorest part of the dodgy end of Aberddu city had never seen the like of it. If you were lucky, fur came from whatever died near your house or anything you trapped and ate; normally rats. If anything white and furry had ever lived Aberddu or its surrounding woodlands, then it had long since been hunted into extinction. She picked up the fur with due reverence and rubbed her face in it. It was deliciously soft as it looked and had a faint savoury smell about it. Perfect. She wrapped the treasures in the fur and stashed them all in her bag.

"Let's go," she murmured to Angel who was trying to fit a candlestick into her satchel.

"Why?" Angel grunted sourly.

"We're done," hissed Clara. Angel scowled at her but didn't argue, she was used to Clara calling the shots in this regard, she had an undeniable knack for it.

They made their way carefully back to the landing and had their feet on the top step when they heard the noise behind them. It was a low, menacing growl. Clara cursed under her breath. The spell had worn off. Angel, who had no idea what had made the sound, hesitated. The rumbling growl grew into a more purposeful snarl and there was the sound of a large claw scraping at wood. That was the moment when Clara realised with horror that she had been too distracted by watching Angel close her door to shut the one she had come through herself. It was hanging unlatched, and whilst the dog was having little success opening the inward swinging door, it was only a matter of time and persistence.

Even if the beast didn't succeed in getting its claws around the edge of the door, the noise it was now making would doubtless draw attention. Clara started forward down the stairs, snatching at Angel's sleeve to pull her away. Caught off balance, Angel wobbled and tried to right herself. She missed her footing and tumbled forward down the wide staircase, rolling head over heels over head over heels, her bag clanking on every step it hit, scattering stolen goods as it went. Clara let out a silence, hoarse gasp and scurried after her. A fall like that could be fatal, never mind about the consequences of the noise. Thankfully, by the time Clara reached the bottom step Angel was stirring, dazed and bruised but not seriously damaged. Clara didn't pause to find out what help Angel wanted, she simply hauled her to standing and started dragging her towards the drawing room. Above them they heard the unmistakable sound of a large dog hitting a door and from behind them, in the bowels of the ground floor came the uneven rolling footsteps of a large man topped up with cheap booze. They didn't pause to find out who was coming, they just kept moving as fast as they could, caution abandoned.

The footsteps grew louder and were accompanied by a stream of inebriated grumbling. "Bloody useless dog," and "Could have taken it with them" were the only intelligible phrases. Then, just as Angel and Clara reached the drawing room door there was the crashing sound of four and a half stone of frustrated canine breaking through a door and a shout of

"Oi! You! Stop!"

Why anyone shouts 'stop' at people who are clearly trying to get away is a mystery and in this case it was about as effective as you would expect. Clara and

Angel flung themselves through the drawing room door towards the still open window. The dog descended the stairs at speed, barking frantically, joining the sound of boots on flag stones. The dog burst into the drawing room just as Clara was shoving Angel and what was left in her bag through the window. Later, Clara liked to imagine she could smell the sour stench of the beast's breath and hear the gnashing of its jaws as it dived across the room towards her. In truth she imagined most of it, her attention was almost completely focused on trying to escape with at least some of what they had taken intact. She vaguely heard the drunken shouting of the man as he followed the dog through the door. She didn't stop look back as she dropped her own bag carefully into a bush below the window, even in this turmoil making sure she was careful with the fragile enamel. She hooked both legs through the window and was about to push herself down after her bag when she felt the hot, clinging breath as the dog lunged forward and sunk its teeth into her behind. She let out a shrill shriek of pain, given their current situation there was no point in swallowing it.

"Run," she hissed at Angel through gritted teeth as she wrestled with the animal. "Take my bag." Angel, still befuddled from her fall, was at least cogent enough to take the hint. She snatched Clara's satchel and legged it. Clara wriggled in the window, trying to turn so she could put a hand on the dog. Gambling on the fact that the beast would slacken its jaw if it fell asleep again she cast another sleeping charm on it. It worked instantly, the dog flopped and its grip loosened. Clara was through the window almost before the sleeping dog hit the floor, where the momentary enchantment broke and it awoke even angrier than before. But by then it was too late, Clara had sprinted away into the darkness, adrenaline over-riding the searing pain in her buttock for now. The large drunk man swore loudly and kicked out at the still furious dog, who returned the favour by sinking his teeth into the man's ankle. The scream echoed across the garden but Clara was too far away to hear it.

Tabitha was sitting up in her bed, soft white linen sheets on a feather-stuffed mattress - brushing her hair out. She felt like a princess. Bella had been as good as her word, she had dressed Tabitha up like a 'real lady' and Metcalfe had been indulgent enough to let her stay up until the very end of the evening. She had a full stomach and the warm, comfortable and unusual sensation of contentment and security. Bella had just left, after reclaiming her jewellery and tucking her in. She had to admit, as she let a yawn take her over, that she didn't want to go home tomorrow. She didn't care how much money they could make out of this scam, if Tabitha could have a life like this then she didn't want to go back to being Min. Ever. As she blew out the candle and slid down into her heavenly bed she wondered to herself if there was a deal to be had. Maybe Maurice was thinking the same thing too. She closed her eyes in a darkness that didn't threaten her and drifted into a sweet dreaming sleep.

Chapter 17
Home Again

It was an uncomfortable journey back to Aberddu, not just because of the shocking state of the northern Albion roads. Tabitha had had her eyes opened to what life might be like. She had only been partly joking when she had asked Lady Arabella if she could go home with her instead. She absolutely did not want to go back to a cold house, a scratchy mattress and a diet of pease pudding and scrap ham.

She had made it quite clear to Daddy Maurice that she thought he should make an effort to court Lady Arabella but Mulligan had not been impressed. When Min had pushed the point, Mulligan had cut her off with a cruel, disdainful laugh. They had not spoken since. Luce, who was driving, had barely spoken to anyone all weekend and was even less impressed by the swollen silence behind her than she had been by the grooms' lustful badinage and ribald humour. Silently she wondered if this was all worth it. When all was said and done, what was she going to do with all that money anyhow? She could hardly become a lady of leisure, what would she do all day? She might even be better off getting a job as a stable hand. She was good at it. She'd be fed, clothed and housed and if she didn't pretend she was a boy she might get to sleep on her own.

She looked up at the sky, they had left Metcalfe's after lunch and if she was any judge they were about an hour or so away from Aberddu by now. The woolly clouds were heavy enough to hold the heat of the day, promising a warm evening, but thankfully not bulging with rain. She snapped the reins and drove the horse a little faster. Regardless of the weather, she just wanted to get home.

Clara was lying on her front on the kitchen hearth rug where she had been all day. She had a damp rag pressed against her bite, it was the only thing she could think of to ease the pain and itching. She couldn't see the ragged wound unaided, but she could feel that it was becoming stiff and pestilent. She could only imagine the array of different colours that were now blossoming on her arse-cheek. It wasn't in Clara's nature to complain, but she had gained a very painful injury doing a job she hadn't want to do in the first place.

Angel, who was nursing a sprained wrist and some very nasty bruising, had been less than sympathetic to Clara's plight. Perhaps she was also regretting it, because she was more sullen and resentful than usual. This morning she had dumped a bowl of cold oatmeal in front of Clara, pushed off and hadn't been back into the kitchen since. Clara wasn't desperately bothered, she had been drifting in and out of sleep most of the day, but now it was getting dark and she was chilly and hungry.

She felt the chill of the door open and someone stamped in to the kitchen. Clara, unable to see who it was, assumed it was Angel by the lack of greeting.

"I sold the stuff," said Angel's voice from somewhere behind her. "We did okay."

"okay?" said Clara, they should have done better than okay. "How much is okay?"

"A hundred," said Angel sounding smug as she came across the room.

"A hundred?" repeated Clara, unable to hide the scorn in her voice. "Is that all?"

"What do you mean, all?" spat Angel.

"Tha Jade statue was worf double tha' alone," began Clara, "ne'ermind that enamel work! Who'd ya take i' too?"

"Johnny," said Angel as though it were a stupid question

"Johnny?" squealed Clara, her indignation turning into a rising rage.

Forgetting momentarily about her wound, she rolled over so she could see Angel properly. As the festering bite met the stone hearth a wave of overwhelming pain folded over her and she fell back on to her front, howling.

"What is hell is your problem?" hissed Angel, appearing over her all of a sudden.

"It 'urts, a'right?" she managed through her tears of agony. "It 'urts."

"Well, shut it, you'll attract attention," snapped Angel stalking away out of Clara's vision.

"I don't care," wailed Clara, one hand clamped to her bottom.

"Well, I do," snarled Angel coming back into eye line to drop a cold, wet rag on Clara, causing her to yelp at the sudden unexpected contact. "It's your fault anyway," Angel carried on as she flung herself down at the table. Judging by the thudding sound that followed, Clara guessed she had dumped a heavy bag on the table too. "If you'd take more care with that dog, none of this would have happened. My wrist's killing me, thanks for asking, and I'm aching from head to foot thanks to you."

"Thanks to me?" screeched Clara, struggling against the urge to sit up and give Angel what for.

"Yeah," replied Angel as she emptied the contents of the bag on to the table top with a clatter, "I didn't push myself down the stairs did I?"

"It wasn't my fault you were jus' standin' there like some bleedin' numpty!" retorted Clara, anger starting to overtake the pain. "I should'a left you for that dog and saved me'self."

They were now shouting at each other so loudly that they didn't hear the cart rolling into the yard.

"Maybe you should," bellowed Angel back at her, clearly no longer bothered about attracting attention. At that point, the kitchen door swung open and the sour faces of Mulligan and Min appeared.

"What the bloody hell are you to arguing about? I could hear you in the yard!" demanded Mulligan, his deeper voice cut the shrill shrieking dead. Neither Clara nor Angel answered. "Why are you lying on the floor?" was the next question. Clara noticed he had adopted a stern, almost fatherly, tone with them. She was unimpressed.

"I was bitten by a dog," she said doing her best to keep eye contact and maintain her dignity from her prone position. "On the behind." She pointed to the wet rag that was plastered over the wounded cheek.

"What's this," asked Min, pushing herself into the conversation. She was pointing at the coins that Angel had emptied on to the kitchen tables.

"About a hundred guilders," came the sour reply from Angel, who had bristled at the accusatory tone in Min's voice. "Not a bad night's work all in all."

"What?" screeched Clara and Mulligan at the same time. Clara followed it with, "It should'a been at least double tha'" and Mulligan, after a moment's pause said, "what work?" Angel didn't respond, so Mulligan persisted.

"What work?" he repeated slowly, in a dangerously quiet voice.

"We did a job, las' night," explained Clara, even though Mulligan's poorly contained anger was directed almost entirely towards Angel. "That's how I go' bit."

"You did a job?" His tone was coldly controlled; Clara was actually quite scared. "You did a job?"

"Yeah," said Angel, "and?"

"And," said Mulligan, his voice growing louder ever so slightly, "I'm pretty sure we agreed that we weren't going to do a job this weekend." By this point he was also shouting.

"*We* didn't agree anything," retorted Angel, "You just decided. Just because you didn't want us to rob your friends." Mulligan's face drained white with fury,

"No," he said, his voice back under control, "you silly little girl, it was because I knew I couldn't trust you not to screw up." He stabbed a finger in the direction of Clara, who had collapsed back on to the rug, cradling her behind. "You had no plan, no clue what you were after, you were bloody lucky to get away still intact. Mostly intact," he corrected himself after another glance at Clara, who had started tearing up in pain again. "Don't you get it? You could have blown the whole thing. Whose house did you do over anyway?"

"Metcalfe's," was the one-word reply from Angel, arrogant and scornful.

"Oh good gods," was the only response Mulligan could bring himself to make. "You really are stupid," he said after a few silent moments.

"If that's what you think," spat Angel, "Maybe you don't want your share of the money?" Mulligan just looked at her.

"You really are a piece of work," he said.

It had taken Luce this long to park up the cart and care for the elderly nag. Watching him munching down his oats made her realise how hungry she was. Unlike Mulligan and Min, who'd had a three course lunch with wine, she'd had a rock hard piece of bread, some rather dry cheese and half a cup of cider. She was ready for supper, hopefully Clara had cooked up something hot and filling. She had heard the raised voice from the stables, but hadn't really paid any attention to them. As she crossed the yard she started to wonder what the barny was over. She couldn't really hear the details of the exchange because by this point only Angel was audible. As she scraped her boots on the back step, she heard the words 'you really are stupid'. As she stepped into the kitchen, she saw Clara, pale, clammy and in obvious agony on the hearth, Min standing well back from the whole scene twiddling her hair vapidly and Angel with a handful of coins.

"You really are a piece of work," said Mulligan and Angel let out a shriek and flung her handful at his face. Mulligan didn't react at the coins hit his face. Bitterly, Angel sneered and stalked out of the room without another word.

"Come here Min," said Mulligan, slightly more roughly than he needed to, "Clara needs a cleric." Min didn't move, she just looked at him with wide eyes and a quivering lip. "Come here," he growled again before he realised this was the wrong thing to do. Min burst into tears and ran out of the room in the same direction as Angel, although no doubt heading for her bedroom. Mulligan looked after her with exasperated resignation, and then bent down and carefully lifted a still-whimpering Clara on to his shoulder.

"We may be a while," he said to Luce by way of a woefully inadequate explanation, "you might as well go to bed." Then he carried Clara out of the back door and into the fast-falling twilight. Luce stood just inside the door in her stocking feet looking around at the empty kitchen, the pile of coins on the table and the floor and the bloodied rags in front of the guttering range, and wondered briefly what had just happened. Then, her stomach rumbled. Perhaps horse-oats were as tasty as they smelt, maybe the old nag wouldn't mind sharing. She put her boots back on and trudged out to the stable. The horse was better company anyway.

The next few days were extremely uncomfortable, particularly for Clara - who in spite of her injury had not been excused her usual duties. Even though her rear had been neatly dealt with by a comfortably round priestess from the Life Temple who had a long grey plait and the sparkling eyes of the truly devoted, she was still in some discomfort. Mulligan, still in his Maurice Fortescue get-up, had walked across the city to the Temple District with the bedraggled and wincing Clara in his arms. Covered in coal dust and still in her working clothes she looked like a cleaner version of her old self. Mulligan had gone for the Life Temple because the sight of a well-to-do man clutching a wounded urchin would provoke nothing but sympathy there. Other temples asked questions, but the wonderful nuns of the Order of the Chalice, who ran an orphanage and took in the most unsightly sick, would just assume he was a kind man who'd found a waif. They hadn't even put out the collection plate as a hint. They'd treated and fed her, and when Mulligan had assured them that he would see her home they let her go without query.

By the time they had got back to the house that night, it was just after midnight and raining. The kitchen was dark, but the coins on the kitchen table had gone and so had Angel. She hadn't been back since. Min had taken to floating about the upper floors with her nose in the air and her hair in ringlets, wearing a long white cotton night-gown Arabella had given her. She only spoke when necessary. Luce had basically moved in with the horse. Clara didn't blame her.

The unpleasant atmosphere at home was by no means the most uncomfortable thing about the week for Mulligan. The fortnight following a country house weekend was something of a social minefield. There was a considerable etiquette involved when it came to return invitations, notes of thanks and similar. It was not considered seemly to make any sort of contact for the first two days after returning - unless of course you had either suffered a mysterious illness or lost something of value; in these circumstances it was acceptable to have the head of your household staff contact the head of the host's staff to convey information and whatnot relating to the unfortunate events. However, on the third day it was imperative that you sent a note of thanks, hand written – Mulligan couldn't work out how else it would be written - and delivered direct to the host or hostess. The note, as well as extensively thanking them for their hospitality also required a 'return invitation' of some kind. Mulligan had nearly choked when he discovered this. Arabella, who had not really bothered to chat much of the weekend, had at least had the patience to explain it all to him. Mulligan hadn't as yet had the guts to tell Clara.

Mulligan had gone to great lengths to make sure he did everything right. He had about ten days to get everything straight and still be within accepted protocols. It wasn't simply a matter of dropping a casual invitation to afternoon tea; before he could invite them all over he had to get some furniture and someone to make the tea. And some tea. And all the necessary china, and other things that would make it look like they actually lived in the house as opposed to just the kitchen. Sparse was fine, but in the set up they had furnished only the bits that might be seen and left it at that. He had been in town some months now, and if he really had been a gentleman he would have certainly acquired some stuff.

As he walked across the city, heading for the Guild District he started compiling a mental list of what he might need, where he could get it and who would deliver it discretely and possibly under the cover of darkness. The last thing he wanted was that noisy old baggage Lady Sutton-Colney lifting her abalone-shell handled pince-nez up to her piggy little eyes and musing,

"I heard you received a large delivery in the week, dreadfully exciting," in such a hoity-toity southern Albion drawl that it was barely possible to understand her.

It was just as well he had put on Mulligan's clothes this morning he thought to himself as he walked. He usually wore them when he was about his business in the less salubrious areas of the City, particularly if he was hoping not to get overcharged for something.

Today's first errand was in to the Scribes and Cartographers guild to order a hand-written invitation. It was a couple of groats worth of work, but if he'd turned up in his toff-frocks it would suddenly have cost at least a florin, probably more. After that, he'd have to pay a visit to a Guild of a very different kind, or it's market at any rate. Mulligan's clothes were used to being trawled about the tunnels below the city, Maurice on the other hand would have probably baulked at the smell.

There were bound to be a few people down in the Black Market who could put their hands on the right stuff, even if it was only on loan. A momentary thought amused him as he left the Scribes and Cartographers and turned left down a wide passageway that lead down to the river via one of the better sewer hatches in the area: he would have to be careful about the source of whatever he purchased. There was probably some kind of etiquette that forbade one from inviting people for tea and then serving them using their own stolen china. One thing was for damn sure, he thought as he climbed down the rope ladder, finding it more of a struggle than it had ever been before, Clara wasn't going to do the cooking. He was going to splash out on proper bread, and two kinds of jam and those little fruit and honey cakes that he had grown so fond of. It was the only thing that would make another afternoon with Lady Sutton-Colney bearable.

Mulligan was feeling justifiably self-satisfied when he sauntered back towards the Merchants' District after his day's shopping. It was a pleasant afternoon, and the wind was blowing a tantalizing salty smell off the sea. He was smiling to himself as he slipped into the little alley that would take him within dashing distance of his own back yard without being in site of any of the public thoroughfares.

Unfortunately, his joy was short-lived as the sight of the back gate of his own house made his heart sink. He exhaled loudly. There was no telling what had transpired in his absence. Angel still hadn't reappeared and he wasn't desperately sorry. Min, on the other hand, was becoming impossible. When she wasn't taciturn she was stroppy and it was winding Clara up - with good reason. Mulligan tried to push these woes to the back of his mind. This was business after all and he had better talk to Clara, and anyone else who was prepared to listen, when he got in. Then, he thought to himself, he would decide on which two flavours of jam he would order and keep thinking of that so as not to lose his temper. Of all the things he expected to be waiting for him when he got in, he hadn't bargained on a supper invitation from Lady Sutton-Colney. It was the last thing he needed right now, he had far too much on his mind. He read it carefully and wondered if there was etiquette for making blatantly transparent excuses to avoid these things. It would take too long to find out. He sighed. It would be far easier to just go along and leave as early as possible.

The old boot was in fine form the following evening, when they were all forced to assemble in her salon for supper. All but Tabitha, who had pointedly been left out of the invitation. Min just exhaled in response to Mulligan telling her this and floated back upstairs to her room. She was carrying the blasted raggy-doll around with her everywhere these days. He wasn't quite sure why it annoyed him so much, but it did.

It was a mercifully casual affair with large dishes to pick from, rather than anything involving too much cutlery. Judging by the speed with which they were let at the food, Lady Sutton-Colney was not keen to have them hanging about. The atmosphere in the room was far less relaxed than it had been at the Lodge, and at first Mulligan had attributed that to the fact that everyone was minding their manners. Then, he realised that it was because Metcalfe wasn't really talking. She was dutifully attentive but it was the first time that Mulligan could honestly remember her saying so little. As the evening wore on the wine should have loosened the tension, but it only made things chillier. Metcalfe did not become her usual ebullient self after the booze, she went from pleasantly neutral to tight-lipped and bristling. No one dared ask her what was wrong, Arabella and Maurice sat beside each other in tacit silence picking over their food, their proximity unregarded by Metcalfe. Lord Metcalfe San Clear and Lord Sutton-Colney, ensconced in armchairs either side of a ghastly ornamental lamp, were smoking in companionable silence. Only Lady Sutton-Colney felt the need to fill the void by rattling away. It was somewhat off-putting and Maurice was actually relieved when Lord Metcalfe announced just after the evening ten hour that they had better be going. Metcalfe didn't hang around to take her leave, she simply stalked into the hallway, followed at speed by the footman whose job it was to be waiting by the door with her cloak when she got there. Lord Metcalfe lingered a moment and in his quiet, unassuming way said to his hostess,

"Thank you so much for a delightful evening," this was an outright lie, they all knew it and by this point Lady Sutton-Colney was red in the face with embarrassment. "Truly," he said, taking her hand. "It's been a difficult few days, since the robbery." The word robbery was barely audible, "I'm sorry about Evadne, she's had quite a shock, she's not really herself right now."

It took Maurice a few seconds to realise who Evadne was. Of course, Lord Metcalfe San Clear didn't refer to his wife as 'Metcalfe' but after all this time it suddenly occurred to Maurice that this was the first time he'd heard him refer to her as anything other than 'my wife' to guests or 'Lady Metcalfe' to the staff. There was a pinching twinge of guilt as he looked at Lord Metcalfe's kind, upright countenance and saw the obvious signs of strain around his eyes. He was totally unmoved by the calculated understated sympathies of Lady Sutton-Colney, but he actually felt bad for Lord Metcalfe San Clear. It was the first time he had come face to face with a mark after they had been hit and he didn't like it. He turned his attention back to his glass, which was still half full. Once he reached the bottom of this really very good port, he would head off himself and take the long way home.

It was the best part of an hour later when Mulligan finally meandered in through the back gate to find Luce tacking up the horse. She didn't say anything to him when he appeared, she just started untacking again in sullen silence. Mulligan didn't really care, if she wanted to be like that that was her problem. He was feeling so much better. His hair was tousled and his cheeks tingled from the fresh breeze coming off the delta, mixing the sea and river air. The unique sulphurous brine clung in his nostrils: the smell of this extraordinary city. He had taken off Maurice's coat in the warm evening, like a snake shedding a skin, and was carrying it over one shoulder. He was smiling a cool, wide smile that somehow reflected as a dangerous glint in his eyes. Luce didn't notice. Neither did the horse.

Whilst he had been walking, Mulligan had had the chance to get his head straight and he had come to two significant conclusions. The first was that if his name had been Evadne he would have told everybody to call him by his last name as well. The second was that Maurice Fortescue was on borrowed time. The feelings he experiences as he picked his way from the Sutton-Colney's to the water's edge were feeling that didn't belong to him. He was not some soft, perfumed Albion jessy with a sense of justice and pity. He was turning into something of a sap and he didn't like it. It was bad for business. No doubt about it, it was almost time to cut and run. All he had to decide was where he was going and how much, if any, of the stash he would leave for the girls.

Metcalfe was back on form by the time Maurice and Tabitha were required for a light lunch at home with Arabella a couple of days later . Mercifully, the Sutton-Colney's were 'out of town'. No-one asked why. They would be back for tea with The Fortescues but for now it was a nice reprieve for everyone apart from Lord San Clear, who was forced to smoke his pipe alone.

"Apparently," started Metcalfe, between mouthfuls of cold meat, "there's been an absolute spate of robberies." She said the word spate like a small child exclaiming over ice cream. "Anyone, who's anyone has had it in the last few months." It seemed that the ignominy and loss was a fair price for a part in *the* scandal of the summer.

"Really?" said Arabella, pausing with a forkful of radish in front of her mouth and turning a sharp gaze on Maurice.

"Yes," said Metcalfe, warming to her audience, "Even the Al Rahiris, al-though..." she didn't finish the sentence.

"How interesting," said Arabella blandly, turning back to the salmagundi with little enthusiasm. "Have you been affected Mr Fortescue?"

Maurice shifted uneasily in his seat, and somewhere behind his eyes Mulligan cleared his throat uncomfortably. It was a very deliberately pointed question.

"Ah," he started, putting his cutlery down, "no, no not yet. But then, I guess Tabitha and I aren't really 'anybody'." He punctuated this with an uncomfortable little chuckle. "Nothing worth taking really."

"Quite so," said Lord San-Clear with a dry little cough and a small smile. "No women cluttering up the place."

"Hush you," retorted Metcalfe with an indulgent look at her husband. Maurice let out a little more of his uncomfortable chuckle. "Well, Maurice," she continued with her customary ebullience fully restored, "We shall be able to judge for ourselves soon."

"Yes," said Arabella, "I can't wait." She said this with a chilly tone that made Maurice shudder, he had no doubt she was telling the truth but it sounded very much more like a threat than anything else. Tabitha, sitting beside Arabella, helped herself to another dollop of pickled fish and ignored the grown-up talk.

Chapter 18
At Home with The Fortescues

It was a miracle, thought Clara, that she had any hair left by the morning of The Fortescues' afternoon tea. Angel was still missing, something that seemed not to worry any of the others, and Min was slowly turning into Tabitha. Clara had considered snatching that bloody rag-doll and shoving it into the kitchen range, but she wasn't sure that the ensuing temper tantrum would be worth it.

In light of all this and the taxing social rounds Maurice was required to keep up, the bulk of arrangements for the tea party had fallen on Clara and Luce. The furniture Mulligan had acquired arrived in the back of a coal merchants wagon, covered in sacking. After seeing it, Clara was of the opinion that it should go straight back into the sacks again, because it's only use was as fire wood. She took a deep breath and put it all out anyway. After all, it wasn't her that would have to explain it to the posh-knobs who were going to sit on it. If any of them got lice, it wouldn't be her fault. She had just taken delivery of a bread basket containing half a tea service wrapped in brown paper, and a hideous portrait of some drippy girl trailing her hand in a pond, which apparently was all the rage in Albion, when there was a knock on the back door and she found Truvalle standing on the back step.

"Oh," she said, caught on the hop as she unwound the strips of blanketing that wrapped the tea cups. "Hi. I fought tha horse was okay for 'nother week or so?"

"It is," said the wizard simply. By now, they had developed the kind of working relationship that required absolutely no pleasantries, which suited them both admirably. "I'm here for the furniture and Min's teeth."

"Oh," said Clara again, placing a tea pot carefully on the kitchen table. "Right. The furniture." She was poking about the basket inattentively, looking for something that might be the teapot lid. "Well. Um." She was too distracted to make sense of a plan which no one had told her about. "I'm 'fraid I unpacked it all. It's upstairs."

"Excellent." said Truvalle, inviting himself in and heading straight for the stairs out of the kitchen. "I'll get started them."

"Oh, okay," said Clara, triumphantly snatching up a small parcel in the corner of the basket. "Sure."

It took a few minutes for the significance of the conversation to dawn on Clara. She abandoned the rest of the tea service, picked up the portray and raced upstairs. She got as far as the drawing room door and stopped dead in her tracks. The change was phenomenal; in half of the room at any rate. The wood-worm ridden straight-backed chairs had become fine walnut reading chairs; the old stained table an elegant writing desk. The broken coal shuttle was now brightly polished copper, matching the fire irons. The three chipped tankards had gone, and there were three ornamental vases on the mantle-piece, each with a traditional Kchonese tableau exquisitely etched on to it.

Truvalle was standing by the fireplace, eyes closed and spell-book open on the table. He was quivering slightly. She didn't say anything for fear of causing a problem, she just kept watching as his hands started to twitch and his fingers started to manipulate the air. As he did so, the flea-ridden settle and two lumpy looking straw-padded chairs, that smelt like a cat had pissed over one of them and died in the other, blurred before her eyes and changed shape. The room smelled better, and then suddenly the items came back into focus as an exquisitely upholstered chaise and a pair of winged armchairs.

"Nearly done," said Truvalle, opening his eyes to find Clara gaping at him. "Just a few extra touches here and there. I'd step outside if I were you, just in case." Clara did as she was told, taking the ghastly painting with her. Truvalle was spreading the sacks out in front of the fire place. When he called her back minutes later, he had transformed the sacks into a fine Jaffrian silk rug and there were flowers blooming in one of the vases.

"There," he said simply, as though he'd just iced a cake, "that'll do I think." Clara couldn't even bring herself to nod. He just smiled at her and said, "Is Min upstairs?" This did elicit a nod from Clara. "Oh, and tell Mulligan he's only got this until five, okay?"

"Yeah, alrigh'" uttered Clara because it seemed like the thing to say.

"What a hideous picture," said Truvalle as he breezed past her to find Min.

"Yeah," agreed Clara under her breath, looking about her with a certain amount of discomfort and wondered if Mulligan had asked Truvalle to do the privy as well.

Afternoon tea was traditionally half past three to four o clock, which meant that guests were expected to arrive just after the afternoon three-hour and depart not long after the four-hour. By the time the Law Temple bells rang two o clock, Clara was worn to a frazzle. Luce had been only a certain amount of help, the moment that Mulligan went upstairs to change into Maurice's 'at home' outfit, she had sloped back out to the yard, tucking her hair up under her cap as she went. Clara washed her face quickly in the cold puddle that lurked under the hand pump and pulled her cap on with a grimace. She felt ridiculous in bodice, skirt and cap but it was expected. It was only for a couple of hours she kept telling herself as she sliced into the warm loaves. They had arrived in yet another basket, that had been filled with teaspoons and such at the bottom.

The smell of the freshly baked bread filled her nostrils and made her content. She had torn off a handful and eaten it before she'd even finished unpacking the basket. There was plenty there she reasoned, and she wasn't missing out just because Min was more adorable than she was. She hacked off another large chunk to keep for Luce and herself later and set it to one side before she started trying to slice it. Clara had never cut bread of this quality in her life, she was fighting against its softness and squashed or tore the first half dozen slices. Then she threw caution to the wind and gave up on anything delicate - it was doorsteps or nothing.

By half past two, Clara was completely ready and had already boiled the kettle once. She took it off the hob, manoeuvring the heavy iron pot skilfully with two cloth-wrapped hands and put it on the hearth. She sighed. In the time it had taken her to sort out the furnishings, hanging the paintings, sweep the floor and freshen up the privy, slice the bread, put out the buns and wash the tea service, Maurice and Tabitha had just about managed to bathe and dress themselves. Gods only knew what took them so long. She flopped down in the chair and waited. She didn't need to move until somebody rang the doorbell, and that shouldn't be for a good thirty minutes. Lazily, she reached out to one of the earthenware jars on the table and lifted the covering cloth.

Jam was easily the best thing about posh living. She stuck her nose in to the jar and inhaled the deep, fruity aroma of blackberries. She had spooned a civilised amount out into a small dish - which she had been told by Maurice and Tabitha was how the 'right people' served their jam. That had left about an inch or so in the bottom of the jar. The intense purple sweetness was so inviting that she didn't want to break the joy by tasting it, but after a few moments of ecstatic agony she caved and snatched up one of the borrowed teaspoons. She sniffed every spoonful indulgently, before putting it into her mouth and letting it linger on her tongue until it started to melt away. She scraped the edge of the jar, careful not to waste any of this divine preserve. The unusually large intake of sugar was making her feel slightly nauseated and warm but she didn't let that stop her. In fact, it was only the harsh clang of the spoon on the bottom of the jar that brought her out of her reverie, just in time to hear the door bell, followed moments later by the Law Temple chimes.

Caught unawares, she raced up the stairs, straightening her cap with one hand and still clutching the spoon with other. She hadn't even bothered to wipe the jam from around her mouth when she flung the door wide and said in her best imitation of someone 'talking proper'

"Good afternoon your Ladyship, do come inside and I will take your wrap."

"Thank you," said Arabella pleasantly and did as instructed. Clara chucked the spoon into the corner behind the open door before taking Arabella's fine wool shawl in her sticky fingers and ushering her into the drawing room. "If you wouldn't mind waiting in here," continued Clara, over-annunciating every word, "I shall summon the family forthwith." Arabella smiled warmly and went where she was directed. She didn't seem remotely perturbed by the unortho-dox manner of Clara's door answering. Clara hung her wrap on a hook by the door and stomped up the stairs to yell for Min and Mulligan muttering to herself about having to do everything. She got as far as the first landing, her feet aching, and opened her mouth.

"Mi…" she started at the top of voice before she checked herself. "Miss Tabitha," she corrected hastily, "Mr Fortescue, there's a guest in the drawin' room for you."

This produced both of them at high speed, Maurice glaring at Clara for her total lack of decorum as he trotted past her down the stairs straightening his neck-scarf. Arabella was still standing as they arrived in the drawing room, apparently examining the hideous portrait.

"Bella," squealed Tabitha, as she overtook Maurice at the bottom of the stairs and ran towards her with her arms open.

"Lady Arabella," said Maurice, with far more reserve. "So nice of you to join us. Do sit down."

Clara, who had never met the Fortescues before, was forced to clamp a hand over her mouth to stifle the laugh that was trying to escape. She went back to the kitchen to get everything ready, smirking through her nose. She would have to find a way to compose herself before they rang the bell for the tea things. It really wouldn't do to burst out laughing while serving the bread and jam. When she got back downstairs the kitchen was still empty. Luce was in the yard, using the dry day to scrub the tack with saddle soap. It wasn't as though she could really help out now - even in houses like this one, the stable lad didn't serve the tea.

It was approaching the afternoon four hour by the time that Maurice finally managed to pause the conversation to ring the bell for tea. Having invited everybody for three o clock, they had all swanned up at about half past, apart from Arabella. It rankled with Clara, did rich people think they were too important to be on time? The bread would be growing harder by the minute and she had reboiled the kettle twice.

She had ended up sitting on the stairs, irritably waiting for the doorbell and when it finally rung she had great difficulty being polite to the ample, effervescent woman on the step who buried a startled look upon seeing Clara - who was still smeared with jam - and the tall, solid gentleman behind her who hadn't even looked down that far. She ushered them in with due courtesy and the distinct feeling that the woman in particular was enjoying the spectacle. No sooner had she finished hanging their cloaks than the bell rang again. She grumbled under breath and opened it. Her less than pleasant expression was echoed in the flaccid-looking woman she found on the doorstep, wrinkling her nose with such force that her jowls quivered. She too was accompanied by a tall, amiable gent who gave Clara an embarrassed half-smile, well aware of the grimace that had taken over his wife's countenance. Clara ran through procedure, although the sour-dough woman declined to have her shawl hung up, clutching it to her as she went through into the drawing room. Then, with a certain amount of sulking, Clara went back downstairs to await the jingling of the tea bell.

Upstairs, things were far more convivial. Lady Sutton-Colney, on seeing that Metcalfe had made herself very much at home on one end of the chaise lounge, relaxed somewhat and sat beside her. She didn't say anything, because even though she had been there only a matter of minutes, Metcalfe was already in full flow.

"Oh yes," she was saying authoritatively, "the Militia officers have been very thorough. In fact, they think they may even have a lead!" She imparted this news with delight, unperturbed by its lukewarm reception. "They're watching all the caravans out of the city. Especially Al Rahiri's." She said this with an unspoken 'obviously' after it. "Some of my husband's artefacts are very rare indeed. Easily identified. And it's well-known that those *eastern* caravans take more than their share of stolen goods." This much was true - it was well-known. It was also manifestly untrue. The majority of stolen goods that left the city headed north towards the Middle Kingdoms, where the constant upheaval made it almost impossible to trace things, and then beyond to Paravel where they didn't really care about stolen property as long as it hadn't been stolen from them. However, the caravan-drivers that went North were born and bred in dear old Aberddu and the ones that went east, or south across the Sea of Stars tended to either be obviously foreign like the Alrahiri's or non-humans, and gate guards the world over are nothing if not predictable in their bigotry.

"I mean," continued Metcalfe without noticing the smirk Arabella was directing towards Maurice, or the slight discolouration in Maurice's cheeks, "How stupid do you have to be to believe that you could get away with such an audacious crime?" She paused, but only for effect not for comment. "I ask you, I sometimes think the class of criminals in this city really does leave a lot to be desired." At this point, Arabella produced her handkerchief and started dabbing her face.

"Quite so," said Lord San-Clear and Lord Sutton-Colney grunted his assent.

"I don't know Maurice," she carried on blithely, "You're a relative newcomer, what do you make of this?"

Maurice, who had been hoping to get a word in to announce tea, blinked furiously as he was actually called in to the conversation.

"Oh," he stammered, "Well, yes. It does seem a trifle ill-advised perhaps. Not the sort of thing that happens in Albion." There was more grunting agreement. "It's most unpleasant to contemplate," he continued with all eyes on him, including Tabitha's. "In fact, it's almost enough to make one think of returning to Albion." This statement had the desired effect of closing every mouth in the room. After a momentary pause, he stood up and walked to the bell pull.

"Tea?" he said cordially and tugged the cord.

By the time Clara came clattering up the stairs, with the tea things on a tray that was nearly as big as she was, the Law Temple bell was ringing the afternoon four hour. It was only when she got into the drawing room that it occurred to all three of them, Maurice, Tabitha and Clara that she didn't know what to do with the tray. She just hovered stupidly.

"Ah, thank you," said Maurice, playing for time as he worked it out. "Let's have it there." He pointed at a low rectangular table in the middle of the seating area. Metcalfe shuffled forward in her seat, eyes fixed on Arabella who remained reclining and distracted. After a pause where both Maurice and Clara were trying to work out the correct procedure for getting the tea into the cups, and Clara back to the kitchen, Metcalfe cleared her throat and said, with a pointed and vaguely disappointed glance at Arabella,

"I'll pour shall I?"

With that, Clara didn't hang around. She trotted back downstairs to fetch the food, and the small plates that were apparently a necessity. Clara couldn't imagine why - in her experience crockery was only for things that would escape if you tried to eat them with your fingers. She was so intent on getting everything upstairs as fast as possible that she abandoned any remaining vestiges of decorum, plonking the pile of plates and the platter of bread and butter down on table beside the teapot with no grace what so ever. It was all she could do to slow herself to a walk as she left the room to collect the buns.

They had better not hang around; time was ticking away. The way she figured it she could sink a cup of tea and a slab of bread the size of her face in less than five minutes, taking in to account the fact that rich folk were less likely to be hungry and therefore more likely to chew, that should mean that ten minutes, maybe fifteen at a push, would be sufficient. She was panting by the time she appeared with the plate of buns. There was no room on the table so she just handed them to a mystified looking Lord Sutton-Colney and turned to Maurice, made a clumsy dip of a courtesy and said,

"Any fink else guvnor?" This was met with an urgent glare from Maurice.

"Oh sorry," mumbled Clara, curtsying again, "I mean do you re-quire any fink further your honour?" At this point, Arabella seemed to have a coughing fit.

"No thank you girl," said Maurice imperiously, "We'll ring when we've finished."

"Very good your excellency," finished Clara with a low bow that was met with a strangulated sneeze from Arabella and stunned silence from the rest of the company.

Metcalfe, being an Albion matron, was an adept tea-pourer and had everybody accommodated in no time, passing out cups with gentle commands and well-versed enough in the company to not need to ask preferences. Lady Sutton-Colney, a woman who would have been vastly improved by having to live with children, was busily fussing over Arabella's sudden outbreak of poor health in a way that suggested she was more concerned with contagion control than with any discomfort Arabella may be experiencing. Tabitha, on the other hand, had cuddled up to Arabella on the other side and was giving her a concerned look. Arabella was mostly trying to deflect the attention.

Maurice used this momentary lull to skilfully shift the conversation; engaging the two near silent Lords in a stilted discussion about what to expect from the winter in Aberddu in terms of recreation and sports. Anything to avoid any more discussion of the militia and the crime rate.

When Clara got back down to the kitchen, she stuck her head out of the back door and called Luce in. If the posh-knobs could have bread and jam, so could they. She broke off a chunk and rubbed it around the inside of other the jam jar, not a plate in sight. They made short work of it, gobbling it with abandon. It was just as well that the earthenware jar had a wide neck or there may well have been a fight. Five minutes later, they were dabbing sticky fingers at the crumbs on the table when the back door creaked open and they both looked up.

Angel was standing on the door mat, absolutely filthy and looking utterly exhausted. Luce and Clara, just stared at her. It would have been more shocking if Angel had made any pleasantries or offered an explanation. She just helped herself to a splash of water from the pump and said in her usual disdainful tone,

"Why are there two posh-knob carriages outside? The drivers look proper annoyed."

Clara jerked her head up towards the drawing room and managed to clear enough free space to push out the words,

"Tea party."

Angel acknowledged the information with an almost imperceptible jerk of the head.

"I'm starving," she carried on, "and I need a bath." Clara wasn't quite sure if Angel was expecting her to do something but she had no intention of lifting a finger where she didn't have to.

"Well fire's lit, them bellows are there and the skillet's by the pump in rhw yES. Knock yoursel' out." She said without moving an inch.

"How long's that going to be?" asked Angel gracelessly, indicating upstairs, as she set about the bellows.

"It'd best be done by five," said Clara with a snort. "Tha's when the furniture runs out." Angel clearly didn't care enough to pursue this peculiar statement. She concentrated on the fire for a few moments. Once it was rekindled to her satisfaction, she straightened up and demanded to know if there was any food. She was clearly eyeing the crumbs on the table, but even if Clara had wanted to share the treat with Angel, she couldn't. "There's bread and apples in tha' basket," she said waving a hand, "An' scrag-beef and taters in the small pan." Angel tried to smile in acknowledgement but in the end it was more like a momentary leer. "Scrag-beef's cold mind," added Clara, "and about a week old."

Angel just grunted, she'd had far worse meals. At least she knew what was in this one.

Clara was sitting on the edge of her chair willing the bell to ring again. Time was ticking away and she starting to get twitchy. It must be approaching quarter to five by now and she still hadn't been summoned upstairs to clear the tea things. What the hell were they doing? The tea would be cold by now surely, and how long did it take to eat? She stood up but didn't move away from her seat. She actually had no idea what she was going to do because she was pretty sure charging into the drawing room shouting 'everybody out, before the spells wear off' was probably not a good idea. She was almost certain that she had told Mulligan that Truvalle had said they needed to be done by five, but it was also very likely that he had lost track of time. She ran half way up the stairs, stopped and ran back down again. Angel gave her a scornful look as she ladled warm water in her washing bowl. Pulling herself together in the face of Angel's disdain, she took to the stairs again; this time with a commanding stride, and a determined look on her jam-and-crumb-crusted face. She had to do something. It may well be bad etiquette to barge in and speak to the master now, but she was fairly sure that it was better than letting the magic run out on the furniture so that the guests found themselves sitting on the contents of a rag and bone wagon. That was almost certainly a social faux pas.

"Clara," said Maurice with surprise after she knocked on the drawing room door and walked in without waiting. "I don't remember ringing?" His face was doing a little jig between masterly composure and tense questioning.

"You didn't," she replied tersely, the subtly of his look was completely lost on her.

"Well then," he said, starting to edge from questioning to irritated. "Why are you up here?" He asked through his teeth even though there was no point - the whole company had been watching the exchange with expressions ranging from bewilderment to blatant amusement.

"I need a word," she hissed with equal annoyance. "about the time?" She raised her eyebrows at him and folded her arms in a stance not remotely fitting of her supposed position. Lord Sutton-Colney, who liked to think of himself as a firm but fair master, was sucking his teeth right now. In his household, Clara would have been birched for this kind of impudence and then sacked.

"The time?" repeated Maurice in a whisper, clearly searching for the significance of this cryptic sentence.

"Yes," confirmed Clara, "the time. You remember? It's nearly five?"

"Nearly five?" echoed Maurice in bemusement and then, suddenly, the penny dropped. "Nearly five?" he repeated in a louder, more urgent voice. "Really?"

"Yes." replied Clara tersely. "Nearly five."

"Okay, thank you Clara," he said, clearly trying to pull back his masterly composure. "That'll be all then." He gave her a complex, manic grin that contained too many signals to be sure of any of them. Clara bobbed reverentially and left. Turning back to the company, who had been to a body completely enthralled in the little exchange, Maurice broke out his most apologetic smile and said,

"I am terribly sorry, as Clara has reminded me I am due on urgent business in a very short time. I am afraid that I was having such a delightful time that I seem to have got a little carried away. There's no desperate panic, but I'm afraid we need to draw this afternoon to a close."

If Mulligan could have summed up what he had learnt in the time he'd been working this con it would have largely been this: social graces came down to three things - a posh voice, the right clothes and the ability to tell breathtakingly blatant lies without flinching. He'd honestly had a more amusing time picking through the shit on the city midden. However, he stood in the hall, whilst Clara flung cloaks back at the departing guests, and smiled pleasantly. He helped Lord Sutton-Colney into his overcoat with a charming smile. Tabitha had flung herself endearingly around Arabella's bottom half, had had a gentle kiss bestowed on her head and departed gaily upstairs taking full advantage of her youth. The rich apparently never do anything quickly, and Clara was getting more and more anxious as they hung about in the vestibule straightening collars and taking their leave. She stood behind them, unable to take any further action. All she could do was bounce on the balls of her feet and keep half an eye on the drawing room.

"C'mon, c'mon," she mumbled to herself, drawing another disapproving glare from Lord Sutton-Colney. Maurice was doing a far better job of appearing magnanimous and patient, but even he couldn't refrain from the occasional glance towards the drawing room door. Time was dribbling relentlessly on, five o clock loomed on the horizon like a terrible behemoth whilst Lady Sutton-Colney flapped about with her hat and gloves and Metcalfe adjusted her buckles. Clara snapped before Maurice did and pretty much elbowed her way through to the front door. Wrestling Lord San Clear out of the way, she swung it wide open, cleared her throat pointedly and flourished an arm towards the street. By this point, both the Sutton-Colney's and Lord Metcalf San Clear were looking at her like she had gone mad, Metcalfe was looking at Maurice to see if he thought her behaviour was in any way out of line and Arabella was in the throes of a particularly vicious attack of hiccoughs.

"Thank you, Clara," exclaimed Maurice Fortescue through his teeth, giving her an urgent grimace before looking over his shoulder distractedly.

For a moment there was perfect silence. No one seemed to want to be the first to break out of this blisteringly awkward tableaux. The guests were painfully aware that it was not their place to speak and that they must wait for either their increasingly preoccupied host or his eccentric household staff to say something. However, Mr Fortescue was changing colour almost in front of their eyes; his normally healthy complexion had drained to almost grey, leaving fierce spots of red in his cheeks and under his ears. Ghastly didn't cover it.

The silence was broken suddenly by the sonorous chime of the Law Temple bell as it started to peal the evening five-hour.

"Oh crikey, is that the time?" blurted Maurice, "Dreadfully sorry, lovely afternoon must dash, good bye."

"Good-bye," said Lord Sutton-Colney smartly, eyeing him with concern before grabbing his wife by the elbow and almost dragging her down the steps.

"Yes," said Metcalfe, trying to recover the situation, which had started to remind her of a Bard's Guild farce, "Splendid. Look after yourself Maurice." She leant forward for their customary parting kiss and then changed her mind. The peals had finished, and they were three chimes through the hour.

"Yes, of course," said Maurice, starting to sweat, "You too."

With the forth chime the San Clears turned to leave, followed closely by a barely recovered Arabella. On the fifth chime, they paused on the top step and waved. They were just setting foot on the steps down to the street when there was an ungodly clatter from the drawing room. Maurice vanished inside, leaving the three departing guests staring at Clara with open curiosity.

"Don't worry," she said, trying to sound posh - too little too late - "It's just the cat." And with that, she slammed the front door before anyone else could comment.

She found Mulligan, for in this surrounding he couldn't be said to be Mr Fortescue, standing beside the hideous portrait, staring at a room full of cracked and rotting furniture. The magic Truvalle had used to enchant it had obviously somehow accelerated the decomposition process. The whole room smelt sweetly organic, with an over-riding hint of leaf-mould.

"That went well," said Mulligan weakly as Clara walked up beside him, "don't you think?"

"Yeah," she said, because it was all she could think of.

Chapter 19
Beggars at the Feast

Mulligan looked around him at what remained of his furniture and let out a very loud sigh. It would just have to wait. He couldn't face this right now.

"I need a drink," he said more to himself than Clara, and stalked off to find a bottle of something.

Clara, well aware how this was likely to go, made a cursory effort to start tidying up, piling anything that could be usefully burnt by the door to the corridor. If nothing else, they had gained a few days' worth of fire wood. Mulligan found himself a bottle of cheap brandy and took it upstairs to his bedroom; he didn't even bother with a cup. He had some thinking to do about next moves and escape plans.

It was close to nine o clock by the time Clara summoned everyone downstairs for supper - having returned to the kitchen after an hour or so of tidying to find that no one else had bothered to cook anything. She knew Luce would be hiding in the stables, but she was irrationally angry with Angel - who had been sitting on the hearth by the fire since she had washed and eaten, doing absolutely nothing. Clara didn't know what else she'd expected given the usual pattern of things but she was actually starting to develop a deep hatred of the smug little smirk on Angel's porcelain face. She didn't say anything, she just set about making some food, silently seething.

She did at least make Angel go upstairs and fetch Tabitha and Mulligan; she'd pretty much stopped thinking of Min as Min any more. The four girls were always prompt for meals out of habit; in case their dinner was fed to somebody else. Once upon a time they would have chattered with each other companionably throughout the whole meal, forcing words around mouthfuls as they gulped down whatever constituted food that day. Times had drastically changed however, when Mulligan finally pitched up they were sitting in disparate silence picking over plates of watery stew.

It was plain to see that he was drunk, and not the 'endearingly over-indulgent uncle' type of drunk either. He wobbled down the stairs into the kitchen, his eyes red and his hair dishevelled. His face was curled into an unpleasant liquid leer, a look the girls associated with the piss-heads in the docks; the ones that tried to get their hands on you and wouldn't stop if they did. Even before he approached they knew how he would smell; an acrid mixture of sweat and raw liquor. Min actually flinched backwards as he approached but the other girls weren't afraid, they were just disgusted. Angel actually grimaced at him, then looked away. The gesture didn't go unnoticed. Thankfully, however, Mulligan chose not to say anything. He just sat down at the table with a derisive snort at the world in general and helped himself to stew and bread; not freshly baked soft bread for rich people, this was solid, grainy and filling, it took a certain effort to eat.

The silence continued, although it slid from easy indolence into a sharper wariness. The girls flitted glances at Mulligan more often than necessary, waiting for him to lash out at any moment. They started eating faster, clearly not wanting to hang about.

Angel was growing restless with the lack of conversation, she had been away for several days and now she had returned only a few civil, but distinctly cold sentences had been directed at her. The obvious indifference to her reappearance had wounded her pride slightly, but she was more annoyed at the inconvenience because she wanted to tell them about something. She had held on until they were all at supper, a grand announcement being far more her style than a quiet word here and there. Unfortunately, skittishness caused by Mulligan's lubricated entrance, was hardly conducive to conversation. It was understandable, particularly in Clara and Min, who were both small and not desperately strong (although Clara had a bite on her like a rutting pig), but even so.

She waited until everyone had their mouths full of bread; which could be relied on to keep them quiet for at least a minute, then she cleared her throat.

"So," she said confidently, "We need a new plan." At this Mulligan snorted and Angel cut him dead with an ice cold glare. "I've found us a new mark, unless Mulligan has a better idea." With a painful gulp, he cleared his mouth enough to speak.

"You've found us a new mark?" he snorted. "We don't need a new mark."

"Okay," said Angel turning on him immediately, "Who do you have lined up?" Mulligan stared at her, obviously struggling to focus, and said nothing.

"Well?" she demanded after the pause. Her petulant tone infuriating Mulligan, he turned on her deliberately invading her space.

"I haven't got anyone lined up," he said slowly, with admirable command over his words. "And I'm not going to have." It was Angel's turn to snort derisively. "We're finished."

"What'dya mean we're finished?" snapped Clara, before Angel could respond.

"We're done." spat Mulligan. "It's over. We're going to be rumbled. Tell them Min - you heard it too, they were talking about the militia being involved and tracing Lord San Clear's stuff." Min looked up from her bowl with wide eyes, as though she were actually a seven-year-old terrified to be dragged into this, and nodded faintly. "Thanks to you," Mulligan growled at Angel, "Going off without a plan, making a mess."

"Like I said," hissed Angel, "I'm happy to keep your share of the money."

"It's not about the money," screeched Mulligan, suddenly escalating from disdain to fury. "Do you want to hang? That's what'll happen if they catch us. We'll hang, Every. Single. One of us."

"You're losing your nerve," goaded Angel in a low voice. "It doesn't matter. We can handle this job without you anyway, like we've handled all the others. We'll just do without the window dressing, that's all. Feel free to go at any time you like."

For a moment, the flames of hatred burned in Mulligan's blood-shot eyes, the veins on his neck protruded and he quivered with rage. Min and Clara flinched back out of his arm's reach, clearly expecting a violent outburst, but Angel didn't move. She kept her eyes firmly on him with a faint, infuriating smile on her lips. Mulligan clearly had more self-control than they'd given him credit for, even this inebriated, thought Clara, because frankly right now she would have smacked Angel in the face if she'd been him.

"So," he snarled at length, "What's this oh so amazing plan of yours?" Angel glared at him, and turned away as if to dismiss him, addressing the girls instead.

"I was in the market a couple of days ago, and I got listening to this man who some big idea about a scheme in the Temple District, and it got me thinking," she started, keen to set the scene and settling into a long explanation. "Next week is the Feast of the Warden's Keys."

"Wha?" exclaimed Clara, echoing the confusion on Min's face.

"The Feast of the Warden's Keys," repeated Angel and Luce, more helpfully, supplied

"It's some big fancy to-do up in the Law Temple, aint it?"

"Yeah," continued Angel, looking sour for a moment, "It's *the* big event in the Law Temple, you know, everybody in their starch-frillies standing about looking po-faced for hours. They have some long-arsed ceremony that goes on and on and then they have a banquet thing and anybody who's anybody respectable is invited - you know all the Light Alliance High Priests, Militia Commanders and the High Council." At this point Clara and Mulligan snorted in unison,

"Respectable? The High Council?" interrupted Mulligan with a tone of derisive amusement and was cut off by a razor-like stare.

"Well they're supposed to be," said Angel humourlessly. "Anyway, they're all in there for hours and hours."

"So?" demanded Min, who still couldn't see why she should be interested in a ridiculously long religious observance that she was never likely to be invited to.

"So," continued Angel, starting to lose patience, "One of the big-knobs in the Law Temple lives in some massive great house up by The Painted Bridge, and apparently he has plenty worth getting your hands on."

"Okay," said Luce, nodding.

"What's the catch?" demanded Mulligan, not so easily impressed.

"The catch?" echoed Angel, her voice dripping with scorn, "Why would there be a catch?"

"Well," said Mulligan, speaking with the slow self-satisfied tone of someone who is about to take delight in pissing on someone else's bonfire, "if it's so valuable, and every crook in the city knows where it is and no one's stolen it yet, there has to be a catch the size of Jaffria."

Angel gave him a look that could have shatter cold stone.

"Apart from the fact that the house is owned by one of the big-wig Law Followers?" sneered Angel with disdain, "It just so happens that it's on three different Militia patrol routes. There are clear gaps of only about a quarter of an hour between patrols normally."

"Quarter of an hour?" retorted Mulligan, sobering up fast and ready to pick holes in everything this child said. He had finally had enough of being condescended to by a person who was thirteen years old at the absolute outside. "What exactly do you propose we steal in fifteen minutes?"

"Hang on," interjected Luce, who had taken up the role of the peacemaker, "She did say normally."

"Yeah," continued Angel with narrowed eyes, "normally is the key word here. Obviously, we're not going to rob it on a normal night are we?" She looked at Mulligan as though he had the intellect of an easily confused shrew. "We're going to rob it on the night of The Feast of the Warden's Keys aren't we, when half the Militia will be in the Temple. They're changing all the Militia routes for the night aren't they?"

It was the kind of rhetorical question used by people who are conveying an idea that they want everybody else to hail as so ingenious that it may go down in history. It didn't have quite the desired effect, the only real response she got was a slightly lack-lustre

"Brilliant," from Luce. The other girls didn't make a sound and Mulligan simply grunted. After a pause, where Angel regrouped and tried to work out how to make the plan sound more impressive, Mulligan said flatly,

"Just exactly how does that help us?"

"Because," said Angel pausing dramatically to reach into her tunic and produce a scrap of parchment, "I just happen to have that night's patrol routes right here."

It wasn't much of a surprise that they were generally available for the right price on the Black Market. When it came to information the City Militia had a tendency to leak like a poor-quarter hovel in the rain. Min gazed at it for a few moments, nodded her approval and pushed it towards Clara and Luce who were on the other side of the table. Neither of them were particularly literate and after a few dutiful moments of examining the funny squiggles on the page passed it to Mulligan with a look of bemusement.

"With this," said Angel, pointing to the parchment that was now in Mulligan's hands, "we can make a plan."

Mulligan, who was almost back to full function, scanned the schematics in front of him and let his pernicious greed squash the last remaining shreds of his pride. He nodded. This was indeed the beginning of a very lucrative plan. One more job would be okay, he thought to himself as he took in every detail. With one last job he could buy himself a new life in the Middle Kingdoms and eat out for the rest of his life on the tales of his exploits. Gods only knew what Law Temple big-wigs kept in their houses, but they didn't suffer vows of poverty or charity in the same way as some of the other Light Alliance clerics did and there's no point in having a big house if you've got nothing to keep in it. He didn't really care what it was worth, he just wanted to say that he'd stolen it. Whatever it turned out to be.

"Right," said Angel, in the kind of tone that suggests a final decision, "so we're agreed then, this is our next mark?"

"Yeah," said Luce under her breath, smiling. Clara and Min just nodded and Mulligan, who apparently considered himself to be completely forgiven, replied enthusiastically,

"Absolutely."

Chapter 20
Stuck

Mulligan wanted to swear loudly, but it was probably the worst thing he could do at this point. He should have thought it through really, sending Min and Clara to case the joint was a stupid idea, given that they were easily the smallest of the gang. They had located a back corner in a puddle of grubby shadow that seemed to be just off to one side of the kitchens and was therefore likely to be a store room or boot-hole or so other kind of room that rich people liked to have to show how rich they were. It had what they had described as an 'easily accessible' shutter-covered window. Apparently the big-wig had decided that only front end of his unnecessarily large house needed glass in the windows. Around the back, there was no such extravagance. The ground floor, which presumably housed the household utilities and the poor buggers who were responsible for making them happen, just had gaps in the walls with wooden shutters to keep out the worse of the weather and all of the light. The shutter over this particular gap in the wall was rotten along one edge and had been very easy to encourage away from its hinge. It was at that point that Mulligan's heart sank. If the window behind it had been approximately the same size as the shutter they removed, he would have been fine. It would have been a challenge to get through without going head first, but years of flexibility training had left him with no fear of that. However, the gap was considerably smaller. He had looked at it, looked back at the girls - who were already lining up to squirrel through it - and decided not to say a word. There was no point, because the simple fact was that either he went in through this window or he was demoted to nothing more than a road-side lookout and he did still have a very tiny bit of pride left, shredded and squashed as it might be.

The problem was that he would have fit through the gap with ease, if not grace, if he were level with it. He was a lithe and slender man and could simply have posted himself through face first even with his newly acquired paunch. However, the window was actually about five feet above the ground, which meant that in order to get enough of himself through to start the wriggling process he needed to lift himself up on his arms. Six months ago, before this whole caper, it would have been child's play but since then he let his training slip in favour of large lunches, cream teas and even larger dinners so that he was both heavier and less fit than he had been previously.

He hung back and let the girls swarm up and through the gap so that he wouldn't have an audience. Then, left alone to negotiate the problem, he seriously regretted letting Luce go. What he really needed was a leg up. If he could just get an extra foot in height, he'd be able to poke enough of his top half through to get purchase. After three sweaty, abortive attempts at lifting himself with his arms, it was plain that he wasn't going to be able to do this unaided and he was buggered if he was going to ask the girls for assistance. He could imagine them now, rolling their eyes and tutting under their breath as they waited for him.

He looked about him for something to stand on that would give him some much needed extra height, and his eyes landed on a large metal pail lying beside a trough of some description. Perfect. He fetched it, having emptied it carefully into a drainage channel. He didn't want to know what had been in it, he only wanted the bottom to be sturdy - and it was.

With one foot on the upturned pail, he was finally high enough up that he could push his head and shoulders inside. It was at this point he learnt that there was nothing on the other side of the window, just a long drop to the sacking on the floor and a clear space about a yard across surrounded by cruelly amused girls. He was just going to have to ignore it all and think of the money. With a concerted effort that turned his face the colour of cooked beetroot, he managed to get himself so that he was hanging over the window by the hinge of his abdomen. He paused like this for a moment, panting as he considered his options for landing. There weren't many. Basically, he was going to have let himself fall from here and hope his hands could guide him to safety before the weight of his thigh bones came into play and he found himself in a painful and undignified heap at Angel's feet. He couldn't help wondering, in the moments he hung over the window like a towel on a rail, whether the girls had deliberately moved everything out of the way. It was the sort of malicious thing they would find funny. With one last effort, he managed to get his pelvis on to the right side of the wall and started the slow and ignominious descent floor-wards. In the end, he had to hold on to the fact that whilst he had strained his wrist, banged his head twice and severely bruised himself on the way down, he had at least managed to enter the building without making too much noise.

Lying on his back, he could see that they had been correct in the assumption that this would be a store room; large barrels and crocks lined the walls. From his prostrate position, looking up at the girls standing over him, he had expected to be met with an array of exasperated smirks, but was surprised to find that none of them seemed even faintly amused by his predicament. They just looked vaguely unimpressed and Angel huffed as if to suggest he was already a liability and should have been left outside. None of them spoke, but even in the gloom their body language clearly conveyed their irritation at being kept waiting. Mulligan hauled himself to standing and brushed himself off. It suddenly occurred to him that actually, he had never worked with the girls as a gang before. The palpable tension and focus was impressive. They clearly took the business of thievery very seriously indeed. Presumably, this was why they were all still at large in the community with all their limbs still intact.

Luce hadn't wasted any time hanging about waiting for Mulligan to flop through the hole like a dead fish down a storm drain. Not only had she managed, in the dark, to manipulate the heavy tumbler lock on the door, she had also popped open the deadbolt on the other side using some jiggery-pokery contraption that Mulligan didn't understand. The moment he recovered his composure, she held the door open for them and silently, they filed out into the corridor. Mulligan was the last out, hanging back again and feeling foolish. He was barely out of the way when Luce shoved the door closed and slung the bolt across. No sense in leaving it open to accidentally attract the attention of any wakeful house staff. At the top of the corridor, they paused in a small quadrangle with three other passages leading off it. This was convenient in the extreme; one pair of girls went right and the other pair went left, leaving Mulligan to take the middle corridor alone.

The plan for this job was simple. There were three or four items in the house somewhere that would bring in several hundred guilders between them, and a whole host of less valuable treasures to carry off. None of them had ever been inside the building. Opportunities for casing the house of a high-ranking law cleric were minimal, and had been used mostly on establishing the entry point. So, the plan was this: they would enter through the window, make their way into the house and then split up and search the ground floor as thoroughly as possible. Up and down stairs would be on the agenda but only if there was time. The militia patrol would pass the house a few minutes after the evening eleven-hour and they would return about twenty minutes after the chimes rang twelve. Therefore, as soon as the midnight bells rang, they were to scramble back to the access point and make a hasty exit with whatever they had managed to get their hands on.

In a private residence, it is usually safe to assume that most of the corridors are clear of such charming devises as razor trip-wire, spike pits and pressure released venom-tipped darts because most people don't want to have to disarm four or five devices just to get to the privy. These tend to have more of a place in long lost underground chambers, dilapidated Temples and the lairs of paranoid evil wizards; also pretty much the whole of the tunnel system owned by The Guild Below.

However, this doesn't mean you should blunder down them at random. There are subtler ways of injuring the unsuspecting and alerting the very large chaps that sleep in the hayloft to the possibility of intruders. Luce and Angel were both experienced enough to not take any chances. Angel ran her hands carefully over the walls searching for the tell-tale tingle of a magical signature while, a few steps behind her, Luce scanned the area by the blue-white light of a tiny magical lantern for any sign of mechanisms. They were both visibly relieved when at last they found something at about waist height, ten feet or so down the corridor. The moment the tips of Angel's fingers started to warm and tingle she stopped dead in her tracks and Luce nearly walked in to her.

Almost in silence, they inspected the alarm in front to them. It was a clever construction, but not uncommon. A wisp thin magical force field hung across the corridor between chest and knee height. The force field was so thin that unless you knew it was there, or had extremely sensitive skills in detecting magical traces you probably wouldn't notice that you had crossed it - which was the intention. The force field itself was not a defence mechanism, it was the trigger to a series of warning alarms that would go off in other parts of the house. In all probability, if you hadn't spotted the force field, the first you would know of the alarm you had triggered would be the rough fingers of a slab-like hand lifting you by the elbows and inviting you to a visit with the city militia.

Angel smiled darkly at the devise. Not only was she relieved that she had finally found something, she was actually pleased. You don't bother installing a sophisticated magical trap like this in a corridor that has nothing more valuable that granny's favourite tea service at the end of it. She shooed Luce back, took the lantern and started to examine the trap more closely. It was a matter of moments before she let out an almost imperceptible snort of amusement and reached into the pouch on her belt. A lot of people have no idea that finely-milled flour will stick of magical fields without interrupting them – and as Angel always said that was entirely their loss. She took a small handful from a pouch and blew gently so that it dusted the force field. In seconds, a paper thin white cloud hung in front of them. Then, with a feline grin of satisfaction, Angel dropped to the floor and manoeuvred herself through the foot-wide gap at bottom edge the force field. Without being told, Luce followed suit with far less grace than the sylph-like Angel, wriggling under the barrier on her belly. Their caution and expertise were rewarded three feet down the corridor when they found themselves looking at three gilded doors - one of either side of the corridor and one directly in front of them.

Neither girl was daft enough to assume that the barrier alarm was the only protection on these doors. Angel started with the door on the left and Luce with the door on the right. The first thing Angel checked for was a faint trace of magic beyond the door – which, apart from anything else, would tell her if it was worth the effort of opening it. She was gratified to detect the very edges of a powerful signature that was pulsing from what must be a very potent object containing divine magic; hardly a surprise given the owner of this house was such a high-ranking cleric, but good to have located it all the same. She could also feel a handful of other, lesser, enchantments but the divine magic over-whelmed any details. Pushing these signatures away, she concentrated on the door itself, her eyes closed and her cheek pressed to the wood. She was some-what taken aback when she realised that it was blank, apart from the usual background signatures. Surely a simple tumbler lock wasn't the only thing be-tween her and whatever was throwing out that pulse? She turned around to tell Luce, only to find her on her knees peering into the keyhole on the op-posite door.

"Bloody hell," was all Luce said. She wasn't about explain the shear complexity of this locking mechanism. She was almost certain that it had a fail-safe deadlock. These tumblers allowed you to turn them both ways, but if you chose the wrong way the four tumblers would lock themselves together and trigger an iron pin to secure the door. It was sophisticated, expensive and risky - particularly if you had trouble with your left and right, because it would take a very skilled lock-maker several hours to undo this deadlock once it had been triggered. Luce was muttering under her breath as she felt around the inside of the tumbler with one of her lock picks. Angel didn't like to ask, she just waited for her to look up.

Angel gestured for Luce to hang fire for a moment, pressed her cheek to the door and closed her eyes to check for magic traces. In the limited time they had, it might be best to prioritise. After a few seconds, she straightened up and whispered to Luce.

"Don't bother, there's no magic behind there. Do the other one."

Luce didn't argue with Angel, she just crawled across the corridor to try her luck with the door Angel had been looking at.

Min and Clara were making their way towards a sparsely furnished room they had seen during their reconnaissance. It was either a gallery, a receiving chamber or a ballroom and in any case they had seen a plain door in one of the walls that was likely to be a store room. The girls were prepared to bet that it would contain items of silver, or possibly even gold. They weren't expecting much in the way of alarms; the household silver was unlikely to be protected by anything more elaborate than a simple tumble lock. There had been quite a lot of guess work when they made their very sketchy plan of the building and they'd been working on the assumption that public areas for entertaining were on the opposite side of the sprawling villa to any sensitive documents or valuables. That was why two girls went one way and two the other. It had been a general consensus during the planning, which had taken place whilst Mulligan was out, that it didn't matter where the 'long streak of piss'- as Angel had started referring to him - actually went, because anything he managed to swipe was merely a bonus. Privately Min had wondered exactly why Angel had strong-armed him into coming with them if she felt like that, but she didn't dare say anything.

The long streak of piss had found his way to the foot of a very utilitarian stair case and was wondering what was at the top of it. It the last six months, Mulligan had become something of an expert on the cultural differences of household layouts. As far as he could see from the limited plans Min and Clara had drawn up, this place wasn't typical of Paravelian, Alendrian, Albion or even any of the Eastern styles. Gods knew where the architect responsible for this strange gangling pile had found his inspiration, unless he was trying to pioneer a new style known as 'Early Aberddu Catastrophe'.

Years of experience as a thief told him to be wary of this staircase. A plain wooden stair case like this belonged in the staff quarters - for those lucky enough to be entitled to a bedroom. However, the kitchens and other work rooms were at the back of the house and it seemed very peculiar that the staff would have to parade all the way across to the front of the building to go to bed. Either he was completely disorientated or this was very odd. He had run his hands over the bottom step four times, checking for something that might be amiss but he couldn't find anything.

With gurgling trepidation, he put one foot on the bottom step and with agonizing caution transferred his weight on to it. It didn't so much as creak. Not about to get careless, he lifted his other foot to join it and stood stupidly for a moment waiting for something to happen. When nothing did, he felt even more foolish. Moving gingerly but with slightly more speed, he started to climb the stairs as they wound slowly up and around. They may have been utilitarian bare wood but they were remarkably well crafted and solid as stone. There were small oil lanterns hung from iron wall brackets, providing just enough light to avoid tripping. The risers gleamed with wax polish, but the treads had been left untouched to avoid slipping. Because of the way the staircase curved, it was difficult to tell what he would find at the top. He was just going to take it, very literally, one step at a time.

About three steps from where he assumed the landing would be, he paused and pulled a small copper disc from his tunic pocket. It was about the size of a large coin and fit neatly on the palm of his hand. He rubbed it with his gently with his thumb and almost instantly a small white glow began to build above the disc. When the ball of light successfully filled his palm, he held it up so that it spilled its soft glow on to the floor. Slowly, he moved the light into every corner of the small landing and along the foot of the door in front of him. He didn't like what he saw. It all seemed so suspiciously plain, well-maintained and hazard free. His criminal senses were still twitching as he looked again to confirm that the floor was, in fact, made of the same high quality bare wood as the stair case. Apparently so was the door - or at least the bottom foot of it. It felt wrong.

Focusing his attention on details, he checked for all the tricksy things he could think of like pressure pad alarms, poisoned puddles or bolts that might suddenly fly out of the wall at his forehead. He drew a blank. Closing his eyes to block out the magical light for a moment, he sniffed at the air to see if he could sense any trace of magic, hostile or otherwise. If any had been there to pick up on, the end of his nose would have started to tingle. Nothing but a vague prickle around the very edge of his nostrils that felt like he wanted to sneeze and he wasn't sure he hadn't imagined that. At last Mulligan was forced to concede that it might actually be safe to stand in front of the door, although he was also aware that he might freak out somewhat if it turned out that it wasn't locked.

Back on the ground floor, Angel and Luce were having more success. They had abandoned the door with the complex lock, well aware that they had probably just given up on the strong box but of the opinion it wasn't worth the time. Luce thought it was probably for the best, and Angel always favoured taking personal items from targets rather than money. They had managed to open the door with magic behind it it with very little effort in comparison and had found themselves in the mark's study. Angel was evidently delighted.

On the desk, sitting proudly on a round velvet cushion and covered with a glass dome, was a ring. It didn't look like much, just a plain metal band with five tiny chips of deep blue stone embedded in it. In itself, the ring would have been worth about five guilders to the right collector, Luce hazarded - Clara would know. However, given that this ring was the source of the intense magical energy that Angel had been able to pick up from the other side of the door, she was prepared to venture it was worth a little more than that.

The problem they were having was that while the door had been easy enough to deal with, the glass dome was not. It was buzzing with almost as much magic as the ring inside it. Angel suspected that it was protected by a multitude of different enchantments. Luce was at a loss in this situation. She was used to things that, even if you couldn't immediately see them, still left visible holes, grooves or tell-tale marks. Magic confused her. She would just have to stand back and leave it to Angel, who had a natural affinity for magical signatures.

She ran her hands through the air around the dome, with her eyes closed to aid concentration. She frowned and paused. Luce watched, the moonlight streaming through the windows was just bright enough for her to make out Angel's facial expressions. She found herself wondering if she pulled faces like that when she was picking locks. Angel repeated her usual process three times over before screwing her face into a confused but amused grimace. She had apparently just made a discovery she didn't quite believe. With a smirk, she looked over to Luce and said,

"This is going to need specialist equipment."

With that, she turned around, watched over to the mantelpiece and picked up one of the brass candle sticks, removed the candle and placed it back on the mantle. For a horrible minute, Luce thought Angel was just going to use it to break the glass. Clearly amused by the look of shock on Luce's face, Angel said nothing she just smirked.

Carefully, she lay forward on the desk top, so that her top half was supported but her feet were still on the floor. Then she reached out to the dome with the candle stick and gave it a very gentle nudge. It moved about an inch, taking the cushion with it. With virtually no idea what Angel was doing, all Luce could do was keep her ears open and contemplate the quickest way to make an exit if everything went pear-shaped. Slowly, Angel nudged the dome towards the edge of the desk. Every time she pushed it, Luce inched closer to the door still convinced that there was about to be a cacophony of breaking glass.

When the edge of the dome was hanging two inches clear of the desk, Angel stopped. Deftly, she straightened up and trotted around to the dome. Dropping to her knees, she slid the candlestick up through the gap and with impressive poise, jogged the cushion until the ring bounced and moved sideways. Suddenly, Luce realised what she was doing - no wonder she had been smirking. The magical warding on that dome made it too heavy to lift up and also probably searing hot to the human hand – so something else that stopped you touching it. It would have set the owner back the better part of one hundred guilders and nobody but nobody had told him you could get around it with a bit of stick.

It was painstaking work, and painful to watch but entirely worth the effort when after a few minutes the little golden band tumbled off its cushion and hit the floor with the faintest ding. Luce carefully retrieved it, picking it up with a scrap of cloth just in case before folding it up and tucking it into the poacher's pocket in the front of her top.

The large, empty room had turned out to be a gallery. Clara wasn't surprised; she would have been shocked if it turned out to be a ballroom. Hoity-Toity the Law Cleric would have no use for such things. Even if he had a wife, Clara doubted that Mrs Hoity-Toity Cleric was any more inclined to frivolity than her husband. They probably had a bland receiving chamber somewhere for being condescending to callers, but in all likclihood parties were right out.

The gallery was a very peculiar space, long and reasonably narrow. Three of the walls were lined with pictures and the forth, one of the long ones, was basically only there to hold the dozen or so tall, narrow windows that were the rooms major source of light. The drapes were clearly for show, as

moonlight flooded in, casting grubby blue-grey shadows at intervals along the room, providing the girls with just enough light to see where they were going and to be able to see the faces on some of the portraits, made far creepier in the gloom. Not easily scared, they paused in front of an unflattering portrait of a wild-eyed and almost sheet-white dowager wearing a hideous high-collared floral gown, and wasted a minute or so trying to imitate her bizarre facial expression, which was an unattractive combination of displeasure and dyspepsia.

They didn't linger long, pictures and frames were not what they'd come to steal and there was nothing pocket-sized lying around to take. Even the plant pots were too big. Very aware of the passing of time, the girls scurried along the walls in search of the doorway.

Min found it at the far end. The tall darkened archway was the width of a door with a heavy velvet curtain pulled to one side by a thick braided rope, in the opening. It was impossible to see what lay beyond it. Wary of going too far into the unknown darkness, Min poked her head through and sniffed. Whatever the space turned out to be, it was clearly in use. The air wasn't stale or damp, in fact it had a hint of something pleasingly herbal and slightly astringent about it. She turned back and with a theatrical whisper that carried the whole length of the room, called to her companion. Clara, who had been examining a slight dent in the floor in case it turned out to be a trap door to a secret store of gold or something, started at the sound of her name and dutifully trotted over to her friend.

Together, they contemplated the door way in silence. Then Clara grinned and thumped Min playfully on the arm. Apparently confident that this was the jackpot, and not a door to very large pit of spikes and snakes, she stepped blithely through the archway and vanished from Min's sight - albeit only briefly. There was a scraping sound and the room went from pitch black to murky blue-grey as Clara pulled the curtains over a small squarish window. Min smiled and shook her head, of course - they'd have seen this window when they were doing the reconnaissance and had wondered what this room was even then - the window was incongruous with the rest of the building, very simply framed, strangely placed and low.

The odd, plain little window brought them enough light to explore the room and see what was on offer by way of portable pickings. Judging by the faint smell and the furniture, it was some kind of tea parlour. It wasn't a desperately large room, but whilst it was full it wasn't uncomfortably cluttered. The far wall was taken up by a wide, plain-mantled fire place and there were two or possibly three large animal skin throw rugs covering the flagstone floor. There was seating for a dozen or so people, mainly low, padded benches and stools that formed a horseshoe around the fire place, but there were a couple of straight-backed chairs and a long, highly-polished dark wood settle by the door. There were a number of occasional tables scattered about made - as far as it was possible to tell - from the same wood as the settle.

The décor was understated, not a portrait in sight, just a large well-painted mural on the wall opposite the window that depicted a collection of religious symbols. If the girls had been the kind of people to make that kind of comment, they may well have termed it as 'puritanical chic'. There wasn't even a vase of flowers to be seen.

Sadly, the lack of clutter, whilst a bonus for the household staff who would have to clean this room, was a bit of a disappointment for the girls. No bric-a-brac meant no pickings. Clara, becoming increasingly desperate under the time pressure, was rubbing her hand along the wall in hope of finding something - Min had no idea what. She was fast running out of enthusiasm for this robbery and was very much inclined just to wonder back to the meeting point empty-handed. With a disgruntled grunt she turned back to the door and stopped.

"Clara," she hissed through her teeth, "Clara!"

"What?" mumbled Clara in response without turning around.

"You brought your lock-picks right?" whispered Min. That made Clara looked around.

Min was crouching in front of the settle running her hands along the edge of the seat.

"What are you doing?" whispered Clara, crossing the room carefully to avoid the low-slung furniture.

"You wouldn't padlock something that was empty would you?" was Min's response.

"No."

"And if the contents wasn't valuable, you wouldn't bother either would you?"

"No," said Clara again.

"Excellent," said Min shifting slightly, "hand over those lock-picks."

Mulligan was confused. The door wasn't just unlocked, it was unlockable. To all intents and purposes it was just a few planks of wood on two sturdy bronze hinges with a knotted rope handle that allowed him to pull it open. Cringing back, as though he were trying to avoid too much skin contact in case of contagion, Mulligan pulled the rough hessian rope and let the door swing silently towards him. Nothing happened - apart from the door opening.

The smell of damp stone wafted out to him before he'd even had a chance to look into the room. With caution, he stepped inside the large, windowless space and looked around. The room was bathed in flicking red light from two lamps, slightly larger than the ones that lit the stairs and situated on either end of a low table in the middle of the room. Between them, stood an intricate carving picked out with inlaid stones and enamels. It was no surprise to Mulligan that it depicted the Scales of Justice adorned with other various iconic symbols of the Temple of Law.

On the floor around the table were eight small fur pelts arranged in a circle, behind each was one a simple wooden stool with a leather covered seat. The walls were banked with banners depicting various Temple stories and important people including, Mulligan realised, the mighty Gauntlet of Law being paraded back through the city by the Paladins who had hunted it down during the Summer of Fire.

This was a prayer chamber. Of course it was. What else should a High Priest of the Law Temple have in such a strangely secluded location within his house. Mulligan exhaled. Some people really were on the level - he kept forgetting. Not everybody had something to hide, not all people in power were corrupt and just because the guy was a sanctimonious, pompous twit didn't mean he wasn't an honest and faithful sanctimonious twit. What a dead loss. He'd come all this way up here, and there was nothing worth stealing - he could have taken the oil lamps but even if he put them out now, they'd be too hot to carry for a while yet. Frankly he'd sooner forego the ten or so guilders they'd fetch and not have to live with burnt fingers, not to mention the potential backlash of desecrating a shrine.

The girls were not going to be impressed when he turned up empty handed, but he realised as he made his way back to the staircase, that actually he didn't give much of a monkey's. It was high time he moved on. When he got back to the house tonight, he'd make all the right noises, wait for the girls to disperse to bed and make his exit - with the stash from the fire place. More fool them if they thought he was going to split it with them, that had been off the table for a while now. They really shouldn't have pissed him off.

Chapter 21
The Midnight Peal

Once they had the ring safely tucked inside Luce's tunic, they went about filling their bags with anything else that could be lifted - there was a whole array of desk furniture in various metals with inlaid this and engraved that. It was small potatoes compared to the ring, but every guilder was worth having if they were going to be here anyway. Luce filled her satchel quite quickly and gazed out of the window worrying about the time as Angel took a more discerning trawl through the room. Waiting until the midnight bells seemed to be cutting it fine to her, especially as they were going to have to navigate their way around the forcefield. She turned around to find Angel running her finger along a book case, clearly searching for something specific.

"We should get back," she whispered urgently.

"Why?" replied Angel without even turning around.

"I just have a feeling we're going to need more time than we've got," replied Luce, realising as she said it that Angel was the last person to be receptive to the 'I just have this feeling' argument. As predicted, Angel just snorted and carried on scanning the shelves. Luce was left standing there, twitching and rocking on her heels, seriously pondering whether she should just go without her.

The familiar peal of the Law Temple bells sounded across the city, bringing the day to a glorious end. Luce's heart was racing. That was the signal to return to position. They had this peal of the bells and the following twelve chimes heralding the start of the new day to get from where they were to the store room they had entered from. Even on the Night of the Warden's Keys, when the peal was extra twiddly, it still didn't give them much time.

Angel appeared in the door way just as the bells were starting their final descending cadence, to find that Luce had already negotiated the force field and was waiting for her restlessly, about fifteen yards down the corridor. She didn't say anything, and even though Angel couldn't see her face properly in the dark, she could imagine the look of irritated impatience that was on it. She didn't hurry herself, she didn't really care how irritated Luce got. She just approached the flour-covered field at a steady walk. As she dropped to the floor to slither under the alarm field, she heard Luce let out a grunt of annoyance. Still she kept to her purposeful but unhurried pace, as she stood up Luce turned and started scuttling up the corridor towards the quadrangle. Angel paused for a moment and watched her go with a chilly half-smile, then patting her satchel with satisfaction, she followed.

Mulligan was still empty handed when the bells started to ring. He zipped hastily back to the quad looking about him for a side table that might have a few palm-sized trinkets on it, or a couple of easily-detached wall sconces. He wasn't having much luck. Clearly the posh-knob Law frock who lived here believed in austerity and all that nonsense, or he didn't trust his staff not to filch things and therefore kept everything he liked in a strong box somewhere. With Law clerics it could go either way.

Min and Clara were having a completely different dilemma. They had opened the settle with very little effort, the two simple padlocks were child's-play to them. In about thirty seconds they had had the heavy oak lid propped open and were gazing down at what could only be described as 'the jackpot'. The long seat, which could have comfortably accommodated four people, five if they were skinny or very close friends, was the lid of a deep chest crammed full of silver and gold worship-ware. There were cups, dishes, scales, incense burners, hand-bells, lamps, candle-sticks and snuffers, even a pewter and glass decanter with a suspiciously viscous clear liquid in it.

There was surely enough stuff there to furnish eight or nine temples and still have enough left of over for a roadside shrine and a pious widow's prayer meeting. Whether to steal it wasn't Min and Clara's dilemma, they didn't share Mulligan's fear of spiritual retribution. Their problem was simply deciding on which bits to steal. Being two very small girls, they had a limited capacity even with their two sacks. They'd abandoned the hand-bells immediately as a bad idea and the decanter - because that liquid could have been anything and glass things were a daft notion in this kind of caper, but they were still left with a vast array of choice. When the peal started, they were standing stupidly over the chest, sacks half full trying to select the best items. The sound of the bells shook them into action. Within seconds they had filled any remaining space with whatever came to hand and started back towards the gallery, moving as quickly as they possibly could without clattering.

Mulligan was the first to reach the door. He slid back the bolt and slipped into the storeroom, leaving the door ajar. Moments later, he was joined by Luce, who was clearly fed-up.

"Where's Angel?" he hissed and was rewarded with a gruff

"Coming," for his trouble.

However, it wasn't Angel that appeared around the door moments later, it was a large hessian sack followed by a panting Min and then a second that seemed to have Clara's legs. Sullenly, Luce took Min's sack and nudged Mulligan to take Clara's. The two smaller girls relinquished them gratefully and stood breathing deeply, flapping life back into their aching arms. The midnight chimes continued, there must have been at least eight of them by now.

"Where's Angel?" panted Min stretching.

"Coming," replied Luce through her teeth with a non-committal shrug. In the darkness Min couldn't see the glowering look on Luce's face, but she could hear it.

"We can't wait," said Mulligan as the next chime rang out.

"No," said Luce making a decisive move. She didn't know why she was so uneasy about waiting for Angel but something in her guts was nudging her forward. "Mulligan, you go first."

The window on this side was higher than it had been on the outside, which none of them had been able to predict. The girls weren't phased, there were plenty of things to utilise as steps, but it was easier to let Mulligan went first.

"Come on," growled Luce tugging his sleeve. She practically forced him to use her knee as a step up and with alarming strength helped him to wriggle through the gap far enough to allow his bodyweight to take him the rest of the way. He didn't have time to ponder how the girls were planning on getting up and out, he just heaved himself forward into an undignified heap. He was still sorting himself out when Clara appeared. It was like a well-oiled machine - three girls and two sacks of takings appeared in less than a minute.

The chimes had long since stopped and the night was eerily quiet. The militia patrol was leaving the post on Old Selliar Street right now, and proceeding east towards the Singers' bridge. According to the information that Angel had obtained, they had just under ten minutes to get clear. Mulligan was on his feet holding one of the sacks when Luce stuck her head and shoulders back through the windows and hissed something. Moments later she practically dragged Angel into the yard by the scruff of her tunic.

"Let's go," muttered Luce under her breath and started towards the road that went down the side of the house. They'd calculated that if they could get over the lowish wall on this side of the garden, then they'd not only be closer to home, it'd give them a few yards' head start on the approaching patrol. They didn't run, that would have been foolish, laden down with things that clattered as they were and on uncertain ground with plenty to trip on. They didn't amble though, picking their way across the bare earth of the courtyard and into the shrubs at the base of the wall briskly. Min produced a rope from gods only knew where, looped it around her waist and with the practised surety of a very large spider scuttled up the wall. It was only about eight feet high, and rough enough that Min was able to find purchase to climb.

Clara followed once Min has reached the top and secured herself by sitting down. Deftly Luce followed, the rope anchored by the two smaller girls. When she was on top of the wall, Min and Clara were able to drop down and receive the sacks as they were passed from Mulligan to Luce and then over. Luce stayed on the wall as an anchor for Mulligan to make the climb. He was horrified by the struggle he had scaling the wall, even with the aid of the rope. Not a year ago he'd been a reputed cat-burglar, highly skilled and fit as a flea. He'd have been able to get over a wall higher than this in seconds unaided. Three or four months of rich food and little training and he could barely heave himself high enough. Panting, he lumped himself down on the wall, letting Luce drop so that he could anchor Angel. As he felt the sharpness of bile in this throat from the exertion he decided that, whatever happened after tonight, he was definitely going to start training again.

Chapter 22
The Getaway

It was at the moment when Luce's feet hit the ground that everything started to tumble away into chaos. Min and Clara carrying a sack each had slipped into the bushes and Luce was just about to join them when the silence was broken by the sound of heavy footfalls approaching - the unmistakable stodgy plod of two or three militia officers who want to be heard. The very edge of lamp light flickered by the corner of the wall and quiet but not covert voices floated on to the edge of hearing. Mulligan froze on top of the wall for a second or so processing what he heard and then found himself blasted by a shot of adrenaline. The months of idleness and excess sloughed away in an instant as his instincts took over. With a lightning movement, he dived forward grabbed Angel by the upper arm and yanked her up on to the wall. Then, abandoning all caution and subtly, he dropped down and hit the ground just as the puddle of yellow light from the patrolman's storm-lantern spilled out around the end of the wall. Forgetting himself, he held his arms up for Angel, who lowered herself carefully into them and allowed herself to be placed gently on the floor.

That was the vital, wasted moment. He should have run and left Angel to jump down on her own. He'd have been in shadow then, but instead he was in full silhouette against the wall when the first militiaman rounded the corner and lifted his lantern.

"Halt," bellowed the officer as they are wont to do and Mulligan wondered, as he always did, if that had ever worked.

"Scatter," came the shout from the bushes as Clara cottoned on to the situation a moment or so ahead of the others. Two more officers appeared just in time to see a burst of movement through the bushes as the three girls dumped the sacks and scattered in different directions. One of the officers gave chase in the vague direction of one of the shadows whilst the other two homed in on Mulligan and Angel. Already regretting his mistake, Mulligan didn't pause to see where Angel went he just legged it towards the river bank.

Clara was aware that one of the patrol officers was chasing Min as she headed into the heart of the Merchant's Quarter. The back alleys and cut-throughs were like a rat-maze and Min would had no problem shaking him off. On the other hand, the grim-looking bastard baring down on Mulligan had a far clearer field of chase. Very few people would willingly jump into the river Ddu, particularly this close to the delta - because if the sludge didn't kill you the undertow would certainly give it a try - and Mulligan was heading the wrong way for the nearest bridge.

A sudden, rare moment of human generosity caught hold of Clara and she found herself circling round so that she was behind the brute with a good distance between them. Then she yelled as loud as she could,

"Oi, bugger face, over here."

This had the desired effect of distracting both officers momentarily, as they both turned to see which one of them she was addressing. Mulligan grabbed the opportunity with both hands and took to his heels, heading back into the District with a head start on the officer who suddenly realised he'd been had. Clara didn't hang around to see what became of Angel, she darted off into the darkness with the sound of heavy footfalls behind her.

Min was very quick on her feet, she was also tricksy enough to feint and dart. She had the advantage of familiarity with these alley ways. Normally it would have been enough to shake off a militia officer in less than five minutes, but this one seemed far more determined than usual. Just when she thought she'd lost him by doubling back and scrambling up on to an outhouse roof, she heard the sounds of boots on mud and a barrel-chest heaving for breath. She crouched down and watched as he jogged down the road and then stopped for a moment to sniff the air like a hunting dog trying to get a lock on his quarry.

Min made herself comfortable. If she was lucky, this was about to become a waiting game and she wasn't the one who was supposed to go off shift at dawn. The militiaman stood stock-still, looking around him for maybe thirty seconds, then he took a slow meander back the way he'd come for a few hundred yards and gave the area a more thorough checking. Luckily for Min, the officer that had been carrying the storm lantern had started after Angel which meant that this one was relying entirely on the moonlight. She kept her eyes on him as he inspected every crook and crevice he could find. It was evident from his body language that his sense of urgency was starting to dwindle. He poked his foot into a couple of gaps between buildings and then paused again.

Clearly, he didn't think she was worth the effort. Min smiled to herself and waited for him to slope away. She was a little confused when, instead of turning around and heading back the way he came, he started down the road towards the centre of the Quarter. She could have easily dismissed this observation as irrelevant or the usual assumed idiocy of an average duty officer disorientated in the dark, but the reason Min was still alive had a lot to do with the instincts that didn't dismiss anything. The only reason that the militia officer would be walking in that direction was because it was far more valuable than walking in any other direction, and the only thing Min could think of as being of any interest to the militia in that direction was their house.

Luce was still within sight of the Law cleric's house when the shriek rang out through the quiet streets. She had circled back round after the original split and concealed herself in the shadows at the end of an alley way, wondering if it was worth trying to find one of the sacks. She didn't make a move though. She had a funny feeling about the whole thing, and she wanted to see if her gut feeling was correct before she did anything. From her hiding place, she watched with amusement as a militiaman jogged back into view, having lost Clara in the dark. Luce wasn't surprised, Clara was a master at avoiding Militia custody- unless she was cold, tired and hungry – at which point she was a master at getting arrested for very trivial offences that led to nothing more than a night in the cells.

The shriek was coming from just out of Luce's range of vision, and unless Mulligan had been caught in a very unfortunate way, it was coming from one of the other girls. A moment's patience was rewarded as the Militia officer with the lantern appeared from the opposite direction to the last. He was laden down by a kicking, screaming bundle of flailing limbs and shining white-blonde hair, slung over one shoulder. Angel.

Somehow, Luce wasn't at all surprised, things were slowly swimming into clarity. Min was quick and Clara was devious, but neither of them were a patch on Angel when it came to evading arrest. She knew every trick in the book and she was fast, agile and surprisingly strong for her size. She pinched and she had a bite on her that could make even the burliest of guard's squeal like a small girl. Luce couldn't remember a single hold she hadn't managed to wriggle free from in the years they had been on the streets together. If anyone should have been able to get away from a militiaman with a lantern in one hand, it was Angel.

A deep-rooted impulse told Luce to help in some way, throw stones or make a noise to draw attention, maybe even run forward and kick the lantern out of the guard's hand. The part of Luce that had grown louder during the last few months spent in the stables held her back. Once upon a time, it wouldn't have occurred to her to let Angel suffer like that, but that was when she still innocently believed that they were sisters - that their first thoughts were always for each other. She wasn't that naïve any more. Besides, she was pretty certain that if Angel had been caught by the militia then it was no accident. Unsure what else to do, she took to her heels and fled into the darkness.

Angel's protest, however phoney, was enough to keep a whole officer occupied. That still left two others roaming the night. Mulligan had done the only thing he could think of, he'd practically hurdled Angel and fled into the maze of houses that patch-worked this part of the quarter. You could run all you liked, but in this city if you didn't think about where you were going you would more than likely end up in either flat against the city walls or soaking wet having fallen into the Aragonese straits or even worse the foetid River Ddu. To outrun the militia, you had to out think them. It couldn't be denied that the city militia were well-trained when it came to fitness and fighting, but there was a limit to the number of people with a real sense of cunning who felt the need to join a body of Law enforcement. Those kinds of people tended to favour more prosperous or prestigious careers, or at least ones that didn't involve midnight shifts. Having employed his razor-like wits, Mulligan had vaulted the first wall he had come across that was only just over six foot - which had caused him to vomit a little. He was now in the pitch black, trying to carefully extract himself from a large, heavily perfumed climbing rose without getting sick on his hands. He heard the shriek, but didn't really bother to process it - he hoped it was Angel, or Min, both of whom he had started to seriously dislike. He didn't really care which one it was, no doubt they would all end up in clink soon enough. He wouldn't put it past them to be stupid enough to attempt to snatch back whichever one of their merry band was currently bruising the militiaman's ribs and deafening him.

If he could keep his head he told himself, as he stepped clear of the bush trailing soft white petals in his wake, he would be quids in. Hang on here until either all the girls were pulled in or the patrol got bored, then steal a cloak or something and slip down the back streets to the house. It would take him less than five minutes to pack once he got there, after all how long does it take to stash the money in a satchel, replace the tin and saddle the horse? He might even stop to collect his green frock coat and hose, and snatch a loaf from the kitchen but it wasn't vital. He could be away out of the city and on the road to the Middle Kingdoms just before dawn, when the Eastgate was fully opened. With what they had stashed in their secret hiding place, and the not inconsiderable reserve fund he'd been keeping in his bedroom for emergencies, he would be able to live like a King - maybe even buy himself a Kingdom or at very least a Barony. It wasn't quite the end game he'd been hoping for but it was close enough, and at least this way he didn't have to find a way to get rid of the girls.

Clara was hanging on to a damp stone wall for support and panting. She had run the whole length of the alleyway, even though she had heard the militiaman's footfalls fade away slightly before half way. She'd helped as best she could but she'd also heard the shriek, muffled by her pounding heart. Whichever one of the girls that was, they would have to take care of themselves. She was just going to concentrate on getting herself clean away. What she needed was a sewer hatch, but as she stood trying to reclaim her breath she realised that she didn't know where she was, never mind about the location of the nearest hatch. Going by the buildings around her, she was still in the Rich District but judging by the smell, somewhat closer to the docks. Being the Fortescue's maid there had been no call for her to get this far down the quarter. It was not done for young ladies to be seen unaccompanied on the docks, although she didn't really know why, because all the interesting bars and hookers were on the other side of the river. Perhaps it was because they tended to get in the way of the men unloading things?

She straightened up and paused for a moment. That was it! The other side of the river. She would be able to find a hatch over there no problem. All she had to do was cross the Bridge of Stars and lose herself in the tumbledown chaos of the dockland boozers. Working purely on instinct, she started to pick her way out of the maze of houses towards the river. The streets were still and dark. It seemed rich people went to bed before midnight, or sat in the dark and saved money on the lamp oil.

To Clara this was very strange, the sewers were alive at all times of day and night and the poor quarters barely slept. It made her feel as though she should tiptoe in case she woke someone up. She had to force herself to walk purposefully and at a sensible speed. Dressed in her darks with coal dust rubbed across her face, she was clearly up to no good - the late hour and the complete absence of brushes made it impossible to claim she was a chimney sweep and sneaking would make her look suspicious. There was no guarantee that she wasn't about to walk straight into a large and restless militia patrol, not to mention that every prestigious Law Follower in the city would by now be on their way home after their midnight worship. It was not a good time to be on the run.

Clara attributed the speed with which she found the river bank to providence, although it may have had more to do with smell. She was quite some way upstream from the bridge she wanted but the bank was far better lit than the streets, thanks to the docile yellow glow drifting across the water from the rough end of the docks. Clara just kept walking, picking up her pace a little but resisting the urge to run. there was almost no way she would make it across that bridge without passing someone and if she was any judge, there was likely to be a militia patrol heading over the bridge towards the dockland piss-parties any time now. For a wild moment, she considered dipping down to river to wash her face but she quickly thought better of it. She tugged her hood forward and kept her head down. Drinkers heading towards the inns wouldn't be bothered by one more cloaked figure hurrying on their way.

She was bang on about the patrol, they were approaching the bridge from the opposite direction and looked as though they would set foot on the cobbles almost at the same time she did. The officers had clocked her, no question - that was what law officers did. If she paused, or sped up, or even worse vanished completely, that would draw attention. She had no choice, she would just have to brazen it out. As she approached the patrol and found herself caught in the pool of their lantern light, she could see that one of them was a slightly built Elven woman with an armband that designated her as a medic. Both her companions were nearly twice her volume, heavily armoured and baring door shields.

Clara kept telling herself to walk on, that these officers wouldn't know that she was on the run. The best thing she could do would be ignore them, or nod good evening. The pounding of her blood made it difficult to hear anything else, and she was aware of every inch of her body as she approached the patrol and the bridge. She kept breathing and scurried forward, not daring to look up to see if they were looking at her. She didn't have the guts to acknowledge them as they all set foot on the cobbles, she just kept walking and they kept pace with her. Her heart raced, blood flooded around her body. She hunched her shoulders to protect herself from what she imagined to be the searing heat of their glares, every moment tensed against the inevitable grab of a hand and the 'excuse me miss' that would follow. It didn't come.

On the other side of the bridge the Militia split off right and Clara headed left, making her split-second decision based entirely on getting away from the patrol. It turned out to be a mistake, in terms of avoiding militia at least.

It seemed that there was some kind of incident happening in the docks. Not news as such, except that it was drawing a lot of Militia attention. The patrol that had come over the bridge with her, she realised, had been moving more purposefully than the usual ambling 'all's well' night patrols. Judging by the quantity of green tabards, cloaks and sashes jogging towards her, sometime in the last few minutes the alarm bells must have sounded. She had been too busy to notice whether a faint clanging sounds had wafted across the river.

Luckily for her, the militia were too busy heading towards to the yellow flickering glow to be bothered with a paranoid small-time crook. It was the general response to a rough night in the docks – someone had set something on fire. Now she paused to listen, she could hear the crackle of burning timbers above the hubbub. Curiosity got the better of her. Who would notice one more body in the press anyway? She turned around and started to wander slowly in the direction of the fire, the fuss and the jogging militia.

Curiosity does terrible things to people, but in this case it was going to turn out to be strangely fortuitous for Clara.

Chapter 23
Rumbled

Min picked her way towards the house, darting from shadows to alleys, over walls and on to roofs in an impressive display of dexterity. The militiaman, although basically invisible in his dark green cloak and hood was easily tracked thanks to there being few people about in this part of the city at this time of night. He would vanish from view from time to time, but then moments later he would reappear. She hung back in the alley that ran between FitzAlan, Lord George's town house and the Frandell villa, and just as she expected, he appeared walking briskly, taking the most direct route towards their house. It was just around the corner.

There was no way it was a coincidence. He wasn't flapping at the bees any more, he was making a line straight for the hive. They'd been rumbled. This wasn't an accident. They hadn't just fallen foul of a militia patrol, someone had tipped them off. Min froze for a second or so. She couldn't go home, that much was obvious, but that didn't leave many options.

The Guild Below would have been the natural choice a few months ago, but now she knew what it was like to be clean and fed and she didn't want to go back to what she had been before. Besides, before it hadn't just been her, she'd had the others. Alone she was far more likely to end up dead, even in spite of the fact that she was no longer malnourished and had started to grow breasts. She had been aware for a month or so that she was on borrowed time posing as a seven-year-old. The change in her diet had not only fattened her up, it had also finally allowed the onset of puberty. Becoming a woman would make life

Below far more difficult - for all her bravado she had no intention of going on the game.

She stood pressed up against the cold stones of the wall trying to decide what to do and then a moment of inspiration struck. With a wide, satisfied grin she slipped out of the end of the passageway and headed towards an entirely different part of the quarter.

Luce didn't pause, she didn't hide, she just made straight for the house. As the girl with the best knowledge of the quarter's back alleys and short cuts, she had no difficult reaching the house without bumping into anyone, let alone inconvenient militia officers. She paused in the shadow of an outhouse opposite and looked around thoroughly before she darted out into the empty street, zipped straight down the side of the house and into the back yard. She wasn't interested in ever setting foot in that house again. She had nothing in there to speak of. She wasn't about to risk taking the money, she'd be surprised if it was still there in any case. If she had to guess she would say that either Mulligan or Angel had secretly helped themselves to the stash in the last twenty-four hours and tucked it away for 'safe keeping' until everyone else was in the nick. She didn't care, didn't want it anyway, she'd come for the one thing she valued and she had no intention of hanging about once she'd got her hands on it.

The horse was asleep when she opened the stable door and it woke up with a startled whinny. Luce fed him a pail of oats to calm him while she saddled him up and packed everything she needed into saddle bags. It was a shame, she reflected, as she strapped it all down, that she hadn't had the sense to start stock piling food when she felt things starting to go sour but still, she'd eat well enough on the road. She wasn't sure where that road would lead her, but she felt like it was time she found out.

Most of the city's gates were heavily guarded between midnight and the morning five hour, only allowing foot traffic in and out through the wicket but the Darkgate would open to let mounted travellers and wagons in or out at any time of the day or night - hence why it was called the Darkgate. Once she was out of the city she could decide what to do from there. With one long look at the back of the house that she had come to loathe, she heaved herself into the saddle and with a crack of the reins she and the horse departed into the night.

Clara threaded her way through the crowds, revelling in the noise and anonymity. Apparently, there had been some kind of altercation between the drinkers in a bar called The Ugly Yak and a group of Sea God followers fresh from the Temple. Nobody was really sure what it had been about and approximately eighty percent of the people now involved in the ensuing chaos hadn't bothered to find out. The Yak was well ablaze, the innkeeper - a burly woman with low forehead and a cauliflower ear was standing to one side with a look of fury in her close-set eyes and a wailing hooker under each arm. There were people brawling, thieving and generally causing a public nuisance, and about a dozen militia officers trying to deal with it all at once. Two brave militiamen had managed to arrest the entire goblin crew of a cargo ship called The Moribund Mole and were beginning to regret chaining them all together. At least three more seemed to be enjoying the brawl and were making little attempt to end things - unless they planned to knock out everybody else and then arresting them - and nobody but nobody seemed to be interested in trying to put the fire out.

Clara sniggered. She loved a good bit of public farce and the militia never failed to oblige when they took on the more raucous elements of the docklands. In about half an hour, there would be another twenty officers here and probably twice as many drunks and ne'er-do-wells, and by dawn it would all be over, the cells would be full, the pub would be charcoal and it would be back to business as usual. Clara stood back and enjoyed the chaos for a moment, forgetting she was on the run. Then, suddenly, a hat caught her eye.

A small, bulbous figure wearing a ludicrous pair of patch work trousers, a revolting multi-coloured tunic and a towering top hat decorated with ribbons and feathers was doing a very fine job of single-handedly harassing the two officers that had the chain of goblins.

"Hexcuse me Sar," Clara heard the figure say at the top of its lungs, "am I addressing an Orficer of our City's fine militia?"

Clara had known who that was before she had even her the speech. Pudding! Clara grinned. Funny where fate will lead you? she thought as she waited to see what her *hassociate* did next.

"Unhand me sar!" bellowed Pudding, "My name is Aloueta Confluenza Donkey-grappler, and I am these gentlemen's lawyer. I demand you release me and them at wence!" The militia officer in question said something in response that Clara couldn't hear but was evidently not very polite.

"And I do not expect that kind of lang-oo-age from han Orficer of tha Law!" retorted Pudding, clearly putting on a show now, Clara wondered what she was distracting attention from. "Is that the mouth you kiss your mother with sar? You should be ashamed my man!"

That was when Clara saw it - the back end of the line of goblins were wriggling their hands free of the militia standard-size shackle cuffs. They didn't let the chains drop, they didn't move any unnecessary muscles, they just stood there holding the shackles and trying to look innocent - which was a tall order for a bunch of goblin sailors. By this point, the militia officer had Pudding by both elbows and she was heading towards being shackled herself. Try as she might, she was just too short to wrestle herself free from the now extremely irritable militiaman, who she was sportingly trying to kick in the shin.

Clara was torn by two compulsions at that moment. Her head said run, use the opportunity to sink into the obscurity of the labyrinthine poor quarter with its tumbledown warehouses, grimy passages and damp cellars, but her heart said no. In a flash she made the decision.

"Oi! Guvnor!" she bellowed, stepping out of her shadow and into the middle of the chaos. "That is my hassociate! Would you kindly inform me what hexactly you are doin' wiv her?"

The momentary distraction allowed Pudding to wrestle one hand free of the militiaman's grip and afforded the goblin sailors the opportunity that had been waiting for to drop the chains with a loud clang and start running pell-mell all over the place. That in turn caused the officer to spin round, letting go of Pudding's other wrist and letting out a bellow of frustrated rage as the chain whacked across his ankles. Unlike the rest of the goblins, who had only escaped to cause more chaos and had no intention of making a break for it, Pudding took to her heels, grabbed Clara by the sleeve and dived down the nearest passageway. They didn't stop until Pudding had dragged Clara the best part of half a mile along various narrow alleys and down through a coal hatch in the side of a large red stone building that looked like it might have once been a tavern. The rancid orange light that filled the room was provided by a fat tallow candle in a dirty glass jar. It showed Clara that this was probably some kind of living quarters - the dark mound of scraps and rags in the corner was probably a bed or a nest because Clara doubted it was actually a compost heap. In the gloom, she could make out a chair, a battered concertina and a pot-bellied charcoal stove.

"Welcome to my humble abode," Pudding exclaimed, spreading her arms wide. "Feel free to make yourself at 'ome."

Chapter 24
Shattered

Min was picking her ways through a corner of the Quarter she was only familiar with by daylight. Although she was normally driven from place to place in the cart, she had had the wherewithal to stay alert and now she had a thorough internal map. However, most journeys happened in the afternoon and in the darkness, the quarter looked totally different. It didn't help that she had only been to the house she was trying to find once.

She slipped between two building and found herself in a secluded square. This was definitely the place; she could feel her pulse quickening all over her body. She looked around for the main road into the square and tried to orientate herself. The sweet smell of honeysuckle mingling with wood-smoke masked the worst of the city's other smells and told her she was nearly there.

Arabella was awake. She knew it was after midnight but knowing that didn't help. It was the same every night she was at home, she poured herself a cup of brandy and tucked herself in the window alcove and drew her knees up to her chin. She would sit there, gazing out of the window in her night gown and shawl with her long dark braid hanging in her lap. At first she had told herself that the brandy would help her sleep but she had stopped telling that lie a long time ago, now she just had the brandy to keep her company as she sat gazing out at the darkened square. She didn't know what she was looking for, because she knew it wasn't her husband. It was hundreds of nights since he had last come striding confidently up the street and in at the gate, the moonlight glinting off the buckle of his sword belt, glimpses of his pale surcoat showing beneath his dark cloak. They had returned the buckle with the shield and sword when they came to tell her to stop waiting for him. It was still where she had put in under the stairs.

She took a sip of her brandy, she had the knack now of making a single cup last for several hours. As she took the cup from her lips, something caught her attention - a sudden movement in her peripheral vision, probably a trick of the shadows. She dismissed it. Then there it was again. This time she bothered to actually look. There was someone down there, in the garden, but they were dressed in dark fabric and difficult to spot.

In this city, particularly in this quarter with its current crime wave, it was likely that this person was a thief. Even so, something stopped her from waking the rest of the household in alarm. She had a strange feeling that she was safe from that particular crime wave, and an even odder feeling that she knew who was lurking behind her honeysuckle. She swapped her shawl for her heavy robe and softly took herself downstairs. If she was wrong, she could create enough noise to bring all the servants running in a heartbeat, but she just wanted to be sure first.

Min had no idea what to do now. She knew this was Arabella's garden, she knew that the front door was about ten yards away but she didn't know what to do from there. The chances of her being able to rouse Arabella by banging her little fists on that solid wood door where tiny, and ringing the bell in the middle of the night would bring only a disgruntled retainer with a scowl and a candlestick. What did she say then, shivering on the door step in her ragged tunic with coal soot on her cheeks? She could be as polite as she liked but there was no way that the retainer would do anything other than shut the door on her or shout for the militia. The only feasible thing she could do was hide herself until morning and hope Arabella made an appearance early in the day, before she was spotted by a do-gooder and arrested. She pulled her arms inside her tunic to try and warm herself and curled up into a ball under the honeysuckle.

She was just wriggling herself into a comfortable position when a light appeared in one of the windows beside the front door. Panicked, she leapt up to take flight but tripped over her own feet, numb with cold, and tumbled on to the path. She was furiously trying to untangle her limbs to make a break for it when the heavy door creaked open and flooded the night with the soft flicker of an oil lamp.

"Tabitha?" came the whisper, floating into the night. "Tabitha, is that you?" Arabella's voice didn't sound surprised or angry, just curious. Min stopped panicking and, with a deep breath, heaved herself to standing. The she stepped into the light.

"What are you doing?" came the question with slightly more urgency, "It's the middle of the night," Arabella continued, as though Min hadn't realised, "Tabitha come here, come inside, you must be cold."

The look of concern on Arabella's face was something Min had never seen directed at her before. She was struck by a sudden rush of gratitude and vulnerability, she was cold and exhausted and she dearly wanted to go inside. She stepped forward and stopped. It wasn't right, Arabella didn't know who she was inviting into her house. She thought Min was Tabitha Fortescue, a well brought up if somewhat peculiar Albion child. She looked up at the kind face of a woman she had already robbed once and said the only thing she could think of.

"My name's not really Tabitha."

"I know," said Arabella softly, holding out her hands, "Come inside and tell me who you really are."

Min was so surprised she was lost for words, she just let Bella sweep her up in her arms and guide her into the house.

Bella took Min into the kitchen, pumped the bellows to raise the fire and started ladling milk into a pan. She waved Min into a seat at the kitchen table and Min sat gratefully, her arms folded on the table in front of her. After a few minutes of silence, whilst Bella was busy warming milk and finding bread and apples, Min said in a low voice,

"But how did you know?" Bella stopped and put the bread knife down.

"I recognised you," she said, wiping her hands on a cloth and passing Min a slice of the bread.

"What?" said Min, holding the bread, suddenly starving but too confused to eat it.

"From when you and your friends, robbed me," she explained without malice. "and left me in an alleyway? Don't you remember?"

Min just nodded, she didn't have the words to explain anything else.

"But," she said after a minute or so examining the bread, "if you knew that, why were you so kind to me?"

Bella didn't answer immediately, she pulled out the chair opposite Min and sat down. She reached out her soft delicate hand and put it on Min's grubby, calloused one and squeezed gently.

"Has anyone else ever been kind to you?" she asked. "Looked after you?" Min just looked at the table. "Did you rob me for the fun of it?" Min kept her eyes fixed on the wood grain. "Did you enjoy it? Did you really have a choice?" Slowly, without looking up she shook her head.

"Well," said Bella quietly, "I think I'm going to give you a choice." She put an apple down in front of Min. "Now, Miss Fortescue, tell me what your name really is?"

It took Min two attempts to force out enough sound of her throat for Bella to actually hear 'Min'. Then she looked up, at Bella's sweetly smiling face and mumbled,

"but I'd prefer it if you would call me Tabitha, if that's okay?" Bella's face creased with a flurry of emotion, and Min realised that both of them were crying. Bella reached over, gently dried the tears from Min's cheeks with her thumbs and said,

"Tabitha it is then." Then she leant forward and kissed the girl's grubby forehead.

When Mulligan had the time to reflect on things later, he realised that it had all gone wrong the moment he paused to allow himself a smug smile. He'd successfully heaved himself over a wall and picked his way across the quarter back to his house without mishap. He hadn't seen a single militiaman; he hadn't even trodden in a puddle. The smug pause had occurred as he looked out of the end of a passage, at the street his house was on, and sniffed the air. The smell of burning on the breeze told him that this glorious city had provided him with a diversion when he needed it. He wasn't going to scuttle through the shadows or run, he was going to walk with his head held high. There was no hurry. The girls had scattered like shot from a sling, and had probably gone to ground in the Guild Below.

Even if they had fetched up back at the house, they were probably on the rug in front of the range counting their loot. He had no intention of stopping to find out, he was going in through the front door, up to his room to grab a few things and then straight to the stables to hitch up the cart and ride off into the sunset. Actually, it was going to be the sunrise, when it finally appeared, but still. At that moment, Mulligan smirked and congratulated himself - in retrospect he should have known better than to waste that time.

The street was in darkness, apart from a few night-lights glowing in upstairs windows. Luckily, the moon provided enough illumination to walk unhindered through the crisp and clear autumn night. Cobble-stones were one of the things he'd never managed to master about living in the rich district. If he tried to hurry or couldn't see his feet he would likely catch a toe and go arse over tip into the gutter - which he could live without right now. He swaggered down the street, enjoying his last moments as an Aberddu toff.

In less than an hour, Maurice Fortescue would be no longer. He'd always have the heavy green frock-coat and sable hose, but he would have to kiss goodbye to everything else. He was going to miss the cuisine, particularly the fine spirits. Mind you, with the tidy sum he would have in his purse in a few minutes, he'd be able to swan into some tin-pot little country and act the Baron. He smirked. Finally, Mulligan Parks was going to hit the big time.

He walked up the steps to the front door with the languid confidence of a rich home owner and unlocked the door. It swung open into the dark hall way with a pleasing squeal. He stepped inside and stopped dead, something was making him uneasy but he couldn't place it.

He was pretty sure he hadn't heard anything; it was just thief's paranoia he decided as he headed for the drawing room. Even so he stepped cautiously, conscious of the sound of his footfalls. The drawing room door was slightly ajar but not enough for him to see in. With the toe of his boot, he nudged it and it swung open. He found himself looking at an empty room and feeling slightly foolish, but he didn't go striding in because he wasn't actually stupid. For a fleeting moment he would have given anything for a thin-bladed dagger, a palm spike or even just a mirror on a stick. Fighting to keep his breathing tightly under control, he booted the door again with a sudden jerk of his foot. The door shot back and rebounded from the wall behind. There was no resistance, no anguished screech of surprise or pain, no one hiding there.

Mulligan let himself take a deep breath, and with inscrutable self-assurance strode across the room to the fire place. He set about removing the fire irons, the bricks were cool to the touch. It had been a while since there had been a decent fire in this grate, the cold ashes coated his knees as he crawled into the hearth. Working by feel, Mulligan wriggled until he was as far into the gap beneath the flue as he could get and carefully extended his arm up the chimney. It couldn't be too far up. He'd replaced it not long ago. He ran his palm over the familiar flaws in the brick work, feeling for the tell-tale cracks and crumbled bits that would tell him he was nearly at the gap. Finally, he had his hand on the small round tin. It slipped easily out of its hiding place.

Cursing the paunch he didn't used to have, he carefully extracted himself from the chimney breast. He'd made the mistake of hurrying in this position before and tonight was not the night for a bloody nose. It wasn't until he had retrieved his last limb and sat back on his haunches that he took notice of the small tin in his hand. It was lighter than he remembered.

With fumbling fingers, he pushed the top open and found himself looking at the sight he had been dreading. The tin was completely empty, not even a brass button in there to keep the rust company. Stupidly, he stared at it for a moment and then with a sudden outburst of rage, he flung it into the shadows at the corner of the room. That was when he realised that the shadows in the room had changed since he had squirmed into the fireplace. Before he could react, a voice behind him boomed,

"Temper temper Mr Parks," and he felt the hairs on the back of his neck tingle as someone loomed over him.

Mulligan was still alive because his reactions were like lightning. Instead of looking around to see who was behind him, he sprung to his feet and darted forwards. As predicted, the looming man behind him had leaned forward to snatch at his shirt, but Mulligan was already out of grab range. Slightly unbalanced, it took the larger man a few seconds to right himself, buying Mulligan enough time to make a break for the door.

For a blessed moment, Mulligan thought he'd broken free and then he realised that the drawing room door was no longer wide open. In fact, it was tightly closed and standing directly in his path was Angel, her arms folded. She met Mulligan's panicked look with an icy glare and a tight, satisfied smirk - like a cat with a shrew that has nowhere to hide.

Desperation took over, he grabbed her by the shoulders and tried to fling her out of his way. She was stronger than he'd imagined, and it took more effort than he'd expected. He let out an inelegant grunt as he shoved, and she skidded across the floor.

She was back up on her feet, uninjured, in time to see the militia officer reach out and slam a slab-like hand hard on to Mulligan's shoulder.

"You are total scum-bag, Mulligan Parks" he snarled, hot spittle spraying across the back of Mulligan's neck. "We know all about you, oh yes, we know all about you, you filthy pig. Victimising orphans, pushin' them about just because you can. There's a word for people like you. Imprisoning children, beating them, enslaving them to do your dirty work. Keeping them in squalor." The booming voice had become a quiet, menacing hiss in Mulligan's ear. He opened his mouth to object volubly to the charges, then suddenly caught sight of Angel. The face that looked back was so far from the familiar chilly, shrewd-eyed bitch he was used to, it was almost like looking at a different child. Almost. A change in attitude and body language had turned her into a soft-eyed innocent with baby-features to rival Min's. She wore a look of heart-stopping terror on her face and, to Mulligan's amazement, she was actually tearing slightly. In that moment, the penny dropped. Angel had set him up, she'd baited him and cornered him and now she'd released the hounds.

"Where's the money, you little bitch," he shouted at her, unable to hang on to his composure a second longer. "What have you done with it?"

Far from the shrieking retaliation he'd expected, he saw an instantaneous flash of cruel amusement in Angel's eyes just before she flung herself bodily at the officer's leg, howling for all she was worth, red-faced and snotty. If he hadn't been so maniacally angry, Mulligan would have been impressed. The officer, who had both of Mulligan's wrists in a vice-like grip, was not. With a swift jerk, he twisted one of Mulligan's arms up his back, causing Mulligan to emit a yelp of surprised pain.

"Don't like that do you?" barked the officer, "bullies never do, you maggoty low-life scum. Should have thought of that before you started taking 'vantage of children. The noose is too good for the likes of you. I hope they burn you, or maybe the Death Temple'll want you for one of their ... rituals."

The look of grim delight in the officer's eyes was lost on Mulligan as he frantically ran through his limited choices. Angel was still crying, wiping her snot trail on the officer's tabard and periodically allowing herself a glance of vicious delight at Mulligan, just to rub it all in. He tried to wriggle free of the officer's grip but he was out of shape, and he was more likely to do himself serious injury that actually get free.

When the drawing room door started to open, Mulligan looked up hopefully - maybe Clara or Luce had come home and would help him out - and then as he saw the shape of another militiaman come in to view and he finally gave up. It was a long walk from here to Gallows Hill, and he'd be spending some of the time in the cells, he was bound to think of something to save his neck. As he allowed the officers, still snarling insults into his ears, to escort him away in shackles, he didn't once look back at Angel. He wasn't going to give the little bitch the satisfaction.

Epilogue
A One Way Walk

Angel popped her head up out of the hatch, three, or maybe it was four, days below and it was easy to get disorientated. The sky had that fresh morning feeling about it, the late winter air was prickly on her skin. Judging by the smell, she was somewhere in the docks, but she'd come up on the wrong side of the river. She sighed. She had a couple of errands to run, but they could wait for a while. She wasn't going to miss the main event, and if she was any judge she'd have to be quick.

It struck her that she hadn't been in this half of the city for the best part of two months. Whether this was by subconscious design or simple coincidence she had no idea.

She'd forgotten exactly how much she hated the rich district, with its over-large buildings, empty streets, gutters, cobble-stones, gated walls, and rich people. That was why she had spent so much time back Below. Maybe, if she had liked it more, they'd have been pushing that same tired ruse until Mulligan burst out of his trousers completely. It was pure luck on her part that her ticket to freedom had been almost a direct result of her need to escape from the posh-knobs for a few hours. She'd never considered how many people Below would pay you to grass on other people Below. Nor had she realised how much the militia would pay for the same information: a double whammy. It could have been a triple whammy if she'd had the sense to stash those promissory notes somewhere more creative. She had been back to check several times, but the old saddle had definitely gone. Still, you couldn't have it all.

She hurried down the cobbled streets as fast as she dared, wary of tripping. The Singer's Bridge wasn't too far from here once she got to the river bank. She had no real interest in her surroundings as she made a beeline for the bridge. She didn't look up to greet the two people who were walking down the street in the other direction, she just glanced out of the corner of her eye at the mother and her daughter, the hoods of their winter coats pushed back to show the rosy complexions of the well-fed who can walk for pleasure. There was something familiar about them both, but Angel didn't pause to take a second look, she just ignored them as they kept walking, arm in arm, chuckling between themselves as they headed home. By the time she reached the river bank, Angel was nearly running she could see the crowds starting to gather already. The bridge was filling up and she didn't want to miss anything.

Clara loved a crowd, there was so much profit to be made. A public hanging always generated people with little taste looking for entertainment - which was perfect for her and Pudding because they were very bad at entertaining. So far on today's programme, they had forgotten nearly all the words to 'You Can Tell She's a Lady by What She Charges', fallen over trying to dance a traditional Paravelian tarantella and failed to make a rabbit appear out of Pudding's hat. They had made 3 groats - better than a clip round the ear, which was what they'd made last time. Things were looking up. Clara was just pushing her way through to the next bit of the crowd, primed and ready with an epic recitation of 'Algie and the Thirteen Foot Noodle', when she was distracted by the sound of cartwheels on cobble stones. It was time for the big event, the poem could wait until afterwards. Panting, Pudding was elbowing her way towards her and they stood side by side watching the rickety cart approach from Blackwall Prison.

The ride up One Way Walk to Gallows Hill was always done at a subdued pace, mainly so the public could get a lingering gaze at the next neck for the noose. It also gave them extra time to throw things and jeer. Clara had no idea who was up next, they'd done the murderers first, so interest was waning by this point but there were still plenty of people to shout abuse as the cart rattled on. She craned her neck to see, and was horrified to find herself looking at Mulligan. It was true that she hadn't really given him a moment's thought since that evening she had first set foot in Pudding's humble abode but, for all that, she didn't wish him this.

On seeing the look on her partner's face, Pudding removed her hat with a flourish and held it up to her chest, then with the other hand she smartly saluted. With a weary smile, Clara copied her - it was the only tribute she could pay. When Mulligan passed by the pair, he almost smiled. Clara acknowledged him with the faintest nod. Then she turned to Pudding, clapped an arm across her shoulder and said,

"This calls for a drink! Let's see if the Ugly Yak been rebuilt yet."

About a hundred miles from the Aberddu Darkgate, Luce was sitting in a stable attacking the saddle bags with a leather brush. She was biding her time. It had been three days after she'd left when she had patted her pocket and found the ring. Now it was safely sewn into the hem of her tunic - and there it would stay until the trade fares started again in the spring. She could get through the winter without it, she would just have to be careful. Once the saddle bags were dubbin to her satisfaction, she turned her attention to the saddle itself. It was about time she sorted out the uncomfortable lump under her left thigh. Someone had obvious attempted to mend some damage there - you could see the slash they'd sewn closed - and had done a very poor job. She had every intention of riding at least another fifty miles or so, and for the sake of her thigh she was going to try to sort it out. With incongruous delicacy, Luce ran her blade through old stitches and slowly peeled open the leather. No wonder it was uncomfortable; someone had stuffed it with a load of paper instead of straw. With gentle fingers, she pulled the clump free and, seeing that at least one sheet had writing on it, she lay them all flat. Even though Luce couldn't read, she knew exactly what she was looking at. Now all she had to do was find someone who would honour 'Auld Clarensi United Treasuries' promissory notes and life would be rosy. In fact, she liked the word rosy so much she thought she might actually change her name.

# # #

About the Author

LG Surgeson is a writer and teacher from Mid Wales, UK. She lives in a cottage full of fairy doors by a river in the middle of nowhere with her long-suffering partner and their two cats: Ocean and Terminal Curiosity. She prefers it to the real world because it smells better and you can see the sky. Her other hobbies include quilting, gardening, sleeping and wearing a dent in the sofa. She writes in the time she saves by ignoring the housework. The cats like to help. They aren't good at it.

LG was born in South Africa in 1980 and emigrated to the UK with her folks when she was just four years old – hence she's no idea what it's like to be actually warm. She grew up in Dorset on the South Coast of England, and having decided that this was neither rural nor cold enough she packed herself off to university in Aberystwyth in 1998. She's been there ever since. LG claims it's because she loves Wales but some have suggested it may have a little to do with the six-hour train trip back to her folks. She successfully qualified in a fancy pants mathematics masters in 2003 that can basically be boiled down to 'why does jelly wobble and custard get thicker when you stir it'. The following year gained her teaching certificate. Since then, she's been gainfully employed in schools trying to convince teenagers that maths, or at least maths teachers, aren't evil – well not very evil any way.

As a writer, LG started at a young age. Her first masterpiece was a book about a naughty black and white cat that she penned at the tender age of seven or eight. It was lovingly illustrated by her mother. After that she was hooked and has had books on the go ever since. It took her until 2011 to work up the courage to unleash her work on an unsuspecting world. The Freetown Bridge was released as an e-book and was met with a warm reception. Since then,

LG has released 4 more books in her Black River Chronicles, a fantasy series following the exploits of a bunch of misfit adventurers who frequently find themselves being forced to 'Do The Right Thing' when all they wanted was to make a small fortune. The Black River has its own blog, and newsletter written by the adventurers themselves. The series, and LG herself, owe an unending debt of gratitude to the Aberddu Adventures Live Action Roleplay system in Aberystwyth, which she played in and ran for twelve years and on whose game world the series is based.

As well as fantasy novels, LG also writes fiction novels based on various life experiences – predominantly those she has had in her other job as a teacher working with young people with emotion, social and mental health difficulties that lead to extreme and challenging behaviour. (This is often more amusing or heart-warming than it sounds). She hopes these books will touch the souls of their readers in the same way that the experiences have touched her. She hopes to release some of these in the near future, but currently they aren't yet perfect enough to leave her laptop.

As if all this wasn't enough for the unsuspecting readers, LG also writes articles and blog posts on subjects about mental health, the education system and anything else that makes her hot under the collar. She has two blogs for this: Scaling the Chalkface - educational ranting for the terminally exhausted and Good Mental Hygiene, a blog about her own and other people's experience with mental health issues focussing on coping mechanisms and positivity. As well as appearing on her own blog, LGs articles on mental health have appeared in a variety of internet journals.

LG is very excited to be working with Creativia so that she can spread her own personal madness further afield. She hopes they realise what they've let themselves in for.

Lightning Source UK Ltd.
Milton Keynes UK
UKHW041937150321
380411UK00009B/1154/J